WRECK OF THE RAPTOR

AJ BAILEY ADVENTURE SERIES - BOOK 3

NICHOLAS HARVEY

HarveyBooks

Printed in the United States of America

First Printing, 2019

ISBN-13: 9781710723601

Cover design by Wicked Good Book Covers

Author photograph by Lift Your Eyes Photography

This is a work of fiction. Names, characters, businesses, places, events and incidents are either the products of the author's imagination or used in a fictitious manner unless noted otherwise. Any resemblance to actual persons, living or dead, or actual events is purely coincidental. Except Jen and her Greenhouse Restaurant, you can't make up Jen.

Both Jen from Greenhouse Cafe and Rosa from Heritage Kitchen kindly provided their permission to use their characters and locations. The Raptor is a fictitious wreck. The U-1026 is a fictitious wreck as you know… if you've read *Twelve Mile Bank*! The Fox and Hare is a fictitious pub… I wish it wasn't, so someone please open one just like it, you have my permission to use the name. Hasn't been the same since the Triple Crown on SMB closed.

❀ Created with Vellum

DEDICATION

This one's for my dear Dad.
There's a gaping hole in the world, and my life, since he's been gone. A
truly beautiful soul. His influence and example filled my life, and the
pages of my books.

Tony Harvey 1935 - 2019

1

JULY 1974

The bow of the wreck loomed from the edge of visibility like an industrial monster climbing from the depths of the ocean. The first sight of the vessel took Whitey Snow's breath away. Although he had made the dive several times before, it always took his breath away. Unmarked and rarely dived, the 120' freighter had begun accumulating signs of colourful coral growth during her first year on the sea floor. Resting perfectly upright, facing the west end of Grand Cayman, the top of the bow was 70' down; her stern was much deeper as the reef sloped steeply away. Approaching the bow, Whitey barely finned, with the strong current carrying him closer to the wreck as he continued deeper. The wreck of the Raptor was a thrilling challenge; a dive to savour, and marvel at its grandeur. But not for Whitey. Not today.

Glancing up through the gin-clear water, he made sure the small boat at the surface was following his bubbles before he cleared the bow, crossed over the forward deck, and descended into the vast, vacant space of the open cargo hold. Finally sheltered from the current, he kicked briskly, continuing deeper until he reached the floor of the hold, with the superstructure towering overhead. Before him, a door lay half open, wedged so by a steel crowbar.

Whitey checked his tank pressure gauge and the time on his watch before taking a settling breath and slipping through the narrow opening into the dark belly of the ghost ship.

The engine room was alive with shadows cast from the trickle of ambient light leaking in through the door, and a multitude of small fish scattered from the noisy, bubble-blowing creature invading their home. Whitey flicked the switch on his unwieldy Dive Bright aluminium-bodied lantern and illuminated the big diesel engine that once propelled the Raptor. The room was cramped with no space given for a six-foot diver to manoeuvre easily amongst the various pipes and lines extending through the ceiling. Without delay, he gently kicked his Voit fins to glide over the top of the engine, between the lines, and reach the port side of the diesel. Whitey flashed his lantern along the side of the algae-covered metal block until he located an oil filter housing with a clean-looking filter attached. Reaching down, he tried turning the filter with his free hand, but it wouldn't budge. Surprised, as it hadn't been long since his last visit, he repositioned, hanging over the side of the motor to gain a better purchase. He tried the filter again with his long, lean, muscular arm. This time it gave and turned one revolution before dropping away from the housing.

The sudden jerk of the filter coming free stirred up silt and debris around him and movement caught his eye from below the old engine. He froze as a five-foot green moray eel brushed against his bare leg, wriggling its way around him and across the engine room to find quieter refuge. Whitey sucked a few hard breaths through his state-of-the-art Aqualung Alizé single-hose regulator before returning his attention to the filter. Shining the light inside revealed a rag wadded up where the filter element used to live. Resting the light on the top of the engine he freed up his hand to carefully retrieve the cloth. He cautiously set the filter down next to the lantern. It required both hands to unfurl the rag, which contained a thick, greasy mess. Dipping a finger inside the axle grease, he hooked out a small object and used the edges of the rag to wipe it clean. Whitey paused and looked at the silver-coloured key, illuminated by the beam from his lantern. All the plans he'd carefully devised, the plans he'd been sure to be foolproof, were now crashing down around him like a sandcastle at high tide. He'd had two options, as best he'd seen it: die on the boat above by refusing to dive, or die later that day after making the dive. Later seemed the better choice, even if he was simply prolonging the inevitable. They were a long way from shore with currents too strong for him to sneak away underwater; besides, Ainsley was on the boat. He couldn't abandon his best mate, even if it meant he was returning to the surface to meet his maker. At least they'd die together. Just like his shipmates in the war, they'd rather have died together than alone. While he still breathed there was always a glimmer of hope. He thought about replacing the filter but what was the point? He smiled to himself at the irony and, clutching the key, he half pulled, half finned his way back to the door.

The bright glare from the Caribbean sun at the surface made him squint and blink through his oval-shaped mask as his eyes readjusted once clear of the door. Whitey switched off his bulky dive light and scanned the surface for Ainsley's boat. The super-structure of cabins and wheelhouse partially obscured his view, so he began to ascend out of the cargo hold into more open water. At 75' he paused again, kicking to hold position against the current; he rotated 360 degrees, searching the surface. Nothing. Had they abandoned him out here? That made no sense, he had the key. He swung around again, looking up, and suddenly stopped when he made out something floating on the surface, above the stern of the Raptor. It was clearly the outline of a body, dancing slowly with the rhythm of the gentle surface waves. A dark cloud spread away from the body like a ghastly fog and curious fish were circling below, eagerly taking an interest. The sight of the body paralysed Whitey. As much as he'd known this day would almost certainly be his last, the immediacy of someone else's brutal demise was a sharp reality that struck home. Who was it? It had to be one of two people; he could only pray it wasn't his best friend. And where was the damn boat? He swam up farther and desperately searched the waters around him. As he rose to see over the wheelhouse of the wreck, a second sight halted him, and his breathing. He found Ainsley's boat. Slowly descending beyond the stern of the wrecked freighter, the 25' cuddy cabin was disappearing from view, carried away by the currents towards the drop-off, and a long journey down to the sea floor more than a thousand feet below.

2

NOVEMBER 2019

Strings of colourful lights enveloped the perimeter of the backyard, strung from shrub to tree to shrub before finally reaching the bungalow on each side. Eighties English music played loudly, but the sound of the crowd's laughter and chatter still overwhelmed Culture Club's best efforts. Reg Moore sipped from a glass of Scotch whisky over ice, a glow of perspiration on his forehead from the balmy Cayman evening. He scowled at his wife, Pearl.

"I can't take much more of this bloody music," he shouted.

Pearl chuckled and looked up at the broad-shouldered man with his scruffy grey beard and mop of salt-and-pepper hair.

"You'll manage, she'll only turn thirty once; we can probably wait ten years to do this again."

He shook his head but couldn't help a grin creeping across his face as he looked down at the woman he adored. After fifty-seven laps around the sun, she used some product to keep her wavy hair blonde, and she carried a few more pounds than when they married thirty-four years ago. But she was as beautiful as ever, her voluptuous figure still stopped traffic and he loved the fact she'd always been oblivious to the effect she had on men. Except for Reg.

He made sure she knew the effect she'd always had on him. He leaned down and kissed her forehead.

A young, tall, lean Caymanian man pushed through the crowd and halted abruptly in front of Reg and Pearl.

"Boss, it's time, don't you think? Can we give her her present now?" His accented voice burst with enthusiasm matched by the expression on his sweaty face.

Reg grinned and nodded, "Alright Thomas, get someone to turn down this shitty music. I'll go get it."

Thomas left as keenly as he'd arrived, and before Reg had reached the back door to the house, the music volume turned down and the crowd noise lessened as they sensed something happening.

Pearl called out, "AJ? Where's the birthday girl?!"

Shouts and cheers gave away her location and Pearl burrowed her way through the crowd in that direction. Her diminutive size made it impossible to see over anyone, but soon an opening appeared, and AJ Bailey was reluctantly held in the middle by Thomas and AJ's boyfriend Jackson.

"There you are!" Pearl laughed.

"You sneaky buggers are killing me, you know I hate all this fuss." AJ's pretty face looked flushed from a mixture of drinks, dancing and embarrassment. In jean shorts and a tank top, with a toned and tanned, slender figure, she didn't look like a woman who'd grown up on the Sussex coast of England. Purple streaks highlighted her short blonde hair and tattoos adorning both arms made her look more like a pop star than the daughter of a barrister and company CEO.

Reg easily split the crowd, his big frame parting the seas like a warship and his deep voice hushing the cheers.

"Alright you lot, quieten down, we're gonna really embarrass her now."

After some laughter, the group grew silent and Pearl put her arm around AJ. Reg fumbled with his words to start – he was not a man given to speeches.

"You lot know this girl means the world to Pearl and me. Not having brats of our own, she's the closest thing we've got..." He clenched his teeth to keep a tear from giving away his emotion that everyone could see anyway.

"Anyway, her mum and dad, who couldn't make it over tonight, got together with Pearl and I, and young Thomas here, and got her something special to help her get over the fact she's turning thirty and is officially summiting the hill, if not going over it."

Laughing, he presented a small, brightly wrapped gift box to AJ, who did have tears on her cheeks. She took the box and threw her arms around Reg, giving him a big hug to a cheer from the crowd.

Releasing him she studied the box. "Thanks Reg, touching speech, up to the hill part." She smirked at him.

"Well open it!" Pearl urged.

AJ tore into the wrapping paper to reveal a cream-coloured cardboard sleeve with a gold crown on it. She slid the sleeve aside and held a green case with a smaller gold crown emblazoned on it.

"Bloody hell," she whispered to herself as she opened the hinged lid of the box.

A shiny Rolex Submariner watch glistened up at her with silver and gold band and traditional blue face.

"We knew you'd never buy anything like this for yourself and figured it was a good way to remind you of your incredible accomplishment finding the U-1026," Reg said softly, his face beaming with pride.

AJ stood speechless, staring at the gorgeous watch as Thomas stepped forward holding a mobile phone out in front of him. On the screen were Beryl and Bob Bailey, AJ's parents.

"Do you like it my love?" Bob smiled through the Internet video call.

AJ looked up, not having noticed the phone before, and stammered through tears, taking the phone in her other hand.

"This is beautiful, Dad. It's too much, you guys..." She looked around at everyone staring at her. "You shouldn't have, but this is the coolest thing ever!"

Her mum leaned a little closer to the phone on their end as though it would bring her closer to her little girl. "Take it out and look at the back."

AJ handed the phone back to Thomas so she could free up her hand and remove the watch from the plush, cushioned box.

"What time is it there? It must be three in the morning!" she asked as she removed the watch and turned it over to see the back of the case.

"It is, but this is worth it," her mum whispered.

Inscribed in the case were the words 'From U-1026 with Love'.

AJ shook her head slowly in disbelief. Handing the box off to Pearl, she slipped the watch over her hand and clasped its bulky weight to her wrist.

"This week we dive the sub – I can take the watch down to see her."

3

MARCH 1974

The view from the full-length windows of the living room extended across Huánuco to the beautiful mountains bordering the city. From where the sprawling house and grounds nestled in the foothills of the opposing mountains, the Río Huallaga could be clearly seen winding its way through the middle of the long narrow town in the valley. The morning sun set the mountains alight with a rich golden glow and glistened off the river where the waters followed the valley in a slow arc east. At 6,275 feet above sea level, the city had a surprisingly moderate climate, with warm days, cool nights, and a refreshing breeze running through the valley. Late summer in the southern hemisphere meant the peaks in the distance were clear of the long-present winter snow.

Whitey sipped his lemonade the housekeeper had insisted on making him from fresh lemons, and admired the view some more. He would turn forty-seven later this year and despite being incredibly fit and lean for his age, the travelling still wore him out more than it used to. He'd started at Grand Cayman's Owen Roberts airport, hopped to Kingston, Jamaica, which at least was a small jet these days instead of the old twin prop. After a day in Jamaica, he'd flown to Miami, Florida, where he could get a non-stop to Lima, Peru. From Lima it was a small prop plane that had brought him into Huánuco the previous night for a few hours' rest before the car picked him up to bring him to the Caveros' estate that morning. Whitey had been working for Mariano Cavero for a few years, but he still got a small knot in his stomach each time he met the imposing man. At 5' 7" and seventy years old, the Peruvian wasn't physically imposing, but he carried an aura of power and strength that made him the centre of attention in any room. When he walked in, whether it was in his own home or a large restaurant, heads turned and conversation lowered. A presence entered the room, and everyone felt it.

A deep, cheerful voice boomed from across the living room and surprised Whitey.

"Good morning my friend," Mariano bellowed in Spanish.

Wearing white linen pants and a beige cotton dress shirt, Mariano strode across the expansive room with his arms outstretched, looking like he was welcoming a movie star aboard his yacht. Whitey smiled and managed to put his glass down before he was bear hugged. Mariano released him and slapped him on the shoulder.

"Whitey, so good to see you. Lucía made you a drink I see – are you hungry? She can fix you some breakfast?"

Whitey held up his hands as the man assaulted him with offerings. "No, please Señor Cavero, I had breakfast, I'm good," he replied in fluent Spanish, despite his strong London accent.

"Then let's sit on the veranda and talk, it's a beautiful morning."

Mariano ushered the Englishman out of a door to the covered veranda off the living room, and they settled into a pair of wicker chairs. Lucía appeared out of nowhere, replenished Whitey's lemonade, and placed two coffees on the table between them.

Mariano nodded in her direction before speaking, "Gabriel will be sad he missed your visit, he's with his brother in the northern valley taking care of some things for me."

Whitey's connection to the family had come through Gabriel, and although they were fifteen years apart in age, he'd become firm friends with Mariano's son. He certainly felt more comfortable when Gabby was present for these meetings.

"Next time hopefully. We talked about taking a week in the Caribbean somewhere but we've both been too busy," Whitey replied.

Mariano laughed heartily. "Good, it means you're both making me money! You'll have plenty of time for beaches and girls, and plenty of money to spend on them. All in good time."

"So, let us talk business my friend, what did you learn on this trip?" Mariano continued, his tone turning serious.

Whitey took a sip of coffee, hoping the caffeine from the strong Peruvian beans would sharpen his tired mind; he knew what was riding on this conversation.

"As we thought, Jamaica is a mess, the PNP are supported by Castro and the Russians and it's rumoured the CIA are funding the JLP to counter. Both sides are paying groups and gangs to press the voters their way, and there's going to be more protests and uprisings, like they had in the sixties." Whitey knew this wasn't necessarily how they both thought, but he needed to use all the subtle persuasions he could.

Mariano frowned and nodded so Whitey continued, "The Cayman Islands are much more interesting; as you know, they ditched the Jamaican dollar in favour of their own currency two years ago, and in April it will be locked to the US dollar. That's when it gets really useful: it's rate will be 1.2 to 1."

Mariano held up a hand, "1.2 Cayman dollar buys one US? That's not so good."

Whitey leaned over. "No, 1.2 US dollars for one Caymanian."

The old man grinned and nodded slowly. "Okay, okay, that's strong." His expression changed, his grin fading. "But how stable are the islands? They're so close to Cuba, Castro could take them in a heartbeat; what's to stop them ending up like Jamaica?"

Whitey managed a confident smile. "No way Castro makes a move, they're a British sovereignty island. Cuba invades, the British defend, and the Americans are just dying to get involved. Castro isn't that crazy. The islands are politically stable, there's no unrest from the people, and everyone is pulling their cash from the Bahamas and Jamaica and moving it to Cayman."

Whitey leaned in farther. "They dropped all their government restrictions on amounts of money in and out, it's wide open. Best of all, they're not corrupt, the government is straight up; they just want to establish themselves as a financial destination."

Mariano laughed. "I don't know I can trust anywhere that's not a little corrupt. How do we buy off the officials?"

"We don't need to!" Whitey countered. "That's part of the beauty, we don't have to drop a fortune paying off anyone."

"Really?" The Peruvian looked amazed.

"Well, we'll pay one local to help us facilitate everything, but it's nothing compared to how much we can move there. Besides, we don't have to launder any of it, zero loss, it's completely legitimate to bring all the cash we want to onto the island and walk right into the bank."

Mariano's eyes look concerned despite the smile on his face. "This friend, what does he do and how do we know we can trust him?"

Whitey sat back and tried to look relaxed. "He's a local I met in the war when we patrolled the islands, great guy, his family are all fishermen. He's made a living facilitating things, started by trading supplies to people like us Navy Jacks; since then he's run the weed import and knows everyone there. He knows who we need to avoid and who we can work with. He'll arrange a police escort from the airport to the bank."

Mariano howled with laughter and waved a hand in the air to interrupt Whitey. "You're kidding?" he cackled. "The police will escort our money to the bank and we don't have to pay them anything? What kind of place is this? This is like... what's Mickey Mouse's place?"

He tapped his finger loudly on the table and looked at Whitey for the answer.

"Disneyland?" Whitey offered.

Mariano roared with laughter, "Yes, yes. Disneyland! This island is like Disneyland!"

4

NOVEMBER 2019

Metallica's cover of Bob Seger's 'Turn the Page' raged from AJ's mobile phone propped on her bedside table. A hand appeared from under the covers, fumbled around frantically searching for the source of the disturbance, and hit buttons until the rock music stopped. A low groan emanated from the other side of the bed.

"No way is it morning yet," Jackson mumbled without moving.

"Barely," AJ managed in response, both still buried under the lightweight duvet.

After a lengthy silence, a slender leg kicked its way free of the sheets and landed clumsily on the floor. In an awkward rolling slide, the rest of Annabelle Jayne followed the leg and stood shakily rubbing her eyes and brushing her hair from her face.

"Today is going to suck," she predicted to no one in particular, and stumbled to the kitchen, which in her tiny apartment was about five steps from the bed.

"I don't want to leave," came Jackson's soft voice.

AJ hit the start button on the coffee maker and turned around, frowning.

"Noooo, I forgot you leave today. Tell them to wait a day. Or a week. Or a year."

Jackson laughed quietly. "I'll make a call."

The sheets shifted and AJ slid back under, wrapping her arms around her tall, American boyfriend.

"Best make sure I remember you properly then," she whispered in his ear.

The sun was starting to brighten the eastern sky as AJ plodded down the jetty next to West Bay dock. The Caribbean Sea was calm and smooth with a grey-blue tone in the breaking light. Mermaid Divers' thirty-six-foot Newton dive boat was already tied to the jetty cleats and Thomas's beaming smile lit up the dock as she approached.

"Good lord, Thomas, how the hell are you so damn chipper this morning? I can barely function," she complained.

Thomas just laughed. "Happy day after your birthday, Boss."

AJ stepped gingerly onto the boat and gave Thomas a quick hug.

"Thanks again for my watch, it's too much, and too much for you to contribute to." She let him go and smiled. "I know what I pay you and it's not enough to help buy fancy watches."

Thomas stepped up to the jetty. "Don't worry, I think my part bought the box it came in." He started towards the small hut they shared with Reg's Pearl Divers crew for storing paperwork and smaller items. "You settle in and drink your coffee, Boss; I'm going to grab some more waivers and greet some people as they arrive."

AJ dropped her rucksack on the console before she frantically grabbed it back up and scurried after Thomas. "Damn it! I forgot I'm supposed to pick up one lady from Harbour View by downtown."

She ran past him up the jetty toward her van.

"Want me to go get her?" Thomas shouted after her.

AJ waved him off as she opened the van door and flung her bag in. "No, I'll do it, it's better I explain I'm late on her first day."

With that, she fired up the fifteen-passenger van she used as her personal transport as well as the business shuttle vehicle, and sped out of the car park, turning right towards George Town.

Driving a little faster than she should, AJ took a long swig of coffee and a few deep breaths. Her head had a dullness and steady ache that spiked with noise, motion, and light. She was not a big drinker, so it didn't take a lot of alcohol to upset her system, and today her system was definitely upset. She decided she'd ask Thomas to do the first dive, as it would be deeper, and she'd do the second. Breathing off the clean, dry air of the scuba tank would actually make her feel better, and she looked forward to an hour of feeling better.

Her thoughts drifted to Jackson, which made her feel a warm tingle through her whole being. But he was leaving today; that made her head hurt again. Jackson worked on one of Sea Sentry's conservation, non-profit boats that had perfectly timed a fuel and provisions stop on Cayman on its way to South America. They were leaving port this morning and it left them both wondering when they'd be together again. Her chest felt like it was being squeezed of all air at the contemplation, similar to Reg's hugs. She wiped the wetness from her eyes as she pulled into a small, dirt car park off West Bay Road.

Striding towards her was a deeply tanned lady a few inches taller than AJ, but equally lean and muscular, despite being five to ten years older by AJ's best guess. She had black hair tied back in a practical ponytail, no discernible make-up, and AJ was relieved to notice she was being greeted with a warm smile. Jumping out, AJ met her at the back doors and the lady dropped her rucksack and buoyancy compensator device, the inflatable vest divers used, referred to as a BCD, in the van before extending a hand.

"Hello, I'm Hazel Delacroix, I assume you're Annabelle Jayne?" the women asked in a firm but friendly tone with a beautiful hint of a French accent.

For a second AJ was stunned by this gorgeous lady. Her confidence, her simple yet powerful beauty, and disarmingly relaxed manner.

"I am, but AJ, I go by AJ," she managed, "and I apologise for being a little late, we had a..." AJ thought through her fog for a moment, "function last night, and I'm one step behind myself this morning."

They got into the front seats of the van and Hazel smiled at AJ. "It's really no problem. I'm here to relax and enjoy the diving; time is not to be watched too closely."

AJ started the van, relieved her new client was amiable, especially today.

"Although, that's a lovely watch if you do need to know the time," Hazel nodded at the Rolex and winked.

AJ beamed. "Isn't it?"

5

APRIL 1974

A cooling breeze met Whitey as he paused at the top of the steps, a welcome relief after the stuffy, smoke-filled air of the flight. He cautiously surveyed the ramp area, clutching the Zero Halliburton aluminium attaché briefcase tightly in his left hand. A light-brown-skinned man in jeans and a white shirt waved enthusiastically from below where he stood next to a large American-made police car. Whitey tentatively waved back and made his way down the steps, the hot Caribbean sun reminding him he was still in the tropics despite the trade winds. His friend, Ainsley Bush, met him with a spirited handshake and a big smile.

"Welcome back to Cayman, man," he said in a Caymanian accent tinged with an American jive talk influence.

Whitey couldn't help being a little nervous. It seemed surreal to be greeted off the plane by a police car intending to escort you straight to the bank with your briefcase stuffed full of illicitly earned cash. He felt droplets of sweat careening down his back under his wide-collared paisley shirt.

"Good to see you Ainsley," he managed, peering into the police car where an officer politely nodded. Next to him in the other front seat was another man in a blazer and tie who eyed Whitey dispassionately.

"Who's the other bloke, Ainsley?"

Ainsley opened the back door of the car and ushered Whitey to get in. "He's customs, man, one-stop shop right here brother, no need to go through the building or nothing."

Whitey was just about to ask about his luggage when a man in a Cayman Airways uniform dropped his suitcase next to him. Surprised and still slightly dazed by the whole scene, he succumbed to Ainsley's urging, and got in the back of the police car. A place he generally tried to avoid. Ainsley popped the boot and tossed in the suitcase before sliding in the other side of the expansive car.

"Gentlemen, this is my good friend Whitey Snow..." Ainsley began as both men turned around from the front. "He's a respected businessman from the UK who's steered his South American clients to do their banking business here on our wonderful island."

The policeman, a dark-skinned man with a friendly face, just nodded again, and the customs official extended a hand.

"Welcome to the Cayman Islands, Mr Snow. May I trouble you for your passport so we can get you on your way?" The man smiled politely.

Whitey passed the man his British passport and glanced over his shoulder at the queue of arriving passengers stretching out the door of the unimposing low, blue building with a white tin roof. A small sign with red letters mounted over the door read 'Grand Cayman Owen Roberts Airport'.

"Thank you, Mr William Snow," the customs official announced, reading his given name before stamping a page and handing Whitey back his passport. "Enjoy your stay, sir." With that he exited the car and the policeman pulled away.

Ainsley grinned at Whitey and slapped his leg. "Relax my brother; everything is cool, man."

Once they pulled out onto the road that ran around the runway towards town, Whitey started to relax.

"Did you get me a room, mate?" he asked.

"Of course, man, ocean view in the Holiday Inn right on the beach. Wait till you see the view by the pool, man." Ainsley beamed, winking.

Whitey grinned. "Plenty of time for that, mate. Let's get this safely tucked away first, eh?" He tapped on the briefcase.

"Sure thing, man. Dwayne here is heading to the Cayman International Bank and Trust, ain't you Dwayne?" Ainsley indicated the policeman, who nodded amiably once again.

Whitey brushed his moustache, the nerves of the first entry into the country behind him; now another wave of concern took over. When he'd thought over his plan for weeks on end, it all seemed simple and easy. Now that he was here and about to take a risk that would undoubtedly cost him his life if it went awry, it felt overwhelmingly real. The Caveros weren't people you crossed, but they were also fickle in their use of key employees outside the family. Whitey had seen what they did to men they simply suspected of doing them wrong. He needed an insurance policy, and if this played out right, he'd have his.

The police car pulled up outside a modern building two streets inland from George Town harbour. An expensive sign on the building spelt out the name of the financial institution. Whitey looked around. On the same small street he could see a dozen more buildings with similar signs. The financial industry was certainly booming on the little island.

Dwayne the policeman finally spoke. "You gentlemen good from here?" he offered in a deep, smooth Caymanian accent. Whitey wondered if he was the island's version of Barry White.

"Thanks Dwayne, tell Barbara I'll be by for some conch gumbo this weekend," Ainsley replied as he stepped out of the car and waved to Whitey to follow.

"Are you sure this is secure Ainsley?" Whitey asked, clutching the case and looking around them.

Ainsley laughed and Dwayne didn't try very hard to hide a

smirk. "Dwayne, what's the big-time crime you've busted anyone for this year?"

"Had to lock up ole man Tibbetts last week, you know the weird uncle on Miss Celia's side. Got himself all liquored up and couldn't understand why his key wouldn't open his front door," Dwayne chuckled. "Scared the hell outta Mrs Wainwright, who's house it actually was. That about the biggest bust, couple of traffic tickets."

"Get out of the car, Whitey. Unless some pirate's rising from the grave, ain't no one on this island gonna mess with you." Ainsley flashed his white teeth in his almost permanent smile.

Whitey, still not completely convinced, got out of the car and thanked Dwayne before closing the door. He followed Ainsley inside the bank where across the reception two nicely dressed female tellers smiled at them from behind their counter. Ainsley led him to the side where several offices had open doors.

"Well good mornin' Sheila," he greeted a lady with an impressive afro in the first office. "Have my man here I told you about, needs some special attention from a special bank lady." Ainsley laid on the charm like treacle.

Sheila shook her head as she stood and extended a hand to Whitey. "Despite you associating with this fellow, we're happy to have you come bank with us, Mr...?"

Whitey accepted her firm handshake. "Whitey, Whitey Snow."

She grinned at his name. "Well, Mr Snow, how can I be of assistance?"

"Needs to open an account, has a cash deposit to get things rolling," Ainsley enthusiastically explained.

"Well, actually, slight change of plan," Whitey smiled sheepishly at his friend. "Do you have safe deposit boxes Sheila?"

Ainsley looked surprised but Sheila nodded approvingly. "Of course, Mr Snow, what size box do you need?"

"Pretty big I reckon," Whitey replied.

6

NOVEMBER 2019

AJ helped Hazel hand her gear over to Thomas on the boat and greeted the rest of the divers who'd arrived while she was gone. Beth and David Freeman were an older couple from New England who had been coming to Cayman for forty years. The Davises, from Ohio, were a family of four and the parents, Maggie and Bill, had been at AJ's party the night before. They looked a little less chipper than usual. AJ had certified their two teenage daughters a year ago and they were raring to go diving. The eighth diver was Ray Blackburn, an Englishman who lived on island and a keen photographer. He often joined them for an occasional boat trip, especially if AJ had one spot open and gave him the local's rate.

After everyone was introduced and gear was stowed, AJ cast the lines off and Thomas eased the Newton away from the jetty.

"Where does everyone feel like going this morning?" AJ asked, mustering an eager smile.

"Back to bed honestly," Bill answered with a chuckle.

His wife nudged him and both girls rolled their eyes.

Beth Freeman shrugged her shoulders and spoke softly, "We'd be happy doing two shallow dives if that helps?"

Ray Blackburn added, "Light's better for me shallow – I'm good with it."

AJ surveyed the group lest anyone looked perturbed. It was standard practice to do one deep dive to around a hundred feet then a shallow second dive to less than sixty. Cayman's steep drop-off around the island made it easy to do a wall dive, then move to the reef that filled much of the area between the drop-off and twenty-feet-deep water.

"If everyone's okay with that, we'll do two longer shallow dives then," AJ announced, checking again for any complaints and seeing none. "Great, let's start at Three Trees, that's always a good one."

Thomas nodded from the fly bridge and eased the throttle forward on the Newton.

AJ decided she would take the first dive after all as they were staying shallow, hoping the dry, tank air would clear her head. She sat next to Hazel who had already set up her gear as they motored towards the dive site.

"Are you sure you're okay doing two shallows? Don't want you to be disappointed on your first day."

Hazel smiled. "It's probably better for me. I haven't been in the water for a few months and I've never been here so safer to stay shallow to start."

AJ studied her face as she spoke; the woman was so beautiful. A classic, subtle beauty that seemed more striking the closer you looked. Her movements and mannerisms exuded confidence. She'd assembled her BCD and regulator on a tank quickly and efficiently before AJ or Thomas could offer to help. But there was something in her eyes that AJ couldn't pinpoint, a sadness or troubled look despite her smile and warm demeanour.

AJ realised she was staring at the woman and quickly found something to say. "You'll enjoy this dive, it's a beautiful part of the reef with lots of life. Where do you normally dive? You live in southern France, right?"

Hazel slipped on a pair of sunglasses before replying, "Yes, I live in a town called Fréjus, it's between Marseilles and Nice on the

Côte d'Azur; no one outside France has heard of it but it's a really old port town with a lot of historical buildings and ruins. I love it there."

"Can you dive off the coast there? I've dived in the Greek islands but never in France," AJ asked.

"Oh yes, it's fantastic diving, we have many small islands along the coast like Hyères and the Port-Cros National Park. Then there's Corsica, of course, which you can reach by ferry from Nice in about five or six hours, so it's good for weekend trips," Hazel replied, her enthusiasm building as she spoke of her home. "But the wrecks…" she waved her hands and shook her head. "We have the best wreck diving, so many, we have war wrecks and ancient wrecks, and…" She slipped her sunglasses back off. "Have you heard of the Rubis?"

"Yes, yes, the submarine, right?" AJ remembered excitedly, the others on the boat now listening to the women's animated conversation.

"That's right, it was a French sub used in World War Two and sunk for sonar practice after they retired it, I think in the early fifties. It's off Saint-Tropez area. It is magnificent. Strong currents and deep, so it is not for beginners but you have to see this wreck. It's at forty metres." Hazel paused to convert the number.

"About a hundred and thirty feet or so," AJ interjected. "I speak both systems." She laughed.

"Yes, of course, so it's deep, but so worth it. Perfectly upright and still in pretty good condition, although the deck is collapsing on top of the pressure hull. It's not safe to go inside, although there are open compartments you can look in and still see instruments and controls." Hazel took hold of AJ's arm. "Like your submarine here I suspect?" she blurted.

"It sounds similar," AJ agreed. "Ours is a bit further off the coast but only a few years different in sinking."

Hazel shook her head. "Oh, I would love to dive your sub, that would be incredible," she uttered softly.

"We go out there once a month but there's quite a wait list I'm afraid," AJ said sympathetically.

"Maybe another trip and I'll plan ahead more." Hazel smiled. "But you have other wrecks here too, yes?"

AJ stood up as Thomas eased back on the throttle, indicating they were approaching the dive site.

"Of course, we have some wonderful wrecks here – how long are you staying for?"

"A week or two," Hazel replied casually.

AJ hopped up on the side of the boat, making her way to the front to tie into the mooring. "We can dive them all if you stay for two weeks."

7

APRIL 1974

Whitey lay back in the lounger, let out a long sigh, and finally felt he could relax. The pool at the Holiday Inn wrapped around in a curving pattern, forming an island in the centre, where a palapa housed the outside bar. Three arched footbridges gave access to the bar or you could step from the pool itself. Beyond a low brick wall, the white sand beach stretched fifty yards to the edge of the Caribbean Sea, its light blue and teal water glistening and sparkling in the afternoon sun. A radio station played music from speakers at the bar. 'The Air That I Breathe' by The Hollies sounded strangely out of place on the tropical island, a contrast to the usual calypso and reggae.

Whitey turned and smiled at Ainsley, who looked as relaxed as he always did on the lounger next to him. "This doesn't get old, mate."

Ainsley beamed back. "No man, lived here my whole life and can't ever say I'm tired of it."

A shadow moved over Whitey, screening him from the sun, and a soft voice spoke in a friendly, accented tone.

"Can I get you gentlemen a drink from the bar?"

Whitey peered through his Ray-Ban Ambermatic Aviator

sunglasses as the lenses adjusted their tint to the change in light. Before him, tray in hand, stood a pretty, tanned woman with long black hair and strikingly big green eyes. He'd noticed the red miniskirts and form-fitting frilly white tops on the waitresses, but this girl made the outfit look exceptional.

"I would like a drink my dear, thank you." He turned towards Ainsley. "What you having, mate?"

Ainsley had sat up and was leering at the waitress like he was new to the female species. "Red Stripe... please," he mumbled.

Whitey turned back to the woman who was waiting patiently. "Havana Club over ice for me please." He tipped his sunglasses down his nose to allow her to see his piercing blue eyes. "May I know your name as you're taking such good care of us?"

She smiled warmly and her cheeks flushed almost imperceptibly. "Isabella, but most people call me Izzie."

Whitey nodded and returned the smile. "Well I'm not most people and I love your name, so I'll call you Isabella if that's okay?"

She grinned. "I don't mind at all."

Whitey extended a hand, subtly flexing his chest and arm a little to accentuate his athletic physique.

"Very nice to meet you Isabella, my name's Whitey, and this is my friend Ainsley." Neither of them looked Ainsley's way, who continued gawking from his lounger.

She shook his hand, her eyes momentarily flicking from his face to his shirtless chest before returning to his eyes. "Nice to meet you too," she said softly, deftly balancing the tray while shaking hands. "I'll get your drinks for you," she added and turned, walking away with a gentle sway to her walk.

Whitey relaxed into his lounger and pushed his glasses back up his nose nonchalantly. From the corner of his eye he carefully watched her saunter to the palapa with a final glance back over at him as she reached it. She did everything with grace and subtlety, not the giggly, clumsiness of a flirting teenager, and he liked that. He guessed she was probably in her late twenties, and the accent was Hispanic, but not the South American he'd become used to in Peru.

"Man, she really dug us, brother," Ainsley observed as he sank back in his lounger. Whitey grinned and was surprised Ainsley wasn't wiping drool off his face.

Women had never been a problem for Whitey Snow. From a young age he'd discovered his good looks and fun-loving personality made him popular with the girls, and a guy other guys liked to hang out with. He joined the Royal Navy as soon as he was old enough in 1945, only a few months before hostilities ceased in Europe. He was one of the few they kept around, and he did eight years before deciding he'd had enough of bouncing around the world on grey ships. Too many ports of call held more interest than he could satisfy on a brief stop, so at age 26 he shed the uniform and headed to Thailand, a place he'd become enthralled with. Living was cheap, women were plentiful, and Whitey found his talent for trading smokes and liquor in the service made a lot more money in the free market.

"You got a boat, Ainsley?" Whitey changed the subject.

"A boat? Of course I got a boat, we're on an island brother, everybody's got a boat."

Whitey laughed. "Okay, so where do you keep your boat?"

"Near town, it's moored overnight just off the beach," Ainsley replied.

"What does this boat of yours do all day then?" Whitey asked curiously.

Ainsley hesitated a moment. "Well, it's actually my brother's boat, so it's out fishing during the morning."

Whitey laughed again. "I see, so if we wanted to go diving, would your brother let us take this boat, that everyone on the island has, except you."

Ainsley scoffed. "Man, it's the family boat, every family on the island has a boat. Of course I can use it, just gotta go out when he's done fishing. Or on Sunday, he don't fish on Sunday."

"Perfect, cos we're going diving," Whitey added.

"Diving? Like under the water?" Ainsley sat up.

"Yeah, you know, scuba diving." Whitey looked at his friend. "You never been diving? This place is supposed to be the best diving in the western hemisphere."

Ainsley shook his head animatedly. "Hell no I never been diving man, that ain't right, we need air and the air's up here not down there. I'll take you out on the boat but I ain't doing no diving, man."

Whitey laughed incredulously. "That's funny Ainsley, that's like living in the Alps and hating skiing."

Ainsley lay back down shaking his head. "I ain't skiing neither. I'm a Caymanian, brother, we don't do snow."

8

NOVEMBER 2019

The morning sun lit up the reef like a Monet painting and the residents cruised, darted, and hovered about, in a scene akin to a bustling metropolis. The divers descended amongst the throng of activity, and AJ led the group to a crack in the reef forming a sandy-bottomed ravine running towards deeper water. Comfortably wide enough for the divers, she dropped in and gently finned her way forward so the others could follow. Several squirrelfish peered at her from crevices and the long antennae of a lobster probed the water, sensing the movement near its hideout. AJ pointed out the interesting critters so her train of divers would see them too. The ravine widened slightly and the coral to her right had grown over the opening, forming a ledge that overhung the sandy floor. Lying on the sand in the shallow shelter of the ledge was the sleek, mottled-brown figure of a six-foot nurse shark. Contrary to popular belief, many sharks do not have to continually move to keep oxygen-rich water passing over their gills. The nurse shark pumps water through its gills to get the necessary oxygen, and AJ carefully pointed at the flaring gills as they fluttered and moved the water, stirring up a little sand with each pulse. The big, boneless fish watched the passing divers carefully with its beady little eyes, but seemed unthreatened, and certainly not keen on giving up her favourite resting spot.

The ravine opened to a sandy expanse at the end of the coral finger, and AJ allowed the group to gather next to her. In the sandy flats all appeared still except for a few tilefish hovering above their constructed dens and a bed of garden eels waving like strands of hay in the wind. AJ held up her hand to hold the group stationary before finning softly forward about four feet off the sea floor. She paused over an open section of sand, its surface textured in subtle waves by the ebbing tides. Moving slowly, she extended a hand down and pointed at the surface, which appeared to be nothing more than the sandy sea floor. Soon the group began to notice what she was pointing out. An eyeball flicked and moved around, taking in its surroundings, its owner wondering why this noisy, bubble-exuding critter was hanging over its piece of the ocean. AJ eased away to leave it in peace and finned back to the group. As she reached them, the sand all around the eyeball raised up and the stingray, deciding to move on anyway, raised its large flat body with a ripple of its wings, sending sand cascading in waves to settle back on the floor. The grey figure with its long, slim tail glided away to hunt molluscs in another part of the ocean off Seven Mile Beach.

Moving to another coral finger, staying at around thirty-five feet, AJ slowly finned over the reef. Bright yellow tube sponges sprouted in chubby protrusions from several coral heads and AJ scoured the waters in search of something. Rolling on her back and scanning the surface, she found what she was looking for. Pointing through the crystal-clear water towards the sky, she directed the group to the hawksbill turtle taking a few breaths on the surface. The turtle, with its beautifully coloured shell, was at its most vulnerable when grabbing a breath. It used to be from hunters taking the turtles for their meat and shell, a trade the Caymans had been famous for, but now it was from boat traffic. AJ signalled for the group to wait and pointed to the abundant yellow sponges around them. The turtle soon ducked his head below and began swimming awkwardly back down to the reef to continue feeding. Choosing a large clump of yellow tube sponges, he wrapped his flippers around them, using a claw on each flipper to gain a firm grip, before taking a bite from the sponge with his powerful beak. Tiny shards wafted in a cloud around the turtle as he crunched on his breakfast in loud chomps that could easily be heard underwater. The clean-up crew of coral eaters soon swooped in and made short work of the floating crumbs, before the turtle bit down again and removed another chunk.

Ray didn't miss a beat with his camera and added some close-up turtle shots to his stingray-in-flight and resting-nurse-shark collection. The Davis kids did well staying back a bit as they swam about excitedly. AJ made a mental note to remind them not use their hands as they moved through the water. The Freemans calmly observed as always; experienced and wise, they were happy to hang back and let the newer divers get in close, while they conserved their energy and air. They usually surfaced after a long dive with enough air to do a second dive. AJ quietly watched Hazel. She was as graceful in the water as she was above, and moved with polished ease and minimal effort. AJ had noticed she'd pointed out several interesting fish to Ray and had patiently stayed close while he photographed them, taking her assigned dive buddy role seriously. From the way she moved in the water with perfect buoyancy, maintaining her depth effortlessly, and from the gentle stream of bubbles exhaled in a regular, relaxed timing, AJ could tell she was experienced and comfortable.

The hour passed quickly with so much to see, and AJ signalled for the group to begin their ascent, with a three-minute pause at fifteen feet to allow some of the excess nitrogen to work out of their systems. She'd planned to take the second dive, but since both were shallow, she had taken lead on the first, and would let Thomas guide the next one. Breathing from the dry, clean air of the Scuba tank helped clear her head, and for the past sixty minutes she'd forgotten the hangover that had dulled her morning. She looked around at her customers and friends hanging in the water while the three minutes ticked away. All were still and relaxed; even the Davis kids took example from the others and floated motionless, looking down at the reef below for a last glimpse of a rare or interesting critter. AJ felt a warm glow of satisfaction radiate throughout her body and pictured a soft wave of positive energy emanate away into the Caribbean Sea. In these moments she was consumed by the realisation of how fortunate she was.

9

APRIL 1974

Ainsley steered his bright red 1972 Ford Capri Mk1 3000 GXL along North Church Street with the ocean on their right, and thick mangroves and an occasional home on their left. Ainsley tapped out the beat to 'Radar Love' by Golden Earring that played from the car radio. With the windows down, the fresh breeze helped offset the morning heat and Whitey tried not to stick to the black leather seats.

"Honestly mate, what good is this fancy car, here on the island?" he asked his friend, wiping the sweat from his forehead.

Ainsley looked at him as though he'd insulted his mother's honour. "It's a three-litre Capri man, do you know how much it cost me to bring this beauty over from the UK?"

Whitey laughed. "Exactly my point mate, and where on the island can you give this flashy car a real run?"

Ainsley shook his head. "That's not the point Whitey, it's the coolest car on the island man; this beauty pulls skirt like you wouldn't believe."

Whitey smiled and shook his head. "Bloody poser."

Ainsley pulled the Capri into the car park of a white-painted building on the water. A sign on the second floor advertised it was the Lobster Pot restaurant; downstairs displayed it was Bob Soto's Dive Shop.

"Here you go man, Soto's, anything to be known about diving on the island this man knows, started the whole diving thing here," Ainsley effused.

They walked through the propped-open door into the dive shop where a young, tanned man in a tank top and snug shorts looked up from behind the counter. Whitey glanced around at displays of masks, snorkels, various horse collar-style flotation jackets, and some of the new buoyancy compensating packs. Posters on the wall touted products from Aqualung, At-Pac and Scubapro.

"G'day fellas," the man behind the counter greeted them in a thick Australian accent, flicking his long, wavy blond hair from his face.

"My good friend here has a few questions about diving on our fine island, so I brought him here and told him you guys know everything there is to know about that!" Ainsley proclaimed with a big smile.

"Well, we dive in the water rather than on the island, but yeah, I should be able to help you fellas," the man replied with a smirk, looking at Ainsley warily.

Ainsley lost the smile. "Is Bob around man?"

The Aussie shook his head. "Nah, Bob's travelling at the moment." He turned his attention to Whitey. "What can I help you with, mate?"

Ainsley gave up and wandered off to pretend to be interested in looking at dive gear, unimpressed with the man's lack of enthusiasm for his own enthusiasm.

"I'd like to know a bit more about your dive sites, especially wrecks. I'll be visiting here frequently, and I'd like to dive some wrecks," Whitey asked nonchalantly.

"Well, as you probably know we're known for our reefs here, but we've got some ace wrecks as well." He turned and pointed out the double doors open to the water. "Got two right out here mate: the Balboa and the Cali are real shallow, blown apart so they're scattered wreckage but ripper dives." He grabbed a map of the island and laid it on the countertop. "If you're up for more of an adventure there's a new wreck just went down over the winter." He pointed to a spot off the north-west corner of the island. "Here, it's a cargo ship, over a hundred feet long, sitting at a depth of eighty feet or so."

Whitey looked at the spot on the map. "That sounds interesting, gotta be pretty popular, a new wreck like that?"

The man shook his head. "Not really. Like I said, you gotta be up for an adventure, currents are strong where it's sitting near the drop-off. We'll only take hardcore guys out there. What's your experience level?"

Whitey smiled politely. "Navy, some salvage work, bunch of diving in the South Pacific and Australia. I'd be fine."

"Perfect mate, she'd be all right then, want me to sign you up?" The man grabbed a clipboard.

"Sure, when you going out there?"

"Usually we try and get at least six blokes to go, but I know there's a group of four been on about it so if I can sign them up, I'll schedule it and try and add a few more. That sound alright?"

Whitey nodded. "Yeah, that works for me, what's the name of this wreck anyway?"

"The Raptor." The Aussie paused from writing. "Crew abandoned it at anchor further round towards the north. They'd been avoiding coming in the harbour; seemed like they couldn't pay the fees or something. Next thing we know it's listing over. They sent out a tug, cut the anchor chain, and started towing her towards George Town, but only made it to the corner there." He tapped the map again. "Down she went right there mate, quick as you like – she dropped and landed upright on the deeper reef. Crew must have pulled her plug before they bailed. Two fingers up to their owners I reckon."

"Blimey, and she's upright you say?"

"Yup, sitting right there, but I tell you the currents are ripper man, they'll tear you off and take you out over the deep stuff." He slid his finger across the map away from the island. "So, what's the name for the booking mate?"

"Whitey, Whitey Snow. I need some gear too, I don't have my stuff with me."

The man's eyes lit up at the prospect of selling equipment along with a charter. "Bonzer, we got all the latest stuff, mate. I'm Curly by the way." He extended a hand across the counter.

Whitey shook his hand firmly and asked, "I heard about the new Scubapro buoyancy compensating packs, can you show me one of those?"

The Aussie quickly came around from the counter and pointed at a glass display case behind him on the way. "You betcha, and you gotta try Aqualung's new single-hose reg mate: top of the line, you'll totally dig it."

10

NOVEMBER 2019

Reg stepped from the pier onto the deck of Mermaid Divers' boat with two ice-cold Strongbow ciders in hand. AJ was just zipping up her rucksack ready to go and gladly took the drink from Reg.

"A little hair of the dog for ya," he said with a grin.

She sat down on one of the benches under the fly bridge and Reg took the other side.

"I'm just knackered now, I drank about five gallons of water, and breathing off the tank does wonders. A good night's sleep tonight and I'll be right as rain again," she said and took a gentle swig of the cider.

The bottle looked like a kid's toy in Reg's big paw, and his first swig drained half the contents. They both sat quietly for a few minutes as the boat bobbed gently against the jetty and the breeze eased the heat of the early afternoon sun.

"I'm bloody thirty, Reg," AJ finally blurted out.

He looked at her blankly. "So? You're a spring chicken, thirty's nothing girl."

AJ shook her head. "It's not nothing Reg, it's a big deal. Twenties are brilliant cos you're old enough to do what you want, but not too old to be expected to be completely responsible. Thirty is serious. I don't think I'm ready to be serious about very much. Plus all the marriage and baby rubbish – so much is expected of you in your thirties."

Reg chuckled, which sounded like a deep rumble you'd expect during an earthquake, his beard fluttering.

"What a load of nonsense. First of all, you've been responsible since I first knew you, when you were what? Sixteen?" AJ nodded and Reg continued, "Since then you've run dive boats for me, set up your own business, found a long-lost submarine, and helped save a whole reef system from two governments... if you think you've spent the last fourteen years being irresponsible I can't wait to see what happens when you get serious." He pointed his empty bottle at her and grinned.

AJ laughed. "I suppose, when you put it like that."

"Damn right," Reg added.

"But you know what I mean Reg, some birthdays are milestones and they mark a change, or at least an expected change."

"Are you saying someone expects you to get married? Cos I don't think your mum and dad do, and you know Pearl and I don't think like that. Bugger anyone else." He looked at her, puzzled.

"My mum would love to see me married, or at least settled down with a fella. Babies and all that. Pretty sure she still thinks I might be gay. I don't think she'd care if I was, but she hates the idea that she might not know everything about me. Guess it's the barrister in her." AJ put her empty bottle in the side of her rucksack to take off the boat and shrugged her shoulders. "My dad is pretty relaxed about it all. He'd really like Jackson, if they ever get to meet with everyone's crazy schedules."

"Pearl and I like that fella of yours a lot, if that means anything. It shouldn't really." Reg looked thoughtful. "It shouldn't matter what we think if you think he's right. But I'm just saying, we like him a lot, so if you do screw it up, we'll probably still have him by for tea and a chat." He tried to keep a straight face but couldn't manage it and they both laughed.

"Thanks Reg, thanks a ton."

"Look, here's the deal, age doesn't mean a damn, apart from two things." Reg leaned forward and held up a finger. "First, the older you get, the less time you have to do things that mean something." He held up a second finger. "And the second is, the older you get, the harder it is physically to do some of the things that mean something." Reg sat back and let AJ think about his words a moment.

"You've done a lot of things that have meant something Reg, I don't think you should worry about doing more," she finally said.

Reg shook his head and his mop of brown and grey hair wobbled about. "Maybe. We felt like we were doing good things in the Navy but who knows in the big scheme of things. After that, all the salvage stuff, I was involved in a few things that meant something, but mainly I helped other people make a lot of money. What we do now, training people to dive, and taking them diving, I think is a great thing. It's a magical world under there, as you well know, it transports you away from the mess the world is becoming. People need that escape. If it can help people clear their minds, simplify their thoughts, and see some of this madness for what it is, just a destructive waste of humanity, then I think we do something good."

AJ was surprised by Reg's speech. He usually kept his thoughts to himself, and a sentence was the most he spoke at any time. His passion was inspiring and made her feel good about what she did for a living.

"Well, I'm pretty sure you're gonna live until you're a hundred and fifty so you can keep on doing good things and straightening out people's minds, Reg," she said, chuckling.

He smiled. "I want to live one minute less than Pearl, that's all I ask. Selfish of me I know, but as fantastical as this world is, and as wonderful as my life is, it ain't worth a thing without that woman in it. Now, I hope that's a hundred and fifty years, but we'll see."

AJ shook her head and fought back a tear that threatened to roll down her cheek. "You romantic old buzzard," she mumbled.

He grinned and waved a hand. "Don't be accusing me of that crap now, you'll ruin my reputation."

"I miss Jackson, Reg. I think he might be the one I want to die a minute before," AJ said quietly.

Reg got up, moved over to her and gave her shoulder a tender squeeze. "I figured he might be," he said softly.

He then stepped from the boat to the pier and turned around, ducking down so he could look AJ in the eye with a wry grin on his face. "Just remember, either way, we're still having him over for tea."

11

APRIL 1974

Isabella Alonso had been on her feet since eight o'clock that morning, and after seven hours of walking back and forth on the concrete deck surrounding the pool, her favourite new platform sandals weren't as comfortable as they were stylish. The bartender was taking his time between serving guests and filling her next drink order, so she was glad of the break. This was her third year on the island and in some ways it felt like home, in others it seemed like a place to spend a few years and move on. Maybe it was working in a hotel where everyone was transitory, including most of the staff. With four years' experience working in a hotel in her seaside hometown of Mojácar, she'd had no problem landing the job on Cayman. But at twenty-eight, she felt the pressure of settling down, especially when she spoke to her mother. Growing up in an old Spanish town, steeped in Catholic traditions, she was considered rebellious for leaving, wild, and almost certainly promiscuous for travelling abroad on her own. Her bold and confident manner didn't help quell such rumours. In contrast, by seventies standards at least, she was actually quite conservative. But the old women of the Moorish town over-looking the Mediterranean Sea would consider nothing short of virgin-until-married to be acceptable. Still, she missed the tiny streets winding through the whitewashed homes, the marketplace on Saturday mornings, and the family gatherings every Sunday. It was home and she hadn't been back since she'd started work on the island, the flights were too expensive, and she wasn't allowed to take time off at the holidays. Maybe it was time to at least make a visit.

The bartender placed two more drinks on her tray, startling her back from her wandering thoughts. "There you go Izzie."

She smiled and thanked him before heading over one of the small walkway bridges to deliver the drinks to a group of English people with their loungers huddled under a large umbrella near the pool. She chuckled at their pale white skin which was already glowing a painful red on their first day on holiday. After distributing the drinks, she surveyed her area for anyone looking for service, glancing at her watch, and willing it to be four o'clock already. She noticed the guy she'd chatted to yesterday was just settling into a lounger by the edge of her service area. Whitey, she recalled his unusual name. He was much too old for her, she thought, he was probably in his forties, but he was really good looking and seemed to be interested in her. Most of the men preferred the younger girls that giggled and flirted and babbled nonsense to them, another reason she was feeling her age. She couldn't bring herself to play those games. But then again, she never had.

"Miss."

The voice came from behind her and she turned. One of the pasty English sunburned group was waving a hand at her.

"You're blocking the view, miss."

She smiled as apologetically as she could muster without laughing and walked over to the guy that, now she looked again, reminded her of Sean Connery. That wasn't a bad thing. 'The Most Beautiful Girl' by Charlie Rich was playing from the bar. That wasn't a bad thing either, she decided.

"Hello again," she said as nonchalantly as she could manage, while trying to look younger and more relaxed in the awkward pose she'd found herself.

"Good afternoon, Isabella," he surprised her by speaking fluent Spanish, "How has your day been?"

"Long, but my shift is nearly over and I'm looking forward to taking these shoes off," she babbled, happy to be speaking her native language.

Whitey laughed. "Well, I hate to keep you on your feet, but I'd love a drink."

"No, no, I didn't mean it like that," she blurted clumsily, but he held up his hand, still laughing.

"Please, I'm kidding with you. Those shoes are pretty groovy though," he said, looking over his sunglasses at her legs more than her shoes.

"Thank you, they're new and I love them, but they're not quite worn in yet for a full shift on my feet." She relaxed and wiggled her foot around, showing off the shoe.

"Havana Club over ice please, Isabella," he asked politely and she remembered she was a waitress.

"Of course sir, I'll be right back."

He smiled with amusement. "Take your time, and please, I'm Whitey; sir is for officers, not regulars like me."

She scolded herself all the way to the bar for being such a bumbling idiot. No way this gorgeous guy is interested in a silly drinks server, and now he thinks I didn't remember his name, she thought. She asked the bartender for the drink and leaned on the bar to relieve the pressure on her feet. She took a few deep breaths and wondered why this guy made her such a mess; she was usually bold around men, and was certainly used to fending off advances. Many men, especially the Americans, seem to think that grabbing a girl's arse was fine when they were on holiday. But this guy wasn't the arse-grabbing type, he seemed like a gentleman. A working-class gentleman.

"Havana Club over ice, Mr Whitey." She placed his drink on the table and smiled. He took his sunglasses off and looked her in the eyes.

"Isabella, I was thinking, once you've finished your shift and had a chance to revive your poor feet, would you consider having dinner with me?"

Despite all her thoughts about how attractive he was, and whether he was interested in her, she hadn't actually thought he'd ask her out, and now she had a problem. "That's very kind of you, but I'm afraid the hotel doesn't allow us to date guests."

"I see," he responded thoughtfully. "Well that's not a problem if we can make it tomorrow night instead."

She was puzzled. "But they'll still fire me if I date a guest, and I do need my job."

"But tomorrow I won't be a guest here anymore." He grinned irresistibly.

"Oh?" she asked, still puzzled. "You're leaving?"

"For dinner with you, I'm delighted to move hotels, my dear." His blue eyes shining with boyish glee.

Isabella thought for a moment. He was certainly a charmer and she hadn't been out on a date in months.

"If you're looking for an island fling, I'm not that girl, Mr Whitey," she frowned at him.

"I wouldn't be interested if you were," he replied, without missing a beat. It didn't feel like the lie he'd usually tell either, which surprised him.

"If they knew you'd checked out because of me, I'd get fired for sure," she offered half-heartedly.

"They'll never know; if they ask me why, I'll tell them my trip was cut short," he countered confidently.

Isabella let out a sigh as though she was reluctant to give in, but happily took some time to swim in his eyes a little longer.

"Okay," she said, and just managed to hold back her smile until she'd turned and walked away.

12

NOVEMBER 2019

The Newton bobbed lazily in the calm water and the divers relaxed and enjoyed the tranquillity between the two dives. The Davis girls swam around the tethered boat, excitedly checking out the shallow reef they'd be exploring on their second dive, while the other divers soaked up the hot sun and made idle chat. It was the same group as the day before, with the exception of Ray Blackburn, so Hazel had buddied with AJ on the first dive, and would go with Thomas on the second. AJ now sat in the captain's chair on the fly bridge, sipped on her stainless steel water canteen, and ate some orange slices Thomas had handed around. Hazel and Thomas lounged on the bench seats either side of the ladder and AJ couldn't help but notice Hazel's lean and fit physique, clearly visible in her two-piece bathing suit. She wondered if she'd look that good in ten years. Hopefully she'd be doing exactly what she was doing now, in which case she might, with all the physical work it took to run a dive boat.

"So, how many lovers do you have in tow, AJ?" Hazel surprised AJ by asking, and made her spill some water she was drinking. Thomas laughed loudly.

"I have one boyfriend thank you very much, one is plenty," AJ replied, feigning indignity.

"Pourquoi?" Hazel countered loudly. "If one is good, surely more is better? There must be so many tasty young men around the island?"

Thomas continued to chuckle and AJ threw an orange rind at him. She was never comfortable talking about her love life and her cheeks flushed.

"Not for this girl, my one is enough," she mumbled.

"So who is this magical one? Where is he? I have to meet this Valentino," Hazel teased.

Between chuckles Thomas managed, "Oh he's not here, he only makes it by the island every few months or so."

AJ glared at him and threw full slices of orange this time. "Nobody asked you Mister Bodden – maybe we should talk about your love life, huh? What's your latest one? Cecilia? You've been talking about her for at least a week now."

Thomas laughed even louder to the wonder of the others on the lower deck.

"Wait a second," Hazel intervened. "Don't try and deflect now, Annabelle Jayne. Once every few months? My God! How can you not have a plaything to fill in? Why is Valentino only here every few months? How could he possibly stay away from you, you're gorgeous, you're the perfect young Aphrodite."

AJ glowed red and stammered, "He works for Sea Sentry on one of their boats, so he's at sea for months at a time. And it's Jackson, his name's Jackson."

Thomas grinned from ear to ear and looked at Hazel expectantly, enjoying how she made his boss squirm with her playful banter.

"Jackson! He must be American? That's an American lumberjack name! Or, or a fireman, like in those calendars you can buy with the firemen not really wearing their firemen's outfits," Hazel said loudly before breaking into laughter herself.

AJ's face glowed like a scarlet beacon, but she couldn't help laughing with them. A clichéd vision of her gentle, peaceful Jackson in a heavy tartan flannel shirt, carrying a big axe around, looking for trees to cut down, was rather amusing, and tears rolled down her cheeks as she sank deeper into her chair. She managed to get herself together enough to make an attempt at turning the conversation around.

"I take it you're not married then, Hazel?"

Hazel pointed to herself and looked surprised, "Moi? Are you crazy? I've never met a man I wanted to spend more than a month with. They become soooo boring after a while." She looked straight at Thomas. "Don't you think so, sexy island boy?"

All three roared with laughter again and Bill Davis called up, "Are you drinking up there? Cos I'm coming up if you are, I could do with a drink."

Hazel peered over the railing to the rear deck below. "Sorry, sorry, we are having a deep conversation about Miss Bailey's romantic life and it appears it is quite amusing."

AJ reached over and gave Hazel a playful slap on the arm. "Hey, my romantic life was just fine until you started making fun of it!"

Hazel leaned back over the railing. "Okay we're moving on to Thomas's love life now; I think we'll be laughing again in a few minutes, so be ready down there."

Thomas leapt out of his seat, blurting, "No ma'am we're not", and slid down the ladder in a flash.

"Okay guys, about time for our second dive!" he said to the group as he landed on the deck, beaming his huge smile.

Hazel turned back to AJ and gave her a wink. "So, if your man isn't in town, could I talk you into dinner? I'm getting bored kicking around on my own every evening. You can tell me all about Jackson and I promise I won't make fun of you anymore."

AJ got up to follow Thomas but paused at the top of the ladder. "Sure, I'd like that, but it'll be my turn to pry out all your secrets."

Hazel laughed. "Fair enough, deal."

13

APRIL 1974

Curly shut down the throttle on the large skiff and coasted in the open water off the north-west corner of the island. A short man with a shaved head sporting a Bob Soto's Diving shirt, similar to Curly's, eyed the coastline.

"What do you think Brad?" Curly shouted at his co-worker.

Brad gave the shoreline a final check in both directions, nodded, and peered over the side of the boat to make sure they were over sand, before tossing the anchor into the water with a splash.

Whitey had been chatting with the other five customers on board during the ride out, sizing them up. Four guys from America talked amongst themselves; they were the group Curly had mentioned in the shop. They'd most likely dive together and shouldn't bother him. The fifth was a heavy-set French-Canadian man who hadn't said much. Whitey guessed he wasn't confident in his English and was doing more listening than trying to converse. He was pretty sure Soto's would want the group to stick close together, as the currents were supposed to be fierce, and he'd be partnered with the Québécois.

The two crew manoeuvred the boat to make sure the anchor was steadfast, then Brad jumped in with a mask, snorkel and fins to survey the location. After a minute of kicking around towards the open ocean he gave a thumbs up and swam back to the skiff, working hard to do so.

Breathing heavily, he climbed back aboard, "We're good, she's slightly west and slightly south of us, which is perfect with the current."

He sat down on one of the benches that ran the length of the boat on both sides and the divers looked eagerly his way for more intel.

"The current looks pretty strong, the fans on the reef I could see were laid over. Surface current is brisk too. Getting to the Raptor should be good but save some gas, it'll be a tough swim back."

Curly clapped his hands together. "Alright men, you heard Brad, if you're good with some hard swimming, let's get geared up." He turned to the Canadian. "You get all that Olivier?"

The man looked back at Curly, slightly startled. "Oui. Uhh, Yes," he replied in a heavy French accent, but Whitey was pretty certain he didn't understand half of what was said.

Curly gave him a thumbs-up and continued to the group, "Look fellas, with the currents and all, we'll try and stick together down there alright?" A few moans came from the Americans. "I know, you're all experienced and used to doing your own thing, but we can't have people getting blown off the site and chasing stragglers around with the boat while the rest are trying to get back on board."

The group nodded in compliance and Curly wrapped up, "Awesome, this'll be a bonzer dive guys, just keep an eye on me and the other blokes. Watch your air and leave plenty for the swim back."

He waved at the sides. "We'll back-roll in fellas; let me gear up and we'll go in a jiffy."

Within a few minutes Brad was the only one left on the boat and divers were scattered in the water as the current pulled them away as soon as they descended. Whitey let the water take him without struggling, and headed down to make sure he met the wreck, rather than being blown over it. He looked around to check the group. The four Americans were close by, a little above Whitey, but Olivier was messing with his gear near the surface and was already losing the group. If he didn't descend farther, he'd miss the wreck that they could easily see ahead of them now. Curly swam back up and waved frantically to get the Canadian's attention, but the man was focused on something out of place with his older-style life vest. As Curly almost reached him he appeared to satisfy whatever the issue was, and looked around nonchalantly before descending rapidly, seemingly oblivious to the group.

The wreck was an impressive site. It indeed sat bolt upright on the reef and had caused a considerable amount of damage to the delicate coral. It must have landed and slid back about thirty feet before grinding itself into a comfortable seat. Behind it, the sea floor sloped away more acutely before dropping off the abrupt wall that surrounded Grand Cayman. If it hadn't found purchase on the reef, it may have disappeared to the depths. It appeared to have been painted a dark blue, but the algae and beginnings of coral growth had already tinted most of the surfaces with a soft brown hue. An abundance of fish life patrolled the big ship, from jacks and barracuda above the cabin structure, to a shoal of yellowtail snappers swirling around the large, open cargo hold. All that was left of the canvas hold cover was remnants that ran down each edge in tatters.

As Whitey drifted over the bow and forward deck he quickly dropped into the shelter of the hold and escaped the current. The four Americans did the same and proceeded to make a lap of the interior, looking for curiosities. Curly guided Olivier in the same direction and visibly relaxed when he saw all his divers in the same locale. Whitey finned towards the rear of the hold and looked for access points into the ship's interior. A metal walkway ran across the top of the hold, with doors leading into the structure and steep steps down into the hold on each side. He made for one of the doors and was surprised when the metal handle turned easily, but the heavy metal door didn't budge at all. Assuming silt and debris had already gummed up the seal he looked around to make sure he wasn't attracting too much attention before heaving on the door with a finned foot against the cabin. The door ground open about halfway, which was plenty for Whitey to slip through and look inside. He cursed himself for not bringing an underwater torch and made a mental note to buy one from Soto's. The hallway was dark, with nothing more than the light from the door he'd half opened. The interior still looked clear of debris as best he could tell. Curly had told him that over the few months after the sinking, divers had cleared the wreck of anything valuable, which wasn't much, then moved on to general house cleaning, removing potential flotsam and loose, floating debris. They'd managed to pump some of the diesel and oil from the tanks and engine, but a lot had escaped before they could get to it. Fortunately, the currents had taken the fluids away from the island into deeper water where they would cause less damage.

Whitey thought about that for a moment. The engine bay might have what he was looking for. But where the hell was the engine room in this old tub?

14

NOVEMBER 2019

AJ kept an eye on the door from her table in the Fox and Hare pub, her favourite restaurant in West Bay. She sipped from her Strongbow cider and thumbed through email on her phone. She looked up when she heard the door swing open and waved to Hazel as she came in.

"Hey there, hope I haven't kept you waiting?" Hazel greeted her.

"Not at all, I was early. Can I get you a drink?" AJ responded warmly.

Hazel sat and hung her small rucksack style handbag over the chair. "I'll have a glass of Chardonnay please."

AJ waved to the bartender and relayed the drink order, to which he gave her a thumbs-up.

"Thanks for inviting me tonight. Being here on my own it's nice to have someone to chat with over dinner. I've spent the last few evenings fending off drunk men in various restaurants." Hazel rolled her eyes.

They made small talk and, before long, the bartender set the wine on the table.

"You guys want some food?" he asked.

"Do you have fresh grouper tonight Frank?" AJ asked.

"We do, he can do it blackened if you like?" Frank replied.

"I'll have that, but Hazel do you want a few minutes to look at the menu?" AJ offered.

Hazel shook her head. "No, no, blackened grouper sounds perfect, I'll have the same."

"You got it," Frank replied as he cleared the menus and left.

"So, what brings you to the island? Just getting away for a bit?" AJ asked politely.

Hazel considered her response a moment. "Just a break I suppose. I'm between work at the moment, so the timing was good."

Hazel sipped her wine and AJ continued, "What do you do for work?"

"Well, I was the manager for a large art gallery in Fréjus, until a few months ago. Now I'm not sure what will come next."

It was the first time AJ had seen Hazel be anything but assertive and confident since she'd picked her up two days before.

"That doesn't sound good – what happened, if you don't mind me asking?" AJ enquired quietly.

Hazel managed a smile. "I'm not sure, honestly. I'd worked for the owner for over ten years. We'd grown the business together and we were doing well. One day everything was fine and the next he called me into his office and said he had to make a change. That was it. No explanation. He apologised, and I of course asked what I'd done wrong. He said, 'Nothing, I just need to make a change.'" She took another sip of wine and looked away, clearly still upset by the incident.

"That's awful, I'm so sorry," AJ sympathised, unsure quite what to say.

"Oh well, new opportunities ahead, right?" Hazel forced a cheery expression. "So, what's on the cards for tomorrow's dives?"

AJ took the hint Hazel was done talking about herself, her work at least. "Well, you're on our smaller boat tomorrow with Carlos and one of Reg's guys. Once a month we get to dive the submarine so we're taking the Newton out there. You'll love Carlos, he's Cuban, engaged to Thomas's sister. I'm sorry the boat to the sub is full, it gets booked up way ahead of time."

"That's okay, I understand. Would be incredible to see it but like I said yesterday, I'll just have to plan ahead and come back."

Frank returned with two plates and placed them on the table. "Get you ladies anything else?"

AJ took in the smell of the fresh grouper rubbed in spices and blackened perfectly. "This looks great, thank you. Tell George I'll bring him some lionfish tomorrow afternoon, we're diving the sub tomorrow."

Frank nodded. "Will do, maybe he'll plan a ceviche special."

Frank wandered back to his bar and the women tucked into their meal.

"You should come to France and dive the Rubis, AJ; you could stay with me, plan some other fun dives, maybe go to Corsica as well," Hazel enthused between mouthfuls.

"I'd love to," AJ replied honestly. "I don't get a lot of time away as you can imagine, but I need to visit my parents sometime; maybe I could combine a trip to France too."

"Perfect." Hazel held up her wine glass. "Santé, we have a plan."

AJ carefully clinked her cider bottle to the wine glass. "Cheers, I like this plan."

She'd only known this lady for a few days, but AJ already felt a strong connection and the idea of diving in southern France was very appealing. She'd slowly come to realise over the years that she was a strong independent female herself but she still looked up to and admired confident women. Some people had a strong presence in a positive way, people noticed when they were in a room and she saw Hazel Delacroix as one of those people. Of course, too many people had a strong presence in a room for all the wrong reasons. AJ had known a few of them too.

"Your parents are in England?" Hazel asked, bringing AJ out of her mental wandering.

"They are, yes, and I'm an only child so I'm fortunate they come here and visit two or three times a year. What about yours? In France I assume?"

Hazel paused a moment. "My mother died earlier this year I'm afraid: cancer. My dad is still in France but I don't see him much. My mother divorced him twenty years ago and I was much closer to her."

Put my foot right in it again, AJ thought. "I'm so sorry about your mum, Hazel. You really are having a bad run of things."

Hazel smiled and AJ's phone rang loudly on the table, startling them both.

"Shit, sorry, I forgot to silence the thing," she said, scrambling to mute the ringing. Looking at the caller ID she said, "I'm so sorry but I should take this."

Hazel waved to her that she didn't mind and AJ answered the phone. "Hey Jonty, what's up?"

AJ's face frowned as she listened to the caller. "Bloody hell Jonty, well I hope you're okay?"

She listened some more, still frowning. "Sure, I'll get you the next opening but you know it'll be next year right?"

Another pause and she winked at Hazel. "Okay Jonty, I'll sign you up for the next available and add you to the wait list. You look after yourself and you should go to the hospital as soon as you hang up, mate."

AJ shook her head as she listened to the response. "Okay, well take care, thanks for letting me know, bye for now."

AJ hung up her mobile and looked at Hazel, still shaking her head.

"Everything okay?" Hazel asked, looking concerned.

AJ laughed. "That was a bloke called Jonty Gladstone." AJ paused trying to decide how to describe the man. "You know what, it would take too long to describe Jonty; the important part is he has a concussion. Well, he's pretty sure he has a concussion. Either way he has to cancel tomorrow."

Hazel looked at AJ in anticipation.

"Want to dive the U-1026 tomorrow?" AJ said with a grin from ear to ear.

"Oui! yes, yes!" Hazel gushed, jumping up and hugging AJ across the table.

15

APRIL 1974

Whitey slipped back out the doorway of the cabin and shoved the big door as far closed as he could manage. He checked around again for the other divers. The Americans were over the other side of the cabin structure looking at the sister doorway. He gave them an encouraging thumbs-up. That's it fellas, you have a good explore in there, he thought humorously. Olivier was still circulating in the hold, where apparently Curly felt he was safe, as he'd moved on to looking through the wheelhouse windows above. Whitey dropped back down into the expanse of the empty hold and spotted another doorway dead centre of the rear wall. He wondered if he could get that lucky. Moving past a curious mutton snapper he arrived at the door. Again, the handle moved easily; these fellas must have kept the hinges and locks well greased, he thought, and heaved on the handle. This door came open far more easily. Three sharp bangs rang out through the ship and startled Whitey. Looking around him he saw Curly floating above by the wheelhouse with a big metal clip in one hand and waving at all the divers with the other. He was calling the dive. Damn it, Whitey cursed, he just needed a few more minutes. He waved back at Curly so he'd worry about someone else and looked around for the other divers. The Americans were close by Curly but where was Olivier? He spotted him, still in the front of the cargo hold, staring up at Curly but not moving. Whitey quickly finned in his direction and, looking up at Curly, gave him an okay sign that he'd retrieve his buddy. Curly seemed satisfied and gathered the other four to start the struggle back to the skiff. Whitey reached Olivier, who looked at him blankly through his big oval mask. Whitey signalled with both thumbs that they were to ascend and Olivier nodded his acknowledgement, or at least an acceptance that he'd been communicated with, Whitey wasn't sure. The other five were just clearing the hold above, and he signalled again to Curly that he had Olivier with him. Leading the way, he rose up the wall of the hold but angled towards the starboard side, with the Canadian following dutifully close behind. Just before he came out of the hold where the current would hit them Whitey checked up until Olivier was alongside. He'd worked them over to the side of the ship with only a narrow walkway along the edge of the hold, and a railing beyond that, before the open ocean. Whitey eased up out of the hold and immediately felt the current pulling him towards the railing. He rotated over to be horizontal and kicked as subtly as he could to hide the effort it was taking. Olivier, once again seemingly oblivious, swam straight out and was instantly whisked away like a child's balloon on a gusty day. He wrapped around the railing for a moment as he flailed and panicked with one fin caught in the small opening between the top and middle rail. Whitey grabbed the railing with one hand and pinned Olivier's fin with the other, which secured the rubber fin to the metal rail, while the corresponding foot slipped out and followed the rest of the Canadian's body as it drifted away from the Raptor, unable to fight the current with just one fin.

Whitey hung on and turned back to thankfully see Curly had witnessed the whole calamity. He felt bad for poor old Olivier, but he appreciated his unwitting assistance in buying him some time. He checked his tank pressure gauge and was pleased to see he had plenty of air left. Would have been a shame to send Olivier on his little ride just to find out he had to surface anyway with no air left. They all judged their dive safety on the antiquated Navy tables for nitrogen saturation, but with Whitey's depth profile looking like a busy day in a hotel lift, he had to go by air pressure remaining to guess he was within safe limits.

Curly was busy signalling the Americans to continue to the boat and appeared to be kicking after Olivier. Perfect, Whitey chuckled to himself, and dropped back down into the hold and finned back to the door at the rear. Pulling it further open he peered inside the ink-black room. The light from the opening was enough to illuminate the first few feet inside, which revealed some heavy framework, and mounted to that was a big diesel engine. Cursing himself again for not bringing a torch, he hurriedly fumbled his way in and let his eyes adjust to the darkness. He knew he only had a few minutes – as soon as the Americans reached the skiff Brad would pull the anchor and take off to retrieve the drifting divers. It would quickly become apparent he was still missing if he didn't bob up as well. The engine room was eerie with shadows cast from all kinds of pipes and lines and he hoped no menacing critters had taken up residence with the door being closed. He tried moving around the side of the motor but there were too many obstructions, so he bellied along the top, reaching down the sides as he went. Towards the back he found what he'd hoped for in a smooth round cylinder sticking down from a casting on the side of the engine. He twisted the cylinder but his hand just slid on the frictionless oily surface. Good enough, he thought, I know where to come to next time and it won't be with a crowd. Edging back over the top of the engine, he slid off the rear and out the door, making a careful point to close it securely.

Sound travels far better through water than air and he could hear the outboard motor of the skiff fire up. Cautious not to ascend too quickly and get the bends, Whitey finned for the surface without worrying about the current taking him. He hadn't been looking forward to the swim back anyway.

16

NOVEMBER 2019

Conditions on the pinnacle close to Twelve Mile Bank were near perfect. A warm, clear day with a gentle breeze, and barely a swell on the open ocean. Rare this far from the island. Mermaid Divers' Newton was tied to a line that disappeared into the blue water to a submerged buoy that was now tethered to the wreck itself, replacing the original line AJ had tied to a piece of dead reef during her search for the submarine. The GPS on the dive boat put them over the buoy and AJ had dived down thirty feet and tied them in. She'd also had a look at the current and visibility below to relay to the group in their final briefing before the first dive.

"Vis is really good today, I could easily see the wreck from thirty feet down, and the current is light. But please don't underestimate the currents here. I know everyone is experienced and used to free descending, but we need to use the line to go down and to come back up. If you get pulled off the site, we have to get everyone else back on board before we can come searching for you in the open ocean, so better to be safe and use the line."

The group nodded, intently listening, a point AJ always noted. The ones that seemed blasé, or too cool to listen to the briefing, were usually a problem on the dive. Satisfied with the response, she continued, using a large waterproof illustration of the wreck and surrounding terrain as a prop.

"The line is tied to the conning tower around mid-ship here." She pointed to the top of the submarine. "Please double-check your dive computers right before we get in. Many of them will reset to air after a period of time, and you can't change the setting once you're underwater. As I mentioned before all the tanks are Nitrox, custom blended to 29% specifically for this dive. The conning tower is at around one twenty and the screws are at one forty-eight. Our maximum depth on 29% blend is 137 feet so you need to be extremely diligent watching your depth if you drop down the sides. All the cool stuff is really on the decks and around the conning tower, so between one twenty and one thirty. A reminder, take a peek in the open hatch but do not go inside the conning tower please."

She paused and scanned the group again: ten focused faces peered back at her.

"Great, Reg, anything to add?"

Reg shook his head, looking down from the fly bridge where he stood watching the briefing with Thomas. "Nope, you got it covered."

"Any questions? Now is the time to ask if you have any concerns." AJ smiled; she knew there were always questions on people's minds but they rarely asked in a group environment. No one raised a hand.

"Alright, Reg's group of five get ready first; my guys, we'll splash about five minutes after so we're staggered on the wreck, helps everyone get to see everything. Stay out of deco, folks. Remember, we'll do a five-minute safety stop at fifteen feet. Let's suit up." She winked at Hazel, who'd carefully listened to every word of the briefing AJ had given on the boat before leaving the dock, and the one she'd just done at the dive site.

"Forty-two metres in metric for maximum depth Hazel," AJ converted for her.

"I switched my computer to feet so I wouldn't be converting

numbers all this trip," Hazel replied with a smile.

"That's smart," AJ responded. She'd watched Hazel, as she did the other divers, for signs of the butterflies or apprehension. A little nervous anticipation was natural, and often helped people focus, but major jitters could be a problem. If someone was so preoccupied with nerves they tended to bumble and make mistakes, forget the basics. Hazel appeared comfortable and excited for the dive. She exuded the calm confidence she'd shown all along, which AJ enjoyed being around. She'd always been cautious forming relationships, romantic or platonic, taking her time to open up to someone, but she felt an immediate bond with Hazel.

Descending down the line, AJ could see the bubbles from Reg's group below them, as the wreck of the U-1026 German submarine started appearing in view. What a magnificent sight it was. The usual plethora of ocean life swirled around the sunken vessel, adding life and motion to the wreck that had lain dormant since 1945, when she was deliberately sunk by her crew. AJ looked back at her group of five divers as she moved swiftly hand over hand down the line, equalising the pressure in her ears as she went. She caught Hazel's eyes and saw the sparkle of excitement and awe in them. She loved seeing people's first reaction to the wreck that meant so much to her, and her family. AJ glanced at the Rolex on her wrist and felt an overwhelming sense of gratitude.

They reached the conning tower about the time Reg led his group of five rearwards, as planned, to look at the gun deck. AJ hung back so one by one her divers could investigate the open hatch that was held permanently ajar by the coral growth and corrosion. As she did every time she guided this dive, AJ imagined Andreas Jaeger and his two shipmates making their escape. They had clambered through this hatch, in the dark, in the midst of a raging storm above, with only a crude Draeger breathing device. She shivered at the thought, as she did every time. Hazel hovered above the hatch with perfect buoyancy and shone her powerful, compact dive light inside. Looking back at AJ she shook her head in disbelief, clearly sharing a similar thought.

17

APRIL 1974

Whitey fingered through Ainsley's box of cassette tapes on the passenger seat of the Capri as he drove down West Bay Road. Finally finding one he recognised that didn't make him cringe he slotted it in, and Derek and the Dominos started playing 'Layla' from the stereo speakers. The temperature had started dipping as the sun lowered in the western sky and, with a smattering of wispy clouds on the horizon, the sunset over the water promised to be another good one. Ainsley had offered up the use of his Capri enthusiastically until Whitey actually drove away in it. Then he'd looked like a father watching his daughter leave on a first date. With the captain of the football team. Who was two years older than his daughter. Whitey thought he might actually be crying.

Isabella had told him to pick her up where the road forked before George Town and Whitey looked around the intersection as he approached. He spotted her leaning against the wall by the cemetery and pulled over to the curb on the right side of the road. He stared in stunned silence at the vision of beauty walking towards him. She wore skin-tight red hot pants and a form-fitting sleeveless silver top, under which there was no evidence of underwear. On her feet were floral-adorned heeled clogs that extended her calves and made her legs look long enough to stretch to the moon and back. She smiled as she walked around the car to the passenger side, and he recovered just in time to reach over and open the door latch and shove it ajar. She slid into the leather bucket seat.

"Hey," she said softly and if he figured her intent was to take the upper hand to start the evening, then game, set and match, she'd won.

"Hey," he managed back.

"So, where are we going?" she asked, slipping her sunglasses on top of her head and pushing her long black hair behind her ear.

Whitey gathered his wits back up, and pulled his jaw off the floor. "Thought we'd treat ourselves to some seafood overlooking the water, you know, take in the sunset and all that."

"Sounds nice," she said and turned to face the road. He realised he was probably supposed to be driving now and pulled away from the curb with a quick glance over his shoulder.

"Have you eaten at the Grand Old House before?" he asked, hoping she hadn't. Maybe he could gain some ground back.

"Wow, that's fancy, are you trying to impress me, Whitey?" she teased him as she thumbed through Ainsley's box of cassette tapes.

He laughed. "Bloody right I am, my dear."

She hit eject on Clapton pretending to be Derek and slipped another cassette in the player and pressed the play button. Whitey held his breath in anticipation of the potential rubbish he feared would be emitted from the speakers. A serious conflict in musical taste, he thought, could derail this relationship within half a mile of its inception. And then he wondered what on earth he was thinking. Whitey Snow wasn't a relationship guy. Whitey Snow was a girl-in-every-port guy. He'd spent less than ten minutes in this woman's presence, and he was already worrying about their harmonious compatibility? Elvis Presley's unmistakable voice started into 'Suspicious Minds' and Whitey turned and looked at the beautiful woman sitting next to him.

She smiled. "Do you like Elvis?"

"I'm usually a Led Zeppelin, Pink Floyd, Deep Purple kind of guy," he replied without emotion.

"Oh," she said quietly.

"But this is the King, baby: who in their right mind doesn't love the bloody King?" He laughed and she laughed along, clearly relieved. They made their way through George Town waterfront and along South Sound road singing at the top of their lungs.

The maître d' eyed the pair disapprovingly as they entered the old house that now served as a waterfront restaurant. The man opened his mouth to begin discussing dress codes but Whitey quickly interceded.

"Evening, very nice to see you again. Reservation for two tonight, I have a guest with me for a change."

The older man stammered for a moment and rummaged through the reservation book, thrown off guard and hunting his memory for the name he couldn't recall.

"Snow," Whitey offered politely. "Whitey Snow."

"Of course, Mr Snow, my apologies, good to see you again, this way please." Relieved, the maître d' led them to a table by the window overlooking the ocean, with a trail of turned heads and frowns from other diners. Whitey's flared jeans and loud floral paisley shirt unbuttoned to mid-torso drew attention, but Isabella's outfit raised scoffs and mutterings as the old ladies were disgusted and the old men pretended to be.

Once the maître d' had left them with menus in hand, Isabella asked, "You come here a lot?"

Whitey smiled. "First time, actually."

They both chuckled and she whispered, "I didn't realise we'd be going somewhere so fancy or I'd have worn something different. We're getting a lot of disapproving looks."

Whitey took her hand across the table. "Believe me, your outfit is perfect, you look incredible. You can't go through life worrying about what other people think." He winked at her and took his hand back to look at the menu, but mainly to be sure he didn't make her uncomfortable. Her skin was warm, and soft but firm, and sent a tingle through his whole body. The sun was lowering towards the horizon and ignited the sky above the ocean in fiery oranges and yellows as the water darkened from azure to deep blue. Isabella turned to look at the sunset and Whitey noticed the soft light illuminating her pretty face framed in contrast by her glistening black hair. Her green eyes sparkled and he wished he could take a picture at that very moment. Capture the very instant he knew he may have finally met the one woman who could change his life.

18

NOVEMBER 2019

Reg took the helm of the Newton for the ride back from the U-1026, as AJ and Thomas had guided the second dive. Taking a ninety-minute surface interval between dives and breathing the custom 29% oxygen Nitrox mix instead of regular air, they were able to control the excessive amounts of nitrogen in their bodies, and make two dives for about twenty-five minutes each. The ten divers sat on the benches on the rear deck, enthusiastically chatting about their experience as they rode the open ocean swells that had built since the morning. Among them, and more enthused than most, was Hazel. A dive boat had a way of making lifelong friends from strangers and an epic dive like the U-boat broke down the international, economic, and social walls like nothing else.

"You've dived the Rubis haven't you Hazel? How does this compare?" asked Dave, an Englishman who'd travelled from the UK with his brother Stuart to make this dive.

Hazel pondered thoughtfully a moment. "They're different for sure, the wrecks themselves are somewhat similar, but this one has the reef and so much life around it. The way it is held up," she held her hand in the air as though she were presenting a gift to the sky, "like a trophy on top of this pinnacle, is so amazing and dramatic, I think this is the best dive I've ever made."

Dave nodded in agreement and slapped his brother on the back. "For me, for sure this was my favourite dive ever."

Stuart concurred, "Me too, beats dry suits and two metres of vis any day!"

AJ sat down next to Hazel as the brothers laughed heartily.

"I'm so glad this worked out and the dives went as well as they did," AJ said quietly to Hazel.

Hazel put her arm around her and squeezed her affectionately. "Believe me, you've made this trip so worthwhile. This is just what I needed: some positive experience, you know? A few good things to balance out the shit."

AJ hugged her back, smiling broadly. "Well, you've still got some more time here, right? We'll have to keep those good things rolling."

Hazel laughed. "Not sure you can top these dives, but I'm game to try."

AJ laughed with her. "No, I don't think I've got anything more quite like this to show you, but we have some other fun wrecks."

Thomas stood nearby drying himself with a towel, balancing expertly on the swaying boat. "The Kittiwake is a great dive, I know it's not as crazy as the sub, but now it's rolled over at an angle it's a lot more interesting. The lower decks are in total darkness without any external access holes, so it's pretty good fun down there."

AJ agreed and added, "The Doc Poulson is a great night dive too. It's small but teeming with life – we should do that one night this week."

"Ore Verde is as well," added Stuart, "It's all scattered these days but still great at night."

Hazel nodded with a smirk. "I think we got a little spoilt here today guys, it'll be hard to top this."

No one disagreed. "There's always the Carrie Lee," Thomas

offered, "but you'll need mixed gas, she's too deep for air or Nitrox."

"What's the other one?" Dave asked, trying to recall a name, "You know," he looked at his brother, "the bird name, what's it called?"

"The Raptor?" AJ suggested. "That thing's pretty much off limits, it's about to drop over the wall. The government won't even allow a buoy to be tied to it."

"That's the one," Dave said, slapping his brother's leg, "Raptor. She's not too deep, is she?"

AJ thought carefully about her reply. "It's at the limit depth wise, but the currents are really strong that far off the corner of the island."

"Have you been on it?" Thomas asked innocently.

AJ nodded. "I have. Once. It's a cool wreck but there's no access holes cut in it and the superstructure is hard to navigate inside. The hallways and rooms are really tight. It used to be farther up the reef, when it sank, but the storms have moved it closer and closer to the wall. At least a third of the wreck is hanging over the drop-off; next hurricane and she's gone."

"Bloody hell," Dave said slowly. "Not sure I like the sound of that."

AJ smiled, glad to steer them away from the idea. "No, the Cayman authorities don't like people diving it. More people have died or gone missing diving that wreck than any other in the Cayman Islands."

"Bugger that then," Stuart confirmed and they sat in silence for a minute as they mulled that over.

Hazel finally spoke quietly but firmly. "Sounds like a perfect challenge."

AJ looked at her in surprise. "We don't dive the Raptor, it's too dangerous."

Hazel smiled warmly and AJ thought for a second she would back off the idea. "So, it's deep, but not too deep, and it has strong currents?"

"Yeah, and it's going to tip over the wall any moment," AJ replied a little defensively.

"So, if we don't dive it during a hurricane, it would be similar to diving the U-boat wreck we were just on, right?" Hazel retorted gently.

"I suppose she's got a point," Dave mumbled while AJ searched for a response. "I wouldn't dive the bloody thing though," he added.

"I wouldn't mind seeing it before it's gone," Thomas joined in until AJ glared at him and rolled her eyes.

"But there's no point pissing off the authorities," he hurriedly blurted, trying to dig himself out of the boss's wrath.

"Exactly," AJ said firmly. "They do grant me my operator's licence you know."

Hazel laughed. "Well, I wouldn't want to get you in any trouble." She smirked mischievously. "But of course I wouldn't tell if you wouldn't."

Thomas couldn't stop himself from chuckling and AJ just shook her head. But she smiled a little too.

19

APRIL 1974

The final ember of the day's sun left a hint of blue on the horizon line as darkness descended over the island. The lights from the restaurant faintly lit the water's edge where the Caribbean Sea lapped softly against the rugged limestone known as ironshore. The waiter cleared their plates and left dessert menus on the table.

"I couldn't eat another thing, that was so good," Isabella groaned happily.

Whitey smiled. "Glad you enjoyed it. How about a coffee?"

"That sounds perfect," she replied and after thinking a moment added, "I've been meaning to ask you, where did you learn to speak Spanish so well?"

He'd avoided too much discussion about himself over dinner by asking her about her journey ending up on the island, but he knew sooner or later he'd have to offer some explanation for his own lifestyle.

"I've lived in Miami, at least partly, for about eight years and being in the Navy when I was a lad, I'd picked up bits of several languages; Spanish was one of them. In Miami you'd better speak Spanish if you want to get anything done." He thought carefully a moment before continuing, weighing up how much to divulge. "I travel to South America with work quite a bit, so adding all that up I speak Spanish more than I speak English some weeks."

She listened intently and he knew there would be more questions coming.

"What is it you do for work exactly? You said earlier you work for yourself, but doing what?"

He paused to gather his thoughts. He found it hard to stay focused with her – he felt so comfortable in her presence it would be easy to talk all night – but he had to be careful, for both their sakes. "I've always traded commodities wherever I've been; whatever the local need is, I try and supply the need. So, it's varied from liquor, to furniture, to services. For the past few years most of what I do is supply services to a company in Peru. They do business with people in other countries and they like to meet them in Miami, so I facilitate, or handle, those meetings for them."

He hoped that would suffice but she seemed even more interested and pressed on. "And you mentioned you were in Cayman on business – is that for the same people?"

"It is. I'm setting up some banking for them here. Cayman is becoming a popular place for businesses to keep some of their money."

That seemed to appease her curiosity, and the waiter returning provided a welcome break. Whitey ordered them both coffees and took the opportunity to turn the conversation back to her.

"Where is Mojácar? I've been through most of the Mediterranean, but I don't know that town."

She chuckled. "That's because it's old and small. The nearest big town is Almería to the south and further north is Cartagena, but it's known by some as a place for holidays. We have a few hotels along the beach, which is where I worked after I left school. But the old town is built up a steep mountainside that rises from the sea. You grow up with strong legs living in Mojácar."

He pondered her long, lean legs and the extremely short hot pants she was wearing, and lost his train of thought.

"You seem to know the island quite well, I assume you've been here before?" she said, taking the chance to reverse the questions again.

"A few times over the years," he answered and then figured here was a subject he was safe expanding on and continued. "I first came here at the end of the war. I joined as soon as I was of age, which turned out to be at the very end. They sent me to Jamaica, where I served on a patrol boat that ran around these waters. We'd stop in at George Town and refuel before heading back."

"Patrolling in the Caribbean? I didn't know there was any fighting here?" A slight furrow appeared on her forehead when she asked questions, her intensity and genuine interest clear to see. It made him feel warm inside; most of the women he tended to date would be glancing around the room while asking things they didn't really care about it. He knew he invited that by dating girls that were fine with him leaving the next morning, or more often during the night, and those arrangements had suited his nomadic lifestyle. This felt good: to have a real conversation where they both cared about what was said.

"The Germans brought their U-boats through here a lot and would attack shipping coming up from South America to supply the US." Whitey leaned forward and talked more quietly. "We chased one not far from Grand one day, never caught him, but about a week or so later we picked up three Germans in a rotting dinghy in the middle of the ocean. Two were already dead from lack of water but one lived for a few hours." After all these years he still felt the need to be secretive about the incident. Although he was sure it didn't matter anymore, he'd been told to never speak of it, and rarely did.

"Were they from the U-boat you'd seen? How did it sink?" Her eyes were wide with curiosity.

"Same U-boat apparently, but we didn't sink it. Never found out what happened to it. Poor Jerry died before we reached port, and the only one to talk to him was Arthur Bailey. Great bloke he was, Bailey, he taught me everything on that patrol boat. I was the new kid arriving as everything was winding down, and most of the guys just gave me a hard time, but Arthur treated me like one of the crew. Good bloke. Anyway, after the war, I stayed in touch with a local I'd met on the island and we became good friends over the years. I'd stop by whenever I could, which was once every three to five years, sometimes longer. It's Ainsley's car I borrowed for tonight."

She grinned. "I was born the year after the war ended." Her face was full of mischief.

He laughed. "That bother you? We're a few years apart?" He held his breath waiting on her answer, a point that had to be raised at some time.

"No," she said firmly. "I've enjoyed this, but I wonder when will I see you again? Once every four years won't really work for me."

He smiled and took her hand, this time keeping hold of her warm, soft touch. "I'll be coming back to the island every month for a few days, maybe a week, each time. Now I have a good reason to make the trips longer."

She melted him with her intense green eyes, her whole face beaming.

"I can work with that."

20

NOVEMBER 2019

Thomas and AJ finished washing down her boat, tied alongside Reg's West Bay jetty that he let her share. The sun was losing its intensity as the late afternoon was giving way to early evening, and a few scattered clouds offered some welcome shade. AJ was happy to release the lines and let Thomas take the Newton out to its overnight mooring, a hundred yards offshore in the sandy flats. It was always a long but rewarding day when they dived the U-1026, and she gladly accepted a Strongbow cider from Reg who joined her at the end of the pier.

"Another good day in the books, my dear," he said as they sat down and hung their legs over the side.

AJ squinted, looking into the sun at her boat idling out. "Yup, appreciate the help as always. Good group today, makes it more fun when you don't have to stop people trying to kill themselves in the open ocean."

Reg chuckled in a low rumble. "True enough. Our boy Carlos do okay on your RIB today?"

"Sounded like it went fine. He only had five since Hazel came with us. He said north was a little lumpy, but not bad," she answered, before taking a swig of the cold cider.

"It should get flatter over the next few days," Reg said quietly. "I'll probably move two boats north tomorrow night if it does."

AJ nodded. "I should take mine around too, probably safe to switch them now."

When the north side settled down for the summer they dived outside the North Sound more often, and ran their classes and discover Scuba trips off Seven Mile Beach, on the west. Mermaid Divers operated one boat at a time, seeing as it was only Thomas and AJ, unless they borrowed people from Reg, like today, so she would swap her boat's locations and do her classes in the afternoons. She mulled over the logistics of trading her boats, which meant driving them around the west end of the island.

"Thomas and I can do the switch; he drives the van over to the yacht club, I take the spare key with me, and drive it back once I take the Newton around. Works out pretty good."

That would put the RIB, her smaller rigid inflatable boat, which was fast and manoeuvrable, on the west. It was the ideal boat to take to the wreck of the Raptor, especially as they'd have to grapple the wreck with a hook to moor the boat. Or leave the boat live, trolling around until they came up. She shook her head. She couldn't believe she was even contemplating diving the damn thing.

"When was the last time you dived the Raptor, Reg?"

He looked at her with a frown. "What hare-brained scheme you coming up with now?"

She laughed. "Not my scheme. Hazel's all fired up to take a look at it, and Thomas wants to see it before it slides over."

Reg took a sip of his cider and thought a moment. "I haven't been on it since tropical storm Nate moved it the last time. Arse end is hanging way over the wall now apparently. Next big storm and it's gone."

"I'm surprised it didn't go over in Nate, that blow was worse than most hurricanes on the west. To break the chains holding the Kittiwake and roll it on its side, the swells and surge had to have been huge." She shook her head, remembering the storm and the surprising amount of damage it caused.

"I dived it a few times before Hurricane Ivan. Before my time here it was much farther up the reef," Reg recalled. "Then Hurricane Allen in '80 slid it deeper, and Michelle rolled it a bit I believe, in 2001. Then Ivan shoved it down so the stern was about at the wall. I dived it then a few times, but you pretty much stayed around the superstructure because of the depth. Paloma in '08 stood it back upright, and Nate was the one that put it hanging over like it is now."

"Paloma wasn't that bad, was it? Didn't it miss Grand and hit Brac a lot worse? That was two years before I got here," AJ asked.

"Yeah, that's when the DOE here said no more diving on the Raptor. If Paloma could move it around, then it's too unstable." Reg looked over at her. "Besides, it's the current out there that's as much an issue as the depth. That's why tech training for deep stuff is done on the Carrie Lee, or over the wall farther west. Couple of blokes have got themselves killed getting lost inside the cabins, but more have vanished getting blown off the wreck. Started in the mid-seventies, I think, not long after it went down. Some guys *and* their boat went missing, never seen again."

"Jeez," AJ whispered.

"You thinking of taking clients there?" Reg asked.

"No, no. Well, I guess, Hazel would be considered a client, but maybe just me, her, and Thomas. Take someone else, maybe Carlos, to stay on the boat," AJ replied cautiously. She'd about convinced herself to go, but now she had doubts again. Her curiosity was driving her towards it, especially as the only dive she'd been on the wreck before was cut short when another diver had trouble. She also felt a strong urge to please Hazel and a little pressure to keep up with her enthusiasm to seek adventure.

"I'll go with you," Reg surprised her by saying.

"Seriously?" she asked in shock.

He grinned. "I've learnt by now that you'll bloody well do it whether I'm there or not so I might as well try and keep you from doing something completely mad down there."

She gave him a playful shove. "You big knucklehead."

21

APRIL 1974

Ainsley drove slowly towards the airport and pulled over to the side of the road short of the small terminal building to where Whitey directed him from the passenger seat. Whitey turned down the car stereo and quietened David Bowie singing 'Rebel Rebel' as they came to a stop. He reached over to the back seat and grabbed the Zero Halliburton briefcase he'd arrived with. It was considerably lighter now. Popping the latches, he retrieved a brown, unmarked envelope and handed it to Ainsley.

"Here, this is your cut for handling the logistics on the island," he said softly. "I appreciate your help, mate."

Ainsley looked surprised and carefully opened the folded end of the envelope and whistled when he looked inside.

"Damn Whitey, this is a lot of cash! This is more than I make in my best month hustling weed," he enthused, less softly.

Whitey leaned over and lowered Ainsley's hands holding a wad of cash. "Keep your voice down, mate."

A few travellers were walking into the terminal building but otherwise the only ears nearby belonged to the stray chickens that clucked and pecked around the roadside.

"That's ten grand, you'll get the same every time I bring a case full over. All I need is the police escort, for you to ride me around a bit, and we're gonna need your brother's boat one time each visit from now on."

Ainsley grinned. "Seriously? Ten grand for doing that each time? No problem, man. Come back as often as you like." He nudged Whitey's arm and laughed. "Every week would be great, man."

Whitey smiled at his friend's easy-going style and infectious humour. "It'll be once a month or so, but I'll call you and give you a few days' warning each time. Sorry to call in the middle of the night but it's the only time I know you'll be home to answer." Whitey laughed. "One day the island will catch up with the world and get an answering service you can use."

"What's an answering service do?" Ainsley asked innocently.

"They answer your phone for you and take messages," Whitey replied, even more amused.

Ainsley looked perplexed. "So someone sits around my house and answers my phone when I'm not there? I don't want no one in my house when I ain't there, man."

Whitey roared with laughter and several nearby chickens made the cardinal sin of running across the road away from the noise. "They're not in your house you plonker, they're in an office, your calls get directed there when you're not home."

"We're way beyond that man," Ainsley waved a hand in the air. "We got rid of the operator with the telephone switchboard years ago, man, we're cutting edge here brother, cutting edge."

Whitey shook his head and gave up.

"You know," Ainsley turned serious, "you don't need a police escort from the airport. There's no one here on the island that'll try and rob you man. I'm the biggest criminal here and I just sell some weed and a few imported goods under the radar. Worst that ever happens here is the odd family disagreement that might end up in a fist fight; nobody gonna touch a tourist, believe me."

Whitey sat back into his seat and looked at his friend. "How long we known each other?"

Ainsley took a moment. "A long time, brother – what, 1945? That's nearly thirty years man."

"That's right, thirty years. And since the day we met you've always steered me right. We started back in '45 trading a few boxes of smokes, and you've always taken care of me whenever I've showed up on the island every five or ten years since. Well, now I can take care of you a little bit." Whitey held up a finger. "But, you gotta know, this group I'm working for don't bugger about. That's why I'm taking out a little insurance."

Ainsley looked confused. "How do you mean?"

"They're South American, Peruvian in fact, and it's different down there, it's like the wild bloody west. They buy the police and the officials, so they'll let them do what they want. They got 'em all on the payroll, that's how it works. If I went back and said it don't cost me nothin' to work the system here, they wouldn't believe me. So, I pay you to facilitate, and they don't need to know you don't have to pay off the coppers, do they?"

Ainsley nodded slowly. "Okay man, I get it. But why the boat?"

"That's the insurance part." Whitey grinned. "These blokes are paranoid as all hell; they trust you like family, then next minute they get suspicious you're screwing 'em, and you've got a bullet in the back of your noggin, no questions, no discussions, no explanations. Ruthless buggers." He took a deep breath as he thought about it, and he noticed Ainsley looked a little scared. "Anyway, my insurance is, I'm hiding the safety deposit key. That way they can't just whack me if they decide I'm not on their side, or they won't get their money back. Daft buggers are still worried about the banks here, so they said get a safety deposit box instead, at least to start with. So that's what I did. Except I got two. One is in my name and theirs, one is in my name only. Only thing in the joint one is a note saying 'See Whitey for the other box key'."

"Wow man," Ainsley mumbled, astonished.

Whitey handed him an oddly cut silver key. "Keep this safe. When I get back, I'll deposit the next round of cash, and then you and me are taking a boat ride. I've found the perfect place to hide that key. Believe me, these buggers can't even swim, so the bottom of the ocean is the perfect place to hide the key. The pool they put in at their mansion in Peru has a shallow end and an only slightly deeper end; none of it's more than four feet deep. They walk around in the water on a hot day. So, to get the real key, they'll need me, and need me alive."

Ainsley timidly took the key like it was a burning hot poker. "When you back?"

"Don't worry brother, keep that key safe for a few weeks, then it'll be out of your hands and hidden in the spot I've found, safe as houses." Whitey slapped him on the arm and pointed to the terminal building ahead. "Come on then, I gotta plane to catch."

Ainsley put the car in gear, still stunned. "Okay man, sounds like you've figured it all out."

Whitey grinned reassuringly at his friend. "Course I have mate, don't you worry, ole Whitey's got you taken care of."

22

NOVEMBER 2019

"North tomorrow everyone," AJ announced as Thomas piloted the Newton away from Reg's dock in West Bay. "We'll move the boat this afternoon, so we'll still be on the big boat – just meet us at the yacht club."

She looked over at Hazel, who was setting up her gear while she listened. "I'll pick you up fifteen minutes earlier from your hotel, okay?"

Hazel smiled and nodded. "Oui."

"How about we head towards north-west point this morning?" AJ asked the group. "Maybe see if we can get on Orange Canyon?"

The idea was met with enthusiasm from the Davises and the Freemans so Thomas, who'd been listening from the fly bridge, cut the wheel to starboard, and gently eased the throttles forward.

"AJ," Bill Davis asked, "we were wondering if you'd do a navigation class with the girls? Maybe on the second dive?"

The girls looked over at AJ hopefully and she thought for a moment. "Well, the course is three dives and some class. We can do most of the class on the boat, the only problem is starting today. If I'd known, I would have brought an extra person along. We're required to leave a person on the boat while the other leads the dive, but I can get Carlos to come with us tomorrow. He knows the north side really well," she added, chuckling to herself.

"I can take the group if everyone is okay with that," Hazel said from behind where AJ was standing.

Everyone turned to look at her and she smiled back. "I'm a divemaster; I used to work on the dive boats on my days off in the summer in France."

"That's right, of course," AJ replied. "But you're on holiday, I can't ask you to work. You're here to relax and have fun."

"We'd be fine with it," Beth Freeman added. "She's amazing in the water and we know our way around anyway."

"It would be fun for me," Hazel said happily. "Everyone here is a good diver – I'd just be choosing the directions we'd go, right?"

AJ shrugged her shoulders. "Sounds good then, Thomas will take first dive then we'll see if we can get on Bonnie's Arch for the second. Hazel will guide." She turned to the two girls. "And we'll see if you two can find your way back to the boat. Better get your compasses and we'll make a start."

The girls, Scarlett and Kelsi, cheered and bustled about retrieving their compasses from their BCDs.

"Really appreciate it," Bill directed at both Hazel and AJ. "Next trip we need to put the girls through the advanced course, but this will be a good start. Thank you."

They both smiled and after Bill stepped away Hazel whispered to AJ, "You okay with this? I didn't mean to tread on your toes, but it seemed like an easy solution."

AJ put her hand on the French woman's shoulder. "I'm great with it, I just feel bad you're working on your holiday. I'll ask Carlos if he can come tomorrow so we'll be covered."

"Or not," Hazel replied. "If you're okay with how today goes I'm happy to do it as much as needed. It's interesting for me and I get to really learn the dive sites having to pay more attention." She laughed.

AJ whispered back, "I zone out sometimes, especially on sites we dive a lot and I know really well. Then I freak out when I realise we're half a mile from the boat." The two laughed again but the idea of Hazel helping as a divemaster sowed seeds in AJ's mind. She thought about saying something more, but decided she should indeed see how the day went.

The mooring pin was open on Orange Canyon. Thomas led the group on the deep dive amongst giant orange elephant ear sponges and a myriad of life, including a large loggerhead turtle they followed while it feasted on sponges. They moved over to Bonnie's Arch mooring pin and AJ spent the surface interval working with the girls in preparation for their navigation dive, where they would do a series of exercises using their compasses and identifying natural landmarks. Thomas and Hazel sat up on the fly bridge, away from the group, so he could give her a rundown on the dive site.

Once in the water it felt a little strange to AJ watching someone she didn't know that well take her clients away on their dive. She soon thought no more about it as she led the girls through the magnificent coral arch that prominently dominated an open area of crushed coral and sand. Using the arch as their base point, AJ had Scarlett find and follow a south-east compass heading to keep them in the shallower waters before making three ninety degree turns to return to the arch. So Kelsi couldn't copy the route, AJ had her take a reverse course of her sister's. Both girls did a great job and AJ marvelled at their comfort in the water, and calm, gentle movements. They were both so excitable out of the water, always doing something and chattering, but were placid and serene as soon as they submerged. AJ took a little pride in knowing, as their teacher, she may have had a positive influence on their dive style.

The group reappeared as AJ and the girls were just starting their three-minute safety stop at fifteen feet, so they were all finished and climbing back on the boat around the same time. Thomas helped everyone back aboard, and by the enthusiastic chatter amongst the divers, it appeared Hazel's dive was quite a success.

"Two eagle rays," Beth Freeman enthused. "Came right by us!"

"And the biggest nurse shark I think I've ever seen," her husband added.

AJ loved hearing two forty-year veterans still get so excited over a dive they'd made hundreds of times. She looked over at Hazel. "Sounds like a fantastic dive."

Hazel smiled back and gave her a wink. "We didn't lose anyone at least."

AJ laughed. "Well Scarlett and Kelsi can lead us all tomorrow, they're great navigators, they both did really well." She eased over next to her new friend and asked quietly, "Want to take a ride around to the north after lunch? I have to move the boat and wouldn't mind the company."

"Love to," Hazel quickly replied.

23

MAY 1974

The heat and humidity was no less stifling in Miami than it had been on the island, despite being farther north. The lack of a constant, cooling breeze amongst the buildings of the city, and the heat generated by cars, air conditioners, and countless other machinery fed the muggy air. Whitey was relieved to be dropped off by the taxi in Coconut Grove on the south side of Miami, right on the water. His brown flared corduroys and matching jacket over a brightly striped polyester shirt wasn't the best choice for late-afternoon Florida, but he'd wanted to look hip for his dinner. He paid the driver and turned to look at the lavish hotel. A red Ferrari Dino spider, a yellow Lamborghini Countach and a silver-grey Bentley Corniche adorned the valet parking area.

"Welcome to the Mutiny Hotel and Nightclub – checking in, sir?" came a voice from the entryway and Whitey looked over to see the doorman, dressed in a nice suit, smiling politely at him.

"Visiting a friend actually. Mr Cavero," Whitey replied as he made his way up the steps to the front door.

The man opened the door for him. "Ah yes, we've been expecting you, sir. Mr Cavero has made arrangements for you to have a room for the weekend."

Whitey paused and looked at the doorman thinking they must have him confused with someone else.

"Mr Snow, correct?" the doorman asked, seeing Whitey's expression.

Whitey shrugged his shoulders. He never knew what Gabriel would spring on him next, so getting him a room less than two miles from where Whitey had his own apartment was par for the course.

"That's me, Whitey Snow."

The man smiled and ushered Whitey inside. "No luggage, sir?"

Whitey chuckled. "No, no luggage. Wasn't expecting an overnight."

The doorman didn't miss a beat. "No problem sir, happens a lot here; we have a gift shop to accommodate all your needs."

Whitey looked out of the window of his seventh-floor room across the bay towards Key Biscayne, between him and the open Atlantic Ocean. His room was a splurge of excess with a king-sized bed with purple sheets, a large oval tub in the corner with gold taps, various nautical themed accessories and decorations, and gold patterned wallpaper that bathed the room in a warm yellow hue. Whitey was just wondering what he was supposed to do next, when a hammering knock came from his door.

Gabriel nearly bowled him over as he barged into the room when Whitey opened the door. The man was almost a foot shorter than Whitey with a slight, wiry build, yet his hug made Whitey take a step or two backwards.

"Mi hermano!" Gabriel enthused loudly, slapping Whitey on the back before releasing him and striding into the room, spinning around with his arms in the air, his shoulder length black hair swishing. "Isn't this place incredible!"

Whitey closed the door and laughed, "Yeah Gabby, it's bloody amazing, but why did you get me a room? I only live just up the road."

Gabriel banged on the window. "Your place have a view like this, mi hermano?"

Whitey joined him and put his arm around his shoulders, "No, my friend, it does not." Whitey looked down at the numerous boats moored in the expensive nearby marina, and sailing across the water. "There's some beautiful boats around here."

Gabriel waved a hand at him. "Damn boats, hate the things, man lives on land, Whitey. If we were supposed to be in the water, God would have given us the things fish breath through."

"Gills," Whitey helped him with the English word.

"Si, gills." Gabriel looked up at Whitey with a mischievous grin and switched to Spanish. "Besides, we are celebrating this weekend."

"Oh yeah, what are we celebrating?" Whitey replied, also switching to his boss's language.

Gabriel slapped his back, his whole body shaking with excitement. "Maria is pregnant my friend, we're going to have a baby boy!"

"That's fantastic news mate, congratulations!" Whitey hugged his friend. "You know it's a boy already?" he asked as he released him.

"Of course it's a boy! We don't know for sure, but Caveros always have boys first, and besides," Gabriel turned serious, "an old lady in Huánuco who reads palms and other bullshit told me if you do it from behind you get boys. Maria says her knees are worn raw but for sure it has to be a boy!" Gabriel burst out laughing. "Tonight my brother, we are going to celebrate! My beautiful wife is giving me a son! The club here at the hotel is the best in the world! You have to be a member, rock stars, movie stars, everyone comes here, man. Champagne will flow, and the girls here, holy mother the girls here, my brother." He crossed his chest and looked to the ceiling towards God. "We're going to have more beautiful women than you can imagine."

Whitey sat down on a wooden chair by the small desk in the

room and Gabriel sat on the end of the bed. "So, a little business before we have dinner. How was your trip?"

Whitey nodded. "Good, it all went smooth, no problems. My contact had everything lined up, police escort, the works. I set up a safety deposit box as you asked." Whitey reached into his back pocket and retrieved a key wrapped in a piece of paper. "Here's the key, you and I have one each, box is in both our names, either can access it." He handed Gabriel the key and the paper. "Bank and box number are on there. Whenever you feel happy with the bank there, I'll move the money to an account."

Gabriel nodded slowly. "Good, good, I'm sure the bank is secure, but let's give it a few more trips. My father doesn't trust banks too much. The ones in Peru are a joke; every once in a while some government official decides he's going to be a hero and shuts down the accounts of business men like us. Causes a lot of problems until we can remove the fool."

Whitey shuddered at the thought of what fate befell such a brave soul.

Gabriel continued, "Tonight you'll meet the main Colombian we do business with, he's a quiet one, all business. The crazy bastards are the Cubans, they throw money around like water. Stay away from them."

Whitey wondered how ruthless you had to be to make ruthless people call you crazy.

Gabriel kept going. "Our arrangement with the Colombians is perfect, all we do is move product across one border. As I've told you, we own every official at the border, so for us it's easy. No bullshit shipping product here like they do. The US customs are much harder to buy out, and impossible to get them all on the payroll. Only takes one hardnose cop and you've lost an entire shipment."

Gabriel flippantly waved his hand in the air, accentuating his point.

"Anyway, when I can't be here in Miami, I want you to deal with this guy, so it's important you meet him."

Whitey nodded. "Okay, no problem." He didn't know what else

to say. Since he'd met Gabriel two years before, here in Miami, he'd liked the guy and they'd become good friends. The deeper he became involved, the more concerned he'd become that these men operated at a level he wasn't comfortable with. Buying and selling some weed, and occasionally some blow, to small time operators was one thing, but wholesale manufacturing top-grade cocaine for mass export was a whole different world. One Whitey felt ill equipped to navigate in. These men bought and sold lives like bottles of milk. But here he was, up to his eyeballs with the biggest drug dealer in Peru. Men who didn't understand the word no. The only way out was a bullet. When you got involved this deep, you knew too much to be wandering around outside their organisation. He couldn't tell Gabriel no.

"In two weeks come back to Huánuco for the next shipment, okay?" Gabriel asked, but Whitey didn't take it as a request. "Our shipments keep increasing so we may need to export more than once a month." Gabriel smiled. "And my father has bags of money hidden all over the damn ranch. I want him to move it somewhere safer; maybe your island is the place."

"Okay," was all Whitey could say.

24

NOVEMBER 2019

AJ drove the van along the tiny Mary Mollie Hydes Road with the beach and ocean on their right and parked at the end of the street. Hazel followed her as they both stepped out and walked up to a brightly coloured shack with 'Heritage Kitchen' written over the open serving window.

"Hey there AJ, got some lionfish for me?" Josephine Ebanks, a friendly Caymanian woman with a big smile and booming voice, asked.

"Not today I'm afraid," she replied, lifting her sunglasses to her forehead, "I was teaching and couldn't hunt this morning."

"Ooh, I meant to tell you we saw three or four all on the same coral head," Hazel recalled. "I wish I'd had your spear."

"We'll have to put you through the class the DOE requires to hunt here," AJ told her. "It's quick and easy but you have to have a licence and use the registered DOE spears."

Hazel smiled and put her hands together. "Cool, I have projects to keep you busy for weeks."

AJ turned back to Josephine. "Could we have three fish sandwiches, whatever you have in this morning, and a couple of your lovely fruit juices please?" AJ and Hazel both handed the lady stainless steel drinks bottles.

Josephine nodded cheerily. "No problem." She took the bottles. "I have some grouper, maybe pan sear so it stays hot? I assume you're getting to go?"

"Yes please," AJ answered.

"No problem, my dear, I'll give it a little Cayman kick, make your afternoon more spicy huh?" She laughed and her whole face beamed.

AJ and Hazel laughed and let the chef go to work.

With hot sandwiches wrapped in foil and drinks in hand, they stepped back on the boat tied to Reg's dock. AJ handed Thomas the sandwich she'd got for him, which he set down while he cast the lines from the dock cleats as she scampered up the ladder and started the engine.

She called back down, "Thanks Thomas, keys are in the van."

Thomas pushed the bow away from the dock with his foot. "Thanks for lunch! Have fun. See you on the water."

AJ idled the big Newton away from the dock and unwrapped her sandwich as Hazel leaned against the rail next to her and did the same. They savoured the fresh fish with frequent swigs of the juice to calm the spices Josephine had not held back on. Turning to the north-west, it wasn't long before they were close to where they'd dived that morning. AJ took a long drink of juice as she studied the coastline.

"The Raptor is out here somewhere," she pointed to deeper water off the port bow. "The wall is farther from shore around the point here and the wreck isn't marked by a mooring because they don't want anyone diving it." She glanced at Hazel, who was intently studying the water as though she'd be able to see the wreck somehow.

"Tomorrow afternoon," AJ said quietly. "We'll use my other boat, the one Thomas is bringing around."

Hazel turned with a surprised and hopeful expression. "Seriously? We can dive the wreck tomorrow?"

AJ nodded. "Yeah. Reg and Thomas are coming with us too."

"They're diving too?" Hazel asked cautiously.

"Yup. Thomas really wants to see it and Reg is like my second dad, so he's coming so he doesn't sit at the dock and worry. That okay?" she asked, noting hesitation in Hazel's question.

Hazel's face lit up. "Of course! That's great they want to come. Thank you so much for doing this." She clapped her hands enthusiastically. "It'll be so much fun."

AJ began turning the corner around north-west point. "Feel the current here?" she said as the motor strained a touch more and she pushed the throttle forward a little to compensate. "It's actually pretty mild right now, that'll be good if it stays that way for tomorrow."

Hazel glanced back over at the open water beyond the point. She was wearing a loose tank top over her bathing suit and AJ noticed her skin was tanning quickly since she'd arrived only a few days ago. The woman had a perfect figure, toned and firm but still with feminine curves. The kind of body that appeared natural and eye catching, while hiding the fact it took a lot of work to keep it that way. AJ wondered what she did to stay in such good shape, she couldn't imagine working in art galleries was much of a workout. Hazel turned around and AJ realised she was caught staring.

"What?" Hazel asked in friendly tone.

"Sorry." AJ felt a little embarrassed. "I was wondering what do you do to stay in shape. You look amazing."

Hazel laughed. "That's funny coming from you, you're the perfect girl."

AJ blushed and Hazel continued, "I do some martial arts, mainly jujutsu. I started it to feel more comfortable as a woman living alone, and then found I really liked it. And it was more fun than going to a gym."

"Wow." AJ was impressed. "That's cool, I don't know much about that stuff, I did a little judo when I was a kid, but I really don't know the differences between the styles."

"Jujutsu is similar to judo. It's focused on self-defence moves, holds, throws, and ways to pin someone rather than say, karate, which is kicks and ways to attack. I know some karate too though," Hazel explained. "But I got way too into it all a few years back. I eventually realised the competitions and events were taking away some of the fun, so I went back to just training."

"Bloody hell, you fought in competitions? That's amazing."

Hazel waved it away. "Just local stuff, no big deal."

"So, what are you going to do when you go home?" AJ blurted and realised she was prying a bit much right after the words came out. "Sorry, that's not my business, you have enough going on."

Hazel smiled. "It's okay, you can ask me anything, we're friends, right?"

AJ felt relieved that she wasn't the only one feeling they were becoming close over a short period of time. She felt drawn to Hazel in a way she couldn't explain. The woman was so easy to be around and she was incredibly capable, seemingly at everything, but definitely at diving which was AJ's world.

"I was thinking, if you're looking for a change of pace from the art thing, why don't you work as a divemaster, if only for a while as you work things out?" AJ added more tentatively. "You could do it at home, or even over here, if you like it on the island."

Hazel looked at AJ thoughtfully, seemingly weighing her response carefully. "Funny you say that. After this morning it made me start thinking about it." Hazel shifted her stare out across the Caribbean Sea. "I envy your life here," she said quietly.

AJ knew she was privileged to be able to do what she did, in the beautiful place she called home, but still she didn't imagine someone as strong and confident as Hazel envying her.

"Well, Reg and I are always looking for good help. The young divemasters usually do a season or two and then move on to the next cool place, so spots come up. Not that we're the only ones here," she added quickly. "As you've seen there's plenty of dive operations to choose from."

Hazel smiled but AJ noticed a hint of something else in her expression. She thought it might be sadness. Or maybe she felt awkward being grilled or didn't want to say she'd rather not work with her? She wasn't sure.

Hazel spoke softly. "I would love to work here, and work with you." She stiffened slightly. "But I have some things to sort out before I could consider such a move."

AJ wanted to ask what she meant, but decided she'd probably pried enough.

25

MAY 1974

A mop of long blonde hair sprawled across the table and the sound of white powder being loudly vacuumed up through the girl's nose could be heard over George McCrae's 'Rock Your Baby' blaring over the club's sound system. The dance floor was packed with a sea of humanity sporting every bright colour in winged shirt, flared pant, halter top, tube top, and shorts that redefined short. Whitey looked at the blonde, who couldn't be older than twenty, as she picked her face up off the table and sat back, eyes wide, with remnants of cocaine around her nostrils. Her friend, a similar aged black girl with an impressive afro, leaned over and licked her face clean with a seductive smile towards Gabriel, who watched with a wicked grin, his white suit shimmering under the lights.

The song finished and an MC announced that next would be DJ Jimmy Yu mixing and spinning disco sounds that would blow your socks off. Gabriel leapt up and applauded loudly along with the girls and most of the crowd in the packed club. Whitey felt old. He had no idea what was going on, or what mixing and spinning meant. He yearned for some Bachman–Turner Overdrive or those new guys, Queen – he liked them a lot.

"Whitey, mi hermano," Gabriel shouted enthusiastically, "this guy is the next big thing in the clubs, man, you'll love him, this disco groove is gonna be the bomb. He'll be in New York before you know it!"

Whitey gave him a thumbs up and mustered a "Right on" to appease his boss.

More dance music hammered from the club's strained speakers, but Whitey could tell something different was happening as the DJ wove two different songs, neither of which Whitey knew, together in some kind of blend. He seemed to do it quite skilfully, Whitey thought, as he peered around the smoke-filled club, though the lights flashed and whirled making him slightly dizzy. He'd avoided most of the alcohol Gabriel had been putting in front of him, and years ago he'd decided drugs usually left him in compromised and embarrassing places. He squinted at a booth in the shadows. Shit, he thought to himself, that's John Bonham.

"Gabby!" Whitey reached past the two girls, who were wriggling on the couch to the music and sipping Dom Perignon from the bottle. He grabbed Gabriel's arm. "Gabby! That's John bloody Bonham over there," he said, nodding his head in the direction of the booth.

Gabriel looked over in the direction and shrugged his shoulders. "Who the hell is that?"

Whitey was beside himself. "Who the hell is that? What do you mean, Gabby? Led bloody Zeppelin mate, John Bonham, the best drummer that ever took a bleeding breath!"

Gabriel shrugged his shoulders again. "So? I heard Jack Nicholson is coming tonight and Liza Minnelli is over there pestering Rudy Redbeard Gallo for more blow." Gabriel's face lit up. "I told you man, this place is *the* place to be in Miami."

Whitey shook his head. "How come the coppers don't raid this joint? They'd pick up half the world's dealers and suppliers in one bust."

Gabriel laughed. "You kidding me? It would be a bloodbath, there's more fire power in this hotel than in the whole of Saigon right now. The Cubans have all the Miami cops on payroll anyway, they're not dumb enough to raid this place." Gabriel leaned closer. "But if we ever come in here and don't see some Colombians, or the Cubans aren't here, then leave. You never know when someone will turn and organise a raid to grab a bigger piece of the market. That's why we stay out of this mess." Gabriel tapped his temple. "Gotta always be thinking, my brother."

Whitey nodded and sat back down as the waitress swung by in a large frilly hat and a loose shirt, with most of the buttons undone.

"Anything I can get you Mr Cavero?" she asked, leaning over to give Gabriel a nice view of her cleavage.

Gabriel looked around the table, which appeared to be void of drinks, as the girls finished the champagne in a final swig.

"Two more bottles of champagne, and..." He pointed at Whitey. "Mi hermano, what can I bring you that you'll actually drink?"

Whitey laughed; his boss seemed like he was letting his hair down but he never missed a trick.

"Havana Club, over ice please, my dear," Whitey asked politely.

"That's Cuban rum, sir, we can't serve Cuban rum in America," she replied with a smile, and looked over at Gabriel.

"Oh, of course, sorry..." Whitey began to change his order but Gabriel waved a hand in the air. "It's okay, I'll have one as well, my dear. See Burton and tell him it's for me," Gabriel added, winking at the waitress.

She immediately nodded at the drop of the owner's name and headed for the bar.

Whitey glanced at his watch as he unlocked his room. Three thirty am. He dragged himself inside and heard Gabriel, with both girls in tow, fumbling with his own room key. Closing the door, he took a long deep breath. He was dead tired, and his head throbbed from hours of loud thumping music and breathing thick, cigarette smoke-infused air. He walked to the window and slid it open, savouring the fresh air, even though the night was still muggy and hot. As had happened frequently throughout the evening, his mind wandered back to Grand Cayman and Isabella. Not since he was a young lad in the Navy, first discovering the fairer sex, had he been so taken with a woman. Closing his eyes, he pictured her sitting across from him at dinner, her beautiful long black hair, her perfectly smooth, tanned skin that made his own skin tingle with goose bumps. Her blend of maturity and innocence. He opened his eyes as something large and weighty plummeted through his vision to a grotesque thump on the ground below. Startled, he looked down before he could stop himself. The twisted figure of a human being was lying still on the concrete patio below. A deep scarlet river eased its way downhill towards the swimming pool, faintly lit by the mood lighting surrounding the patio. A man, a living person, had just dropped to their death before his very eyes. He'd seen many things in his time, and been witness to the violence of war, but the suddenness and immediacy of a man being killed in the middle of the night, in the suburbs of a major city, in peacetime, was paralysing. Next door the window slid open, and Whitey looked over to see Gabriel, bleary eyed and shirtless, look down, then up to the floors above. He turned to Whitey.

"Damn Cubans," he said nonchalantly and closed his window.

26

NOVEMBER 2019

With the Newton moored securely at the yacht club marina, AJ found the keys Thomas had left. They'd passed Thomas just after they'd made the cut into the North Sound as he moved the RIB in the opposite direction back to West Bay. AJ pulled out of the car park and started along the narrow road leading back to Esterly Tibbetts Highway.

"Where do you shop around here?" Hazel asked out of nowhere.

AJ laughed. "Where do I shop? If you mean clothes shopping, I don't!" She rolled her eyes. "It's too expensive here. I get stuff from reps who come by once in a while, sale rack at the dive shops sometimes, Cost-U-Less, the island's version of a discount superstore. Why?"

Hazel gave her a mischievous look. "Sometimes it's fun to buy something nice, it feels good."

"Well, Camana Bay is our shopping centre, it's quite fancy, what do you need?" AJ asked.

"Got some time?" Hazel asked. "Let's have a ladies' afternoon, maybe pamper ourselves a bit."

AJ laughed again. "Now? I stink! I haven't showered since we came out of the water this morning."

Hazel waved her off. "Who cares, anyway, you don't stink, it's a tropical island, you're supposed to smell like the beach and the water. Where is this Camana Bay?"

AJ turned left at the roundabout and headed down the dual carriageway. "Couple of miles this way. But I warn you, I'm not a shopper, I'm allergic to full retail pricing."

Hazel grinned. "Stop, ummm…" she searched for the word she wanted in English, "fussing! Yes, stop fussing about it, we'll have fun!"

"Oh, I'm fussy now, am I?" AJ pretended to be insulted. "That's nice. Fine, I'll go shopping with you. Only because I'm dying for a coffee and there's a decent coffee shop there."

Hazel smiled, and they chatted happily as AJ made the ten-minute drive to the outdoor shopping centre.

With coffees in hand they sauntered in and out of a few clothing stores, Hazel thumbing through the racks and displays more enthu-siastically than AJ. Walking into a very sophisticated clothing shop, AJ was hesitant, but Hazel shoved her into the air-conditioned, glass-fronted establishment, to a disdainful look from the elegant lady behind the counter.

"Can I help you?" the lady managed, more politely than AJ was expecting, in an accented voice.

"Française?" Hazel quickly responded.

"Oui," the lady replied in surprise.

Hazel walked towards the lady, setting her little backpack-style handbag on the counter. The two then launched into an animated and friendly conversation that AJ's few years of French in school couldn't keep pace with. She wandered around the shop looking over the clothes, leaving them to enjoy conversing in their native language. After turning a couple of price tags she decided it was better not to do that anymore; she couldn't see spending that kind of money on a piece of clothing. She'd always been a practical woman, far more interested in a useful piece of equipment than anything involving fashion. But Cayman catered to the rich and she was certain there were plenty of visitors and ex-pats living here that happily paid these prices for something they'd wear once or twice. Each to their own she thought, and mentally counted the blouses she had hanging in her wardrobe at home. A summer dress caught her eye. It was navy blue with a large paisley patterned print in reds, yellows and oranges. She held it up against her figure and looked across the room to a mirror. The sleeveless style suited her well with her tattoos and the dress was mini length, without being too short. She really liked the dress but was too scared to look at the price. She hung it back up and turned around, realising the chatter had stopped. Hazel was standing right there with a big smile. "Not a shopper, huh?"

AJ shook her head and whispered. "No! I'm not paying these prices for anything!"

Hazel laughed. "Come on then, let's get out of here."

They headed out with a wave to the lady and Hazel looped her arm in AJ's as they strolled away.

"That dress was perfect for you, looked amazing."

AJ sighed. "It was, huh? But no way am I paying that money, it was probably the price of a wetsuit, and I need a new wetsuit more than a fancy dress."

"Hey there," came a voice from the patio of a cafe they were passing. The two looked over and saw the Freemans having an afternoon drink.

"Hello guys," AJ replied and walked over to their table. "Enjoying your afternoon?"

They offered the women a chair and AJ sat, still holding the coffee they'd bought earlier.

"Like a drink?" David offered.

"I'm fine thanks," AJ replied, holding up her coffee cup.

Hazel smiled and didn't sit. "Excuse me, I think I left my phone in the last store we were in." She started back towards the shop. "I'll be right back."

"I'm excited to dive north tomorrow," Beth said, bringing AJ's attention back to the table.

"Me too," AJ replied. "We moved the boats after lunch, so we're all set, and it was flat calm on the north side when we came around."

"Wonderful, it's always a treat to dive the north wall," Beth said happily. "Hazel said this is her first visit to the island. Where did you two meet?"

"Here," AJ replied, slightly confused. "We just met this week."

Beth laughed and looked at David. "We thought you were old friends, the two of you get along so well."

Hazel walked back up and AJ smiled at her. "Yeah, we do, huh?"

Twenty minutes later Hazel and AJ were back in the van heading towards Harbour View hotel, where Hazel was staying. It was a low-key, older place that was nothing more than a handful of rooms in a couple of buildings on the water, just outside George Town. It was owned and run by a Caymanian family that had done so for years. Rooms were clean, basic, and reasonably priced, which was hard to find with an ocean view. AJ pulled into their small car park and Hazel opened the door and stepped out.

"Fifteen minutes earlier in the morning, okay?" AJ reminded Hazel.

"Sounds good and thanks for this afternoon, really enjoyed tagging along, and dragging you to the shopping centre," she replied.

AJ laughed. "Well, I had fun, so thank you."

"Here," Hazel pulled something from her bag and threw it over to AJ before closing the door.

AJ looked at the plush looking shopping bag in her lap. She opened the bag and froze when she saw the dress she'd admired inside. She stared out the front window with her jaw dropped open. Hazel looked back with a big smile and blew her a kiss.

27

MAY 1974

Whitey stirred from beneath the purple sheets to bright daylight leaking past the edge of the curtains. His head still felt dull, although he hadn't had much to drink, despite Gabriel's attempts. He reached to the bedside table, found his watch, and squinted to read the hands. Ten forty. He'd struggled to sleep after seeing the man on the pavement below. He had double-checked his door was locked, and even propped the wooden desk chair against the handle in case anyone came for him in the night; for what reason he had no logical idea why. But somehow it made him feel safer, despite knowing the chair or the lock wouldn't stop anyone with ill intent. It had seemed like forever for the sirens to wail, and finally arrive outside. He guessed no one was willing, or could be troubled, to call the police after it happened. Probably found by some poor employee, leaving after their shift at the club. That person would also have the image of the broken man forever stamped in their mind.

Whitey rolled out of bed and walked to the window. He hesitated. It's a cruel trick the human brain loves to play, between knowing you don't want to see, and the unstoppable curiosity that forces you to look at the car crash. Or pull a curtain back. He slowly revealed the scene below, and for a second, he thought he may have dreamed the whole event. The pool area was bustling with people, bikini-clad women sunned themselves with the shiny glow of suntan oil, and waitresses circled with trays of drinks. Whitey strained against the bright morning sun to see the place on the pavement where the body had lain. He could barely make out a hint of discolouration in the concrete as a man in black Speedos unknowingly walked across the very spot. He let the curtain fall and stepped back in a daze. What world had he managed to embroil himself in? He'd seen a few things at the end of the war, the ease with which human life could be taken away, but that was war. He didn't know if the man from last night was a good guy, or a vicious criminal. Was he honest? Cruel? Did he have a wife? Children? What he did know was that one minute the guy was living and breathing, with life ahead, probably things to do, maybe a fence to mend at his house, and groceries to pick up. Or children to take to school. And seconds later, after a terrifying drop during which his fate became irreversibly clear to him, everything he was going to do, everything he could have been, was gone.

Whitey walked to the bathroom and splashed cold water over his face. Most likely that guy was a cruel fellow that the world wouldn't miss. But maybe he was just a bloke like himself, he thought with a shudder, and looked at his tired face in the mirror. He needed to get himself out of this mess, he decided as he stared at the forty-seven-year-old man looking back at him. He'd made some wrong turns before in his life and got himself in more than his fair share of pickles. Though this was less immediately threatening, it was far more frightening.

After the war Whitey had spent four years in the far east, mainly Thailand, which was a country in turmoil having sided with the Japanese until the end, when they switched back and made friends with the Allies. The political chaos provided a perfect environment for easy trading of goods, and living was so cheap, Whitey lived like a king. Quality booze was his main commodity, as it was hard to come by, and craved by the European officials and businessmen living there. Australia became his main source, and after much travelling back and forth, he fell in love with Cairns and the Great Barrier Reef off the east coast of the continent. With enough contacts in Thailand, he shifted his base to the north-eastern Australian city, and would have stayed there forever. Unfortunately for Whitey the Australian authorities were less corrupt and a bit sharper than the Thai, and after a two-month stint behind bars courtesy of the Australian government, he cut his losses, jumped on the first boat back to England, and started over.

Whitey loved England. He loved his mum. But his father was a wretched man who'd lost his own father in the First World War and grown up angry and bitter. Whitey could never understand why his mother had ever married the man, but all she would say was "he was different back then". It was hard for her young son to see past the character that would rather spend his weekends down the pub than with his family. He seemed so mad at her, and even more so with his boy. Drunk and hateful, he'd yell at her, and hit Whitey so hard the boy would often be green and purple with bruises. The more his mother protested, the more the man would hit his son, so they learnt to be quiet. In his teenage years, Whitey grew like a weed, and was soon taller and much faster than his father. He could dodge the blows, but feared the man would turn on his mother if he couldn't take out his angst on Whitey. He'd let him get a slap or two in, and that seemed to pacify his father enough to flop in his chair and sleep off the booze. Whitey couldn't wait to join up the moment they'd let him.

Her son returning to England delighted his mother. His father briefly glanced up disdainfully from his newspaper and muttered, "Ah, you're back I see. Well don't expect to stay here. Don't think you can just show up and leach off me." That said, he turned back to his paper. Whitey hugged his frail mother for several minutes before walking out the front door, and vowed to never set foot in that house again.

He would meet his mum for tea and a scone, or sit in the park with her, but he refused to enter the house again. He pleaded with her to leave, but she wouldn't. "What would he do if I left?" she'd ask.

"That's his problem mum," Whitey begged. "The miserable bastard has made his bed, let him lie in it." But she wouldn't.

It was 1966, six years after Whitey had returned to England, when his mother was diagnosed with cancer. Within nine weeks he watched them lower her into the ground. Whitey stood on the opposite side of the grave from his father. They never spoke a word. The next day Whitey talked his way onto a freighter heading for America.

Putting yesterday's clothes back on, Whitey quietly left his hotel room and asked the doorman to hail him a taxi. Ten minutes later he walked into his own apartment, shed the corduroy outfit, stood under his shower, and let the water wash away the thoughts that plagued his mind.

28

NOVEMBER 2019

AJ sat at her modest dining table, under the front window of her tiny apartment. She stared out the window at the reds, purples, and oranges formed on the horizon as the sun sank behind a thin band of cloud far to the west. On the table her laptop made a ringing sound like a phone, and she turned to accept the video call. After a few seconds of scratchy static Jackson's face appeared, his beard a little stragglier than when he'd left her four days ago, but his gentle smile lit up the room and made AJ skip a breath.

"Hi there," she said through a smile.

"Hey. You look like you had a good day?" he replied.

AJ laughed. "I'm that obvious, am I? Guess poker's not my calling, huh?"

"Maybe not," he chuckled, "but I love seeing you happy. Hope it's not because I left?" he said humorously.

"No!" she frowned back. "I miss you terribly already. It's just been a good few days. The dive on the U-1026 went really well."

He nodded, his sparkling eyes staying on hers as she continued, "I made a new friend." She felt like a kid back in school for a moment, rushing home to tell her parents about a new friend in her class.

"Fish or human?" he asked with a grin.

"Actually, a human one, surprisingly," she countered. "She's French, but despite that, this English girl likes her."

"I thought you Brits hated everything French and vice versa?" he asked, surprised. Working with a few Europeans on the Sea Sentry boat, he'd been learning as much as he could about English culture, or at least the tainted version.

"We pretend to, but we like their wine and cheese too much to really hate them. She's from southern France and she's a really good diver – came to the U-boat with us, and this morning she guided a dive for me so I could do some instruction," she babbled.

"Does she have a name?" he asked, still smiling and staring into her eyes. She adored the way he listened to her prattle on. He made her feel like he truly wanted to hear every word she shared.

"Hazel, Hazel Delacroix. She's a little older than me but we've been getting along really well. She bought me this really cool dress today," she reached over and picked up the summer dress from the back of the other chair and held it up in front of the laptop's camera. "Isn't it gorgeous? And it was from one of the really posh shops in Camana Bay, so I think it cost a fortune."

Jackson laughed again. "Wait, when you say new friend, you sure she's not after more than a new friend?"

AJ rolled her eyes. "No, it's not like that." They had been dating long enough and spent enough time apart for AJ to know that Jackson wasn't the jealous type. If either of them were, it was she who sometimes let the demons fog her mind. "She took me shopping and I really liked the dress, so she sneakily went back and got it. There was a French lady running the shop, so I hope she gave her a discount or something cos everything I looked at was over a hundred CI for little blouses and shorts. I was too scared to look at the price of the dress, so I don't know what it was."

"So, what's that in real money?" he teased.

"Ha, ha. Typical American," she teased back. "Well, as I've told you a million times the Cayman Islands dollar is worth more than your goofy, same colour, same size American money."

He laughed and then leaned a little closer. "Hey, I have to run, sorry it's so short today, we're off the coast of Nicaragua, chasing down some turtle poachers."

"I'm so sorry, I carried on about me and never asked about things with you." She held her hand to the screen, wishing she could touch him.

"I'd rather hear about you," he grinned. "Love you, I'll try again in a couple of days, okay?"

"Love you too," she replied and the connection went off. AJ closed her laptop and looked back out the window. The sun was below the horizon, leaving only a trace of pale-yellow light dividing ocean from sky. She was left with a mixture of joy from seeing and hearing her man, and the pangs of missing him terribly. They knew being separated so much couldn't last forever, both needed and wanted more, but for either to give up what they were doing would be too big of a sacrifice. It would be like slicing a piece of their very existence away and expecting to feel complete. She hoped he'd eventually burn out on the long trips at sea and maybe pursue an environmental role on the island. She also felt guilty and selfish even thinking that way: why should it be him to give up his passion? Of course, he worked as a volunteer, unpaid beyond room and expenses, so she figured that would eventually become unworkable. The idea she would shut down Mermaid Divers to join him at Sea Sentry was hard to imagine. She'd let Thomas down, all her customers that returned each year, and so many friends. She felt guilty yet again.

AJ moved to the kitchen and poured a glass of wine. She forced herself to think about something else before she twisted herself in a knot and ruined the lovely chat she'd just had, with the man she was truly in love with. She sipped the Chardonnay and focused on tomorrow. She needed to be prepared to dive the wreck. Reg was coming, and after all these years she still felt a little nervous when he was there. It was like the football game your dad was finally able to come to. She wanted everything to go smoothly, and for that she needed to be organised and prepared. She sat back down and opened her laptop again. Starting a new document, she began making notes, starting with her best estimate on depth. She stared at the freshly typed numbers on the screen. It was indeed a similar profile and challenge to the U-1026. But she had familiarity with that wreck. The Raptor was not a dive to be taken lightly.

29

JUNE 1974

Whitey felt none of the nerves and apprehension he'd experienced the first time he'd landed on Grand Cayman with a case full of money, one month before. He'd been a lot more nervous spending three hours in Miami airport waiting on his connection but now he felt nothing but relief and excitement. Pausing at the top of the steps, he soaked up the hot sun and warm breeze sweeping across the small Owen Roberts airport. Whitey smiled at Ainsley, who was enthusiastically waving and standing next to the same police car that had greeted him before.

The deposit at the bank went smoothly, though he noticed the box was already half full, despite being the largest size they had. The policeman dropped them off at the Royal Palms Hotel, Whitey's new hotel after moving out of the Holiday Inn last trip. The pool wasn't quite so stylish, but the view of the Caribbean was identical, and if it meant he could see Isabella he'd happily sleep under a cardboard box on the beach. Whitey threw his small travel bag on the bed and walked over to the window, pulling the curtains back. A sharp memory sparked in the back of his mind as he did so but rapidly evaporated once he stared out across the cerulean water, filtered through the full palms swaying in the breeze.

"Man, am I glad to be back here," Whitey said absentmindedly.

Ainsley patted his friend on the shoulder. "Good to see you again brother. The island has a way of making all your problems not seem so bad, huh?"

Whitey looked at him and smiled. "It helps for sure." He pulled the curtains the rest of the way back and slid the door open to let the breeze rush in. "I could get used to this, mate." He paused another moment to soak up Seven Mile Beach a little more before striding back over to the bed and opening his bag.

"Okay, down to business," He retrieved a stuffed envelope and handed it to Ainsley, "Here you go mate, here's your cut." Whitey had decided to give his friend his money up front, rather than have ten grand cash on him for a week. He knew the island was safe by now, but it still weighed on his mind, and he was determined to simplify things as much as possible. He knew he couldn't step away from the Caveros easily, but he'd made up his mind to find a way. Somehow Whitey Snow had to evaporate. The key would be wrapping up everything in his life and interaction with the family so they'd have little incentive to search too long or too hard. This would all take time and some planning.

Ainsley took the envelope with a big grin. "Thank you, man."

"When can we borrow your brother's boat, Ainsley?" Whitey asked.

"Any afternoon really," Ainsley shrugged, tucking the bulging envelope in the back of his jeans and letting his shirt fall over to cover it.

"Tomorrow then, let's get it done. We'll need some tools with us too; got some basic stuff we can take?" Whitey queried as he took his few clothes out of his bag. He had learnt already that the island required very little in clothing options: shorts and tee shirts got you through most days.

"Of course, there's some on the boat already, but I can gather up some more things. What do you think we'll need?" Ainsley asked, clearly wondering what they'd be up to.

"A small saw, a prybar, a good hammer, some bigger screwdrivers, and an oil filter wrench," Whitey answered as he put his clothes away in the dresser.

"An oil filter wrench?" Ainsley stared at his friend in puzzlement.

"Yeah." Whitey stopped what he was doing and looked at the Caymanian. "You know, a strap wrench to tighten or loosen an oil filter. But a big one for a diesel engine not a little regular car one."

"Right, a strap wrench, but a big one," Ainsley repeated tentatively.

"You never change the oil on your car?" Whitey asked incredulously.

Ainsley looked at him blankly. "No man, I got people for that. Ainsley don't dive, and Ainsley don't get grease on his hands, brother." He burst into his big smile and held up both hands. "These hands are for loving the ladies, man, soft and sensitive."

Whitey laughed at him. "You big girl's blouse!"

Ainsley feigned insult. "Tools of the trade right here, man," he countered, moving his hands down like he was caressing a curvy lady. "And talking of loving the ladies, are you seeing your Spanish waitress while you're here, man?"

Whitey put his empty bag in the small closet. "That's my plan, brother." He took a deep breath and looked at his friend. "I have to be honest; I've thought about her a lot while I've been gone."

"What?!" Ainsley slapped his own forehead dramatically. "The great Whitey Snow, international lover, mister love-them-and-leave-them has finally met his match?"

Whitey laughed. "Slow down there, Sidney Poitier of the Cayman Islands," he jabbed back, "I'm just saying I'd like to see her again."

"Sure," Ainsley kept on. "All the fish in this beautiful sea" – he waved his hand across the view outside – "and one has finally jumped into your boat."

Whitey shook his head. "Look, I may have thought about her – doesn't mean she's been thinking about me, now does it?"

Ainsley laughed even harder. "You're kidding, man? I've never seen a woman that doesn't love the great Whitey Snow!"

Whitey actually blushed a little. "You're an idiot Ainsley." He grabbed his friend around the shoulders and gave him a big squeeze. "I'm just trying to be like you, Romeo." He leaned over and kissed his friend on the side of his head.

30

NOVEMBER 2019

Thomas piloted the Newton through the cut from North Sound into the open water with ease. Powerless knee-high swells softly rolled through the opening and laid down flat calm once clear. AJ checked in with the Davis girls one more time before they reached their dive site.

"So, you guys are sure you're okay doing the two nav dives here? We'll stay on top of the reef in the shallows for both."

The two girls both nodded enthusiastically.

"Alright then, "AJ continued, "you both did great with your online book work so we should wrap it all up today." She turned to their parents. "Hazel will lead you again if that's cool with you? I'll have her do the deep dive this time."

Bill and Maggie both said they had no problem, and on the way out AJ had asked the same of the Freemans, who were happy as well. AJ moved over to Hazel, who was pulling her wetsuit up, getting ready. AJ helped with her back zipper as she spoke quietly, "Okay, so it's an easy wall dive here. Go down to the pin and check for any current. Head straight north to the drop-off, which is obvious cos the reef slopes deeper in that direction. At the wall, turn into the current and drop to ninety feet. I usually go for fifteen minutes at ninety, then wind up the wall to the top, which is around sixty to seventy here, and turn around. Take your time coming back and make sure you ease shallower up the slope some – make it under sixty for most of the return."

Hazel took it all in and AJ could see she was focused. "What time back at the mooring?" Hazel asked.

"About twenty-five minutes and then everyone can burn the rest of their air around the pin, but it's all fifty or deeper here so they won't get long. Watch deco, it'll get you before air on the north wall, because the pins are deeper. I'll take the kids south to forty feet for their class work."

Hazel nodded again. "And I think Bill uses the most air, right?"

AJ was impressed Hazel had already figured out the group. "Yup, he does fine, but he'll run low first so check his air when you turn. The Freemans are fish, they just cruise and don't use any air unless there's current. If there's stronger current turn before fifteen and watch Beth's bubbles; you'll see if she's struggling a bit."

"D'accord, merci," Hazel said with a big smile.

AJ stepped up to the side of the boat and started forward to the bow but stopped and leaned back over to Hazel. "And watch your nitrogen loading; we'll try for two dives on the wreck this afternoon so you'll need all the no-deco time you can get. I brought regular Nitrox tanks for you to use this morning, they're over there." AJ pointed to two green-topped tanks in the port racks. "Don't forget to set your computer, I'll grab the tester once we're moored up."

Forty-five minutes later AJ guided Scarlett and Kelsi back to the mooring pin where they could spend some time exploring while they waited for the group to return. The girls had plenty of air remaining as they had stayed shallow. After a few minutes Hazel appeared from the east, gently finning against the light current across the top of the reef. Her group of four followed at a leisurely pace, peeking in the nooks and crannies at various reef critters and interesting fish. Once the Davises saw their girls they kicked ahead and joined them as the two teenagers made excited hand signals describing their own adventures, which included much pointing at their compasses. AJ laughed into her regulator. David Freeman looked over at AJ and she could tell he was smiling behind his reg. He made the hand signal for a ray with his hands then held up five digits. AJ clapped her hands slowly together and gave him a double okay sign. Damn, she thought, Hazel's raising the expectations on these dives!

Back on the boat the chatter was all about the group of eagle rays they'd seen, and much hilarity was had when AJ pointed out a group of rays was known as a 'fever'. David chuckled and announced from here out Hazel would be known as 'Hazel Fever the Eagle Ray Whisperer'. Hazel laughed and shook her head. "Just lucky," she claimed.

"Two for two!" Thomas reminded her. "Big pressure next dive, what can you find to one-up a fever of eagle rays?"

They laughed and continued in good humour when they moored up for the second dive on a shallow pin. AJ told the group they were on Blue Peter to which the six Americans looked at her blankly. She explained it was supposedly named after the British children's TV show, which didn't help them in the least bit. When AJ started doing a bad impression of presenter John Noakes telling the excitable border collie to 'get down, Shep' none of the crowd knew what she was talking about, but they died laughing at her.

AJ looked at Hazel, who was giggling to herself off to the side. "Do you know what I'm talking about?"

"Oui, I was actually alive when that silly dog was on the show, unlike you! That's the worst impression ever!"

AJ threw her hands in the air and it took a few minutes to get the group to stop laughing enough to continue with the dive briefing.

31

JUNE 1974

Whitey needn't have worried. He walked to the Holiday Inn along the pale-yellow sand beach and found Isabella working by the pool as usual. Her face lit up when she saw him. They eagerly made arrangements to meet for dinner, and now they sat in the restaurant in the Royal Palms after watching the sun go down from the beach front.

Isabella's blue jeans snugly fit her slim figure down to above her knees, where they flared widely until they met the same floral clogs she'd worn before. Her black hair fell across her gold lamé halter top which loosely covered her chest and Whitey found it hard not to stare at the woman's perfect figure. He sipped his Havana Club over ice and happily listened to her chatter on about the ins and outs of her life over the past few weeks in his absence. He liked the fact she'd taken the time to wear a different and equally stunning outfit for his benefit. He adored the fact she wore the same shoes because she loved them so much. She wore make-up but lightly applied and accenting rather than changing her natural look. Her green eyes shone and sparkled as she laughingly described missing the bus along West Bay Road and sneaking into work a few minutes late. Before long, dinner was finished and Whitey had had enough of the Caribbean calypso ambiance music and suggested they move to the bar.

Elton John greeted them with 'Don't Let the Sun Go Down on Me' and Whitey found them a secluded table in the corner away from the smokers at the main bar. The waitress approached, a local girl with curly black hair and perfect skin the colour of Belgian chocolate.

"Hi there Izzie," the waitress said discreetly.

"Hey Dinah." Isabella got up and hugged the girl. "How's your momma doing?"

"She fine now, thank God," Dinah replied and looked Whitey up and down.

Isabella sat down. "This is my friend Whitey," she introduced with a wry smile and a wink.

"Uh huh," Dinah replied, giving him an approving look, "he sure is." She chuckled and Whitey stood, extending a hand.

"Whitey Snow, pleased to meet you, Dinah."

She shook his hand firmly. "You must be the lucky man she been jabbering about the last few weeks."

Isabella slapped her playfully on the arm. "Take our drink order and go about your business before you embarrass me some more, Dinah!"

The girl laughed joyfully. "Okay, okay, What you be wanting to drink, mister lucky man Whitey?"

Whitey sat down, amused by the women's banter and very happy to hear he'd been the topic of Isabella's conversations.

"Havana Club over ice please, Dinah."

She winked at him. "Sure thing, and you baby, what you having?"

"Cinzano and tonic please, Dinah."

"Bianco, right?" Dinah looked at Isabella's gold top. "That top is so groovy, where d'you get that girl?"

Isabella brushed her hand over her top self-consciously, "I've had it a while, I just haven't worn it out before. I got it in Barcelona when I was home last."

"Knew it." Dinah rolled her eyes. "No way you find something cool as that on the island." With another big smile, she turned and headed for the bar with her best hip-swinging stride.

Whitey chuckled. "She's a gas."

Isabella nodded. "Oh yes, Dinah's the life of any party. Maybe she'd double date with your friend Ainsley?"

"If he hasn't already blown his chance with her – pretty sure he's hit on every eligible female on the island."

ABBA's 'Waterloo' started on the bar's sound system and Isabella wriggled enthusiastically in her seat.

"I love this," she enthused.

Whitey listened as the infectious beat and female vocals made him unconsciously tap his foot.

"Not normally my cup of tea," he said unconvincingly. "Is this the Swedish lot that won the Eurovision Song Contest?"

"Yes! Come on," she urged, "tell me you can keep still when this comes on."

He smiled and noticed his tapping foot. "I suppose." He watched her dance in her seat, her gold top swishing and her face beaming as she mouthed the words, "I do like what it does to you."

"Bet you like the blonde one, all the guys like the blonde," she teased.

He shrugged his shoulders. "Hadn't noticed," he lied, knowing he actually had more of a crush on the brunette.

Isabelle rolled her eyes. "Sure."

"Right now, it's my favourite song ever," he whispered and she closed her eyes as she sang the chorus.

He wondered if she could possibly feel the same way he felt in this moment. This woman consumed him completely. Half of him was more relaxed and content than he could ever remember being. Half of him was overwhelmed with panic and fear that he would lose the best thing he'd ever come across, before it had really even started. If he couldn't break free of the Caveros and change the course of his life, once and for all, this could be nothing more than a passing fling, like all the others. For the first time in his life, that wasn't what he wanted.

"I'm thinking of moving here," he said suddenly as the song finished.

Isabella stared at him, clearly surprised. "You are? What about your work? Don't you need to be in Miami?"

"It would mean getting away from what I'm doing," he said quietly.

Her face lit up. "You're serious?"

"I'm seriously thinking about it. Maybe Soto's would take me on. Complete change of pace, you know?" he said before he could stop himself.

She leaned over and held his face softly in her hands. She slowly moved her lips against his and gave him a long passionate kiss. "I'd like that," she whispered.

Dinah quietly set the drinks down on their table. "I'll just leave these right here for you two, you know, for whenever you take a little break." She smiled as she left.

32

NOVEMBER 2019

The second dive on the north side had gone well and they were back to the yacht club by 12:30pm. It took an hour to refill the air tanks at the dock for the next day and then AJ ran by Island Air in George Town to custom-fill some Nitrox tanks for the afternoon dives. Hazel tagged along as she had nothing better to do and AJ was her hotel ride anyway. With tanks clanking in the back of the van, AJ wound through the tiny back streets of George Town to the small car park off Rock Hole Road and was pleased to find an open spot. She led Hazel around the side of a building from where they could see the blue water across North Church Road, the main road into the harbour front. AJ walked to the front of the building and ducked through a glass door into the Greenhouse Cafe. She glanced up to see a curvy young woman with a determined look striding between the tables in her direction. She felt Hazel tense behind her, but AJ smiled. The woman rolled her eyes as she reached AJ and threw her arms around her.

"Thank God you're here, my morning has been an effing night-mare," the woman said a little louder than perhaps she should, as a few heads turned.

"Hey Jen," AJ laughed, releasing herself from her grasp, "this is my friend Hazel."

Hazel extended a hand but was greeted with a similar hug.

"And this is my wonderful friend Jen, who runs this place," AJ said, but Hazel was undoubtedly too surprised to hear.

Jen let her go and put an arm around AJ's shoulder, walking her through the cafe.

"So, this morning, I'm taking an order over the phone and I turn around and there's a couple standing at the counter and she's elbow deep in the tip jar, pulling notes out! I asked her politely what on earth she was doing and she says, 'we want some local money to take home', like, no big deal. I said that's the staff's hard-earned tip money madam, if you'd like some CI money I'd be happy to give you some in your change. She looks straight at me and says, 'it's okay, I'm putting American dollars in there in exchange'." Jen halted in front of the counter and looked at Hazel and then AJ. "So I took a deep breath, cos you know, I can get a wee bit wound up sometimes." She looked back at Hazel as though she'd know what she meant. Hazel's mouth was slightly open, looking like she was caught in an out-of-body experience.

"I said, madam, the exchange rate is zero point eight in the shops so you're actually stealing money from the tip jar on top of the fact you're using our tip jar as a souvenir store!" Jen walked back behind the counter, her expression still deadly serious. "She's looking at me like I'm speaking Swahili so I looked at the husband and asked, nice as pie, can I take your order? Know what he said?"

AJ and Hazel both silently shook their heads.

"We'll have one coffee but please split it into two cups." Jen waved her arms in the air. "Two cups! And then of course they want the Wi-Fi password, so I gave them a close, but not quite right version, despite it being clearly displayed on the wall behind me." She grinned.

As swiftly as she'd greeted them, Jen's face turned from frantic to smiling broadly and her voice softened. "It's so good to see you and your lovely friend." She looked Hazel up and down. "Kinda quiet, isn't she?"

AJ burst out laughing and Jen joined her, both looking at Hazel.

"Sorry Hazel, I should have warned you before we came in," AJ managed.

Hazel finally came out of shock and smiled. "People really do that?" she asked in amazement.

"Cruise-shippers," AJ and Jen said together.

"And bloody Americans," Jen added.

Hazel looked confused. "You're American, aren't you?"

Jen looked incredulous. "I know, embarrassing isn't it?" She handed them a pair of menus and sent them to an empty table, still in fits of laughter.

"She's funny," Hazel finally said as she settled down to look at the menu.

"I always know when I've spent an evening with Jen. The next morning my stomach muscles hurt from laughing so much, it's better than an hour at the gym." AJ chuckled.

"The food looks amazing," Hazel said quietly, studying the choices.

AJ nodded. "Oh yeah, she's an amazing chef and she changes it up a lot, all fresh local fish and produce too."

"My mother had a small café," Hazel said without looking up, taking AJ aback.

Slightly unsure how to respond she carefully enquired, "What happened to it? The cafe?"

Hazel looked up blankly. "It was in my father's name; technically he owned it as it was his money that started it thirty years ago. But he's had nothing to do with it since they split up, she paid everything back, so it was really hers. Except on the paperwork. They never got around to fixing the paperwork."

"That doesn't sound fair," AJ said gently. "Surely she would have wanted you to have it?"

Hazel nodded. "She did. But he kept making excuses for not

sorting out the papers and then she got sick and that was that." She shrugged her shoulders and looked back at the menu.

"Wasn't he around when she was ill, at least to be around you?" AJ asked before she could stop herself.

Hazel took a moment, thinking before she responded. "He has a new family, he didn't want anything to do with us after they split. We don't talk. He didn't even come to her funeral." She forced a smile. "That's okay, I didn't want him there."

AJ really didn't know how to follow that, so she squeezed Hazel's hand across the table. Hazel smiled but AJ could see there was pain and determination and a whirlpool of other emotions in her eyes. As someone who was close with both her parents and in the uncommonly enviable position of having them still together, it was impossible for AJ to truly understand her friend's position. AJ was closer to her father than she was to her mother, but she loved them both very deeply. The idea of either one of them not being in her life was devastating.

AJ was glad when Jen sprang upon their table. "What are we having, kiddos?"

33

JUNE 1974

Whitey waded into the water with his scuba gear thrown over his shoulder and fins in his hand. Ainsley beamed at him with a mischievous look from the helm of a shiny 25′ cuddy cabin as he eased towards the shore to pick him up.

"That's your brother's fishing boat?" Whitey asked in surprise.

Ainsley couldn't stop smiling. "No man, this ain't his boat, this is mine."

Whitey slung his gear into the boat and used the small swim step over the outboard drive to haul himself up.

"Since when?" he asked as he stowed his gear and checked the two tanks Ainsley had picked up for him at Soto's.

Ainsley fumbled with the controls, spinning the wheel one way then the other. "Since yesterday afternoon, man," he explained proudly, still confusing the boat by pushing and pulling various controls.

Whitey looked at him as they drifted closer to the beach. "Wanna back us up there, Horatio Nelson?"

Ainsley frowned and let go of the wheel and stared at the buttons and levers. "I only driven the thing forward so far, not sure it wants to be backed up."

"Mind if I take a look?" Whitey asked patiently and Ainsley stepped from the helm. Whitey selected reverse on the drive and span the wheel hard to the right. He pushed the throttle open and the boat backed up, turning to starboard until they were clear of the beach and facing the ocean. He selected forward, straightened the wheel, and set the throttles just above idle before stepping aside.

"Thanks," Ainsley mumbled,."I just got it yesterday, still figuring out the nuances, you know." He eased the throttles forward and they motored towards deeper water.

Whitey surveyed the vessel. "This thing's pretty nice, brother. Brand new?"

Ainsley got his smile back. "One year old, man; some rich grey-hair brought it over and then had a heart attack on top of his twenty-three-year-old girlfriend." He laughed. "Apparently his wife didn't have much sympathy and started selling all his toys while he's getting patched up in the States. I practically stole this thing, brother."

"It's a SportCraft isn't it?" Whitey asked.

"Sure," Ainsley replied. "Sportcraft, Sportsman, something or other, this thing's the bomb man, chicks are gonna dig it."

Whitey chuckled. "Best you figure out how to drive it before you run someone over with it."

Ainsley frowned at him.

"And we're going to the north-west point, so head north-north-west," Whitey added.

Ainsley looked over the water and then back at Whitey. "Huh?"

"Jesus Ainsley, thought your family made their livelihood on the ocean? You can't read a compass?"

"I have one?" Ainsley asked, looking at the control panel in front of him. Whitey reached over and tapped the domed compass on the top of the console.

"Oh, right, that thing, I knew that. They make their living on the water; you know me man, I'm just a hustler on dry land. So how does it work?" Ainsley asked.

"See that line in the front?" Whitey pointed to a yellow line on the front of the dome facing them. Ainsley nodded and Whitey continued, "That's called the lubber line. Now see you've got all the directions of the compass rose on there, north, south and all that?"

"Yup. Those numbers the degrees?" Ainsley asked.

"See, you're picking it up. There's 360, you know, degrees in a full circle. If you knew your exact heading from a chart you could line that up. We know we want to head north-north-west so you can line the lubber line up with north-north-west on the inner ring there. Do that and see where we head."

Ainsley started turning the wheel bringing the north-north-west point around to the front of the compass, aligning with the line Whitey had showed him. The boat swung around and faced back towards George Town.

Whitey laughed so hard he thought he'd never stop. "That's the reciprocal brother," he choked out. "The heading should be on the far side of the compass cos that's where we're heading. That's why it's called a heading!"

Ainsley swung the wheel back around, glancing at the beach and wondering who was watching him turn around in little circles in his new boat. "Well that's bogus," he mumbled.

Finally, they managed to navigate their way to the north-west point of the island and Whitey remembered as best he could a few landmarks on the island to line up their position over the wreck. There'd been two large palms to the east he saw lined up. Once they were aligned, he had Ainsley motor slowly straight for them until the cemetery at the top of Seven Mile Beach lined up with the north-west point of the island.

"Here," he said. "Where's your anchor?"

Ainsley looked around and shrugged his shoulders. "They come with one? I've only been at a dock so far."

Whitey shook his head and cussed his friend under his breath. At the rear, tucked behind the engine cover, he saw the metal top of the anchor. Relieved, he grabbed it and was even happier to find it had a decent length of chain attached to a long section of rope. He carried the anchor to the front of the boat and tied the rope into a cleat on the bow.

"Okay, start reversing slowly, I'm going to throw the anchor over, and we'll hopefully grapple the wreck."

Ainsley carefully selected reverse and moved the throttle forward lightly and the boat began to reverse, much to his surprise. Whitey dropped the anchor over the bow and began playing out first the chain, which appeared to be about twenty feet long and then the rope. He tried to judge how much rope he was sending over to get an idea when the anchor had gone too far and was on the bottom, but it was hard to judge.

After a few minutes he shouted back to Ainsley, "We missed it. Hold her steady there while I pull the anchor back in."

Ainsley pulled the throttle back to idle and selected forward on the drive. He gently nudged the throttle forward again until it felt like the boat was holding station against the current that was clearly trying to carry them towards deeper water. Whitey heaved the anchor back aboard and started measuring out the rope by stretching sections across his chest with both hands extended. He knew the human wingspan was close to a person's height, so he rounded to six foot per section. Adding the twenty-five feet of chain to twelve lengths of rope gave him over ninety feet of line, which he figured ought to grab the railing or the cabin structure, allowing for the trailing angle the line would take. He had Ainsley motor forward again and this time they let the current drift the boat back out. With his measured line tied off on the cleat they drifted and waited. After a few minutes he was sure they'd missed it again until the little boat jerked to a stop.

"We got it!" Ainsley shouted, almost falling over when the anchor bit.

"We got something," Whitey said with a grin. "Guess I'll dive down and see if it's a big boat called the Raptor."

34

NOVEMBER 2019

It was mid-afternoon by the time AJ steered her RIB away from the dock and headed north-west. Now, as they finally made their way to the wreck, the atmosphere on the boat was filled with nervous energy. The chatter happened in small bursts, surrounded by bouts of silence, with everyone running through their personal checklists and looking over their gear for the umpteenth time. Carlos, the young Cuban man engaged to Thomas's sister, wouldn't be diving, but he sensed the intensity. He had his own concerns, as he would be in charge of the boat and would have the responsibility of making decisions if anyone was blown off the wreck site. AJ loved the tingling sensation and tightness in her stomach that approaching a technical dive brought on. She knew part of it was the unknown, but she didn't like to think about the part she knew was the danger. After a few scary situations she'd been in over the past couple of years, she'd promised her parents she'd avoid walking into dangerous situations whenever possible. They might consider this one of those situations.

AJ brought the RIB off plane as she slowed on approach to the wreck site. At least her best guess at the site, since she'd been unable to find GPS coordinates for it anywhere.

"Let's check the gas in the tanks, guys, while I do a lap or two and look at the depth around here, see if I can get a ping off the wreck."

Thomas produced their Nitrox tester and started at the first green-topped tank down the row stacked in the starboard racks. Each of the other divers joined him to witness the test on the tanks they'd be using. Each tank was tested by slightly opening its valve and blowing a small amount of gas into the receiver of the tester, which would return an oxygen content percentage. Similar to the U-boat dive, AJ had had the tanks custom-filled to 29%. Once the content was confirmed, the diver wrote the percentage on a piece of tape stuck to the tank and then set their dive computer to the corresponding number so its calculations throughout the dive would be based off the accurate breathing gas. The higher oxygen content meant a lower nitrogen content, which was a diver's nemesis. They were breathing from compressed gas to combat the increasing surrounding water pressure as they descended deeper. If they didn't, the higher water pressure would crush their lungs smaller and smaller as they went down. The by-product was substantially more molecules of the gas entering their system that their body had to dissipate. After a while the body reached saturation and the nitrogen in the system became dangerous, causing bubbles of gas to circulate in the bloodstream. No-deco time was the way divers referenced that point calculated by their computers during and after the dive.

AJ's depth finder showed the slope of the reef down to around 140' before going rapidly off the wall to nearly a thousand feet. Once she'd found the line of the wall, which was also noticeable by the water colour change to a deeper blue, she moved up the slope a bit and ran parallel to that line. It took a couple of passes until she found a spot where the depth pinged 120' fairly consistently and then changed to 90' for a small section before returning to 120. Passing back over to verify, she marked the spot in her GPS. It was either a huge coral head or she'd found the wreck. Reg had left her alone while she ran her search pattern but now joined her at the helm.

"Reg, bow's up slope and pointed towards the shore, right?" she asked quietly.

"Last time I saw her it was. We can only assume she slid backwards on her same path," he replied, squinting at the shoreline trying to recall some landmarks.

"The depth change was right for its beam, so I think it is," she confirmed. "I'm going to try and grapple it coming from shallower; maybe we'll get lucky and hook the bow rail."

She had turned the boat to face the shore after turning back over what appeared to be the wreck. Now they both watched the depth continue shallower until it jumped 30' deeper again, which she presumed was the drop from the bow of the wreck to the sea floor. She marked the GPS again and now had two points she could use to make a line along the length of the sunken boat. Trolling about a hundred yards ahead she turned the RIB around and aimed at the two points she'd marked on her GPS. The depth under keel was 80'.

"Let's try 110' of line Reg," she shouted to the big man, who'd moved to the front of the boat. He nodded and began measuring out anchor line to the grappling anchor they'd brought along which had three big, curved prongs rather than the two fatter flukes of a sand anchor.

The boat drifted deeper as they floated while Reg prepared the line. AJ watched her GPS and once Reg waved to indicate he was ready she piloted the boat back into position ahead of the wreck. With a nod from AJ, Reg dropped the anchor and some of the line in the water off the front of the boat, then played out more line as the anchor sank towards the bottom. This way the extra line wouldn't float uselessly under their boat and get caught in the prop. They could have reversed over the wreck dragging the line behind them off the bow, but it made manoeuvring much more difficult and AJ had decided she'd try this way first.

The GPS showed them passing over the first mark right when

Reg had all the line played out. AJ shut the throttles and let the boat drift with the current, which she noted was probably around two knots. Significant, as predicted. Halfway between her two GPS marks the bow dipped suddenly and the boat began rotating around until they were facing the shoreline and no longer moving. The divers all looked at each other with that jolt of nervous energy as the adrenaline was released in their systems. They were hooked on the Raptor.

35

JUNE 1974

Whitey sat on the port side as close to the cabin, and more importantly the bow, as he could get. He knew the current would try to rip him away as soon as he got in and he needed to get to the anchor line, tied to a bow cleat. He'd considered stepping over the railing on the bow and jumping in, but it was a long drop and he worried about losing gear with a big impact in the water. He shuffled his rear end close to the edge, had a last look to make sure he had everything, and back-rolled off the boat into the Caribbean Sea. The froth cleared and Whitey could make out the side of the boat and the surface as he clutched his Dive Bright lantern and the oil filter wrench firmly in his left hand and used his right hand to claw at the water and orientate himself. Kicking hard with his fins, he struggled towards the front of the boat in search of the line. The surface current was strong and for a moment he wished he'd explained to Ainsley how to extricate the anchor in case he needed to be picked up if was carried away. A few more long, full leg kicks and he saw the taut rope disappearing into the darker water below; a few more after that and he held the line in his right hand with great relief.

The Soto's guys had anchored in a sand patch north of the

wreck and relied on the group's ability to swim back to the line. They had a crew and could easily pull anchor to chase divers around if needed, as indeed it had been. Whitey only had Ainsley, who didn't know the bow from the stern, and would likely run him over if he had to come retrieve him from an open ocean drift. Grappling the wreck seemed a safer plan, but next time he needed to find a better way into the water.

Hand over hand Whitey pulled himself down the line. Almost immediately he could make out the wreck below and realised they'd snagged the railing on the starboard side at the stern of the sunken boat. They'd damn near missed it again but at least he only had to haul himself a third of the length of the boat to the rear of the open cargo hold. When he reached the anchor, caught on the railing, he pulled himself along the starboard side around the edge of the cabin structure which filled the stern section of the boat. With a firm kick he dropped into the void of the empty cargo hold and descended to the engine room door he'd discovered on his dive with Soto's.

The door opened, but not quite as easily as it had done a month ago and Whitey made a mental note to address that. He checked his depth. Just over one hundred feet. He switched on his lantern and entered the engine room, his light throwing a beam around the crowded space and forming wild shadows across the back wall. With the aid of the lantern, he swiftly found the oil filter on the side of the big diesel engine and set the Dive Bright down, shining on the area he needed to work. It was awkward, hanging over the side of the motor, but his long arms could reach and he was sure his large frame wouldn't fit any closer. He slipped the strap of the filter wrench over the smooth cylinder of the filter and pulled the strap tight through the adjuster. It took barely a tug on the wrench handle and the filter began to spin on its thread. Oil seeped out as the filter came loose, making inky black trails floating in the water. Whitey hoped they'd successfully drained most of the oil from the motor or it would soon be like the Sea Star in the Gulf of Oman in the small room. The filter came free of its threads and a few small clouds of oil wafted into the darkness beyond the light beam. He removed the strap wrench from the filter and set it down below where he was working; he figured it could stay there until he came back down. Retrieving the lantern, he carefully turned himself around amongst the lines and cables above the engine and gently finned towards the door. It was awkward carrying both the lantern and the slick filter in one hand; he wished he'd brought a bag down with him. He shoved the door farther open from the inside and it dragged as it met sand and silt built up at the edge of the cargo hold. He left it open – he'd be back down shortly.

The swim back to the line was much easier with the current, he just had to make sure he didn't drop anything, and most importantly, didn't miss or let go of the line. Once he reached the rear railing, he looped his right arm around the anchor line and let the current ease him up the angled rope, held taut by Ainsley's cuddy cabin being pulled by the surface waters. Whitey checked his air pressure gauge and his dive watch for his time underwater. He'd only used a thousand psi and been under for fifteen minutes, so he decided to leave the same tank on his rig for the second dive.

Surfacing at the bow of the little SportCraft, he heard Ainsley jump.

"That you Whitey?" came Ainsley's voice from the cockpit.

"No, it's King Neptune. Of course it's me, you plonker. Get up here and take this stuff from me," Whitey replied with a chuckle.

Ainsley scrambled to the bow of the boat, taking careful steps as the boat rocked lightly under his feet. Whitey handed up the lantern and the filter to Ainsley, who was lying on his stomach in order to reach them.

"What the hell's that?" Ainsley asked, looking at the filter.

"You're truly a man's man, Ainsley," Whitey said in a serious tone.

"Ain't I though?" Ainsley answered, a little surprised.

"No," Whitey replied, shaking his head as he let the current pull him alongside the boat to the swim step.

36

NOVEMBER 2019

AJ led the group as they pulled themselves hand over hand down the anchor line. The current held the line taut against the pull of the boat and the tension in the rope could be felt through their bare hands. If the grapple came free now, they'd have four divers hanging on a line trailing behind a loose boat, drifting with the ocean current. It would be a mess. She hoped the prongs had a good hold on the wreck, and furthermore she prayed it was the wreck she'd hooked. If they descended to find she'd stuck a grapple hook in a coral head, she'd be mortified. A few feet farther and her fears subsided. The dark shape of the cargo vessel loomed out of the depths below a large school of young barracuda that seemed oblivious to the current affecting the divers. The top of the cabin structure appeared at about the same time as the bow. Both had lost their hard lines to the coral that grew prolifically in the nutritious waters rushing over the wreck. They were grappled to the side railing on the port side, behind the bow, where the sheet metal dropped and the side was guarded by a handrail. That railing can't be very secure after forty years of decay in the sea water, AJ thought. As she pulled herself closer, she saw the grapple had snagged the first vertical pole down low which she hoped would be less corroded than the top. The whole centre of the wreck was a gaping cavern where the empty cargo hold had lost any covering it may have had when the boat was unceremoniously scuttled by her crew.

As she reached the railing, AJ scanned the wreck and could see the Raptor was indeed hanging stern over the wall, and at quite a steep angle on the slope to the drop-off. The rusty boat appeared to be clinging to the island by her fingernails. AJ eased into the top of the hold in the lee of the bow, clear of the current, and Reg followed her, looking around. She checked her depth: a hundred feet; everything worth exploring was deeper. With the angle of the wreck, they'd have to continue deeper to stay in the shelter of the hold. She looked at Reg, his thick beard floating around like a creature attached to his face. His eyes were calm, but he shook his head and tapped his dive watch, clearly thinking the same thing. AJ signalled back that she planned to start towards the stern in the top of the hold and watch the depth as she went. The other two had joined them and, seeing her signals, returned an okay sign. With everyone following, she finned her way towards the cabin structure watching her depth drop steadily despite staying towards the top of the hold. Below them they could make out the floor of the hold, which was now littered with clumps of coral growth and humming with fish life. Ahead, the rear of the hold was still lost in the darkness from the shadows of the sides and the cabin structure, but slowly revealed itself as they continued deeper. At 115' AJ reached the base of the cabins at the back of the hold. On either side, narrow, steep steps led from the bottom of the hold to the second level of cabins, which were just above them. The angle the wreck sitting on the sloped reef made it hard to judge depth accurately, and they both kept checking their dive computers for reference. AJ rose to the top of the steps on the port side, the structure shielding the current, and came back up to 105'. The door into the structure was covered in growth but she could make out the handle and tried turning it. It didn't budge at all and she looked around for other options to penetrate the wreck. Reg finned over to the door on the starboard side and tried it with the same result. Thomas hung just above them looking around and taking in the experience. AJ swore she could see his big smile and could hear his joyful chuckle in her mind. She envied his ability to absorb himself so completely in his environment and exude every ounce of elation and wonder in that moment. His positivity emanated into the water and AJ felt the awe and beauty of the old wreck. Hazel must have felt it too as she gave AJ a double okay sign then put her hands together in a sign of gratitude.

AJ looked down into the rear of the hold that was now clear to them as she descended again. A door, dead centre of the hold in the stern wall, was wedged open a few feet. She stared at it for a moment and noticed Hazel followed her gaze. They both checked their dive computers. AJ's read 110' and sixteen minutes' dive time, eight minutes' no-deco time remaining. They still had to return to the line at over a hundred feet and the current gave them no option to go shallower to do that. They needed to start back. She looked over at Reg, who must have been thinking the same as he pointed to the bow. She nodded and noticed Thomas had seen the exchange. She looked back for Hazel. She was below AJ and still looking down at the door in the hold. AJ tapped her tank with a stainless steel carabiner she carried for signalling. Hazel looked up immediately, kicked up to join the group and they started back across the hold together.

Once they reached the line, AJ waited by the anchor until the other three started up the rope. As they reached thirty feet, they began the two stages of planned safety stops. AJ peered up at the other divers. She felt lucky to share this experience with a close group of friends. They were all looking back down at the wreck while they hung like laundry in a strong wind and she hoped they all felt as satisfied and grateful as she did.

37

JUNE 1974

Whitey stabbed at the underside of the marine oil filter with a large screwdriver, punching a series of holes in the perforated metal base. He then took a large pair of diagonal cutter pliers and used them as shears to snip away more of the tin. Eventually he was left with an opening all around the threaded centre tube and was able to gouge out the paper filter element leaving a hollow void in the cylinder. Ainsley looked on, wondering what his friend was up to.

"So, why are you makin' a big mess of that filter thingy?" he finally asked.

Whitey continued to snip and bend the jagged edges until he could safely reach inside the cylinder without cutting himself.

"Hand me the key, the safety deposit key," he asked, ignoring the question for the moment.

Ainsley handed him the odd-looking key Whitey had left with him and made sure he'd brought along.

"Got a rag somewhere?" Whitey asked and received a blank stare back. He reached over to the cabinet under the console where the tools had been and rummaged around for a moment. Sure enough, there were a couple of dirty rags the previous owner had left. Whitey wrapped the key in one of the rags and stuffed the rag inside the filter body.

"That's why," he said.

"Oh," Ainsley responded, still sounding confused. "And now what?"

Whitey looked up at him, squinting against the bright afternoon sun. "I put it back."

"Oh." Ainsley wagged a finger at his friend. "I get it, so the key will be hidden on the sunken ship down there?"

"Boat," Whitey corrected.

"Boat?" Ainsley asked.

"Boat," Whitey confirmed. "A ship is much bigger, the Raptor is a boat. Or was a boat when she floated, now she's the wreck of a boat."

"But isn't it a shipwreck, not a boat-wreck?" Ainsley countered.

Whitey laughed. "Got me there, but while it was afloat, it was a boat."

Ainsley looked thoughtful, "So what's it like?"

"The wreck?" Whitey asked.

"All of it." Ainsley pointed over the side of the boat.

"It's beautiful, brother." Whitey smiled. "Even the wreck, it's like this magnificent mechanical beast lying still down there." He became more animated, his enthusiasm welling as he spoke, "The life down there, there's so much life. From tiny little shrimps and blennies, to the big stuff like the rays and the sharks."

Ainsley was transfixed until he heard 'shark'. "No way man, I ain't getting in the water anywhere near a damn shark."

Whitey laughed. "They ain't interested in you, you're not their food. Sharks are beautiful, man, powerful and intelligent; I love seeing them."

"What if you're bleeding? Don't they go crazy over a drop of blood?" Ainsley asked, grimacing.

"I wouldn't get in the water if I was leaking badly, but they won't attack you if you have a scratch on your finger. Like I said they don't see you as food. Mostly they stay away. If you see one, he was heading somewhere and you crossed paths, or he was curious what all the noise was. Divers make a lot of noise compared to fish."

Ainsley nodded. "Maybe one day I'll try this diving thing. But no sharks and I don't think I want to go near a wreck. That seems creepy. Gives me the willies knowing there's a big ship right under us."

"Boat."

"Ship, boat, pedalo, I don't give a shit man," Ainsley complained. "I ain't getting in the water with nothing weird down there."

Whitey shook his head and gave up. "Got any grease?"

"Huh?" Ainsley gave him another blank look.

Whitey went back to the same cabinet and rummaged to no avail. He opened the little cabin door and squeezed himself through the opening. Looking around there wasn't much in the tiny vee berth. Most of it was taken up with the two converging benches that became a bed when a padded panel was dropped in the gap between them. To his left was a small cabinet that looked like it was intended to be a wardrobe. He swung the door open with little expectation. A few old wire hangers swung from a rail, otherwise it was empty. He leaned in and lifted the left bench top to reveal a handful of brand-new life vests that appeared to have never left that spot. Dropping it back down he lifted the right bench and saw mainly an open space. Stuffed in the front corner was a cardboard box and Whitey shuffled over to inspect it. A can of WD-40, two tin cans of engine oil, unopened, and one small tub of marine shaft grease. Perfect, he thought, Ainsley comes through again. He laughed to himself as he extricated his big frame from the bow cabin with grease in hand.

Ainsley pointed at the tub. "Yeah man, course I got grease, gotta have grease on a boat, everyone knows that."

Whitey grinned at him and slapped the tub into his hand, "Hang onto that while I get geared back up." He stood up and stretched after being cramped for the past few minutes. "And grab the crowbar for me."

"The crowbar? What the hell you need a crowbar for down there?" Ainsley asked without moving.

"I'm gonna beat Davy Jones on the noggin with it. Just get the bloody thing." Whitey turned back and grinned. "Better say goodbye to it too, cos it ain't coming back up."

38

NOVEMBER 2019

AJ listened intently as the other divers keenly talked about the wreck from their own perspectives. She noticed Carlos doing the same and could tell he was wishing he was diving instead of babysitting the boat.

"The angle she's sitting at makes the dive so strange," Thomas observed between bites of fresh mango from the cooler. "You think you're staying level but you're going deeper, quickly; it's a little disorientating, like diving the Kittiwake now it's tipped over."

Reg agreed, "Could get you in trouble too, difference between a hundred feet and one twenty in gas consumption is huge. Easy to run out of time on this dive. It's a similar depth to the U-1026 but the profile is different, or maybe we're just more familiar with the sub."

"I'd like to see what's behind that door," Hazel said, looking at AJ.

Reg answered before AJ had a chance, "I knew you two were gonna start on about that bloody door." He rolled his eyes but was smiling.

"Hey, wait a minute," AJ protested, "I haven't said a word

about any door. You're assuming I want to look too, and I haven't said anything about it!"

"What door?" Carlos asked.

Reg pointed at AJ. "You telling me you're not interested in what's behind that door?"

AJ looked sheepish. "I didn't say that either."

They all laughed and amongst the noise Carlos asked again, "What's this door?"

Thomas finally answered him. "The doors to the main structure are all seized shut by the growth, or locked, or corrosion, whatever, they won't open, but at the bottom of the hold is a door that's wedged open."

"But it's at over a hundred and thirty feet, maybe more," Reg added, "and it'll get deeper if you go inside."

"We're capped at 137' on 29% Nitrox so if it's deeper we just abort." AJ shrugged her shoulders like it was no big deal, but she knew the depth limit was serious. The concentration of extra oxygen being crammed into their system became poisonous at the limit depth for each Nitrox mix and it was critical not to exceed that depth. She caught Reg's eye. He grinned and shook his head.

"Watch your computer, girl," he said gently and looked over at Carlos. "Wanna take a look, Carlos?"

Carlos jumped up. "Seriously Reg?"

Reg laughed and stroked his beard. "Yeah, I'll watch the boat. But don't follow these two daredevils through the deep door, someone's gotta have some no-deco time left to bail them out." He looked over at Thomas. "I'm leaving you in charge Thomas – don't let the girls do anything too crazy, alright?"

Thomas laughed. "No sir, mister Reg, I'll keep a watch on them, no problem." He looked over at his boss who was frowning back at him and he laughed again. "Don't be givin' me the stink eye there, Boss, I got my orders straight from the Big Boss man."

AJ couldn't keep a straight face and cracked up. "Glad you'll have our backs, Thomas." She looked at her dive watch. "Been up forty minutes, let's give it a full ninety minutes on the surface interval to off-gas as much as possible."

They all relaxed a little more, knowing they had some time, except Carlos, who was like a dog with two tails he was so excited.

Reg looked around at the scattering of dive and pleasure boats all at least a half mile from them. "Think we should be hanging out all afternoon over the wreck? We'll take a little grief if DOE sees us here."

AJ looked around too. "I thought about moving away while we were up but seeing how we hit that railing I reckon we were pretty damn lucky to get it first try. Don't really want to have to try again. Might spend all afternoon trying to snag it."

Reg nodded. "True enough." He settled back in his seat and pulled his wide-brimmed hat down to cover his eyes from the sun that was lowering as the afternoon wore on.

"We could tie a line off the wreck like you did on the U-boat," Thomas suggested. "Float a buoy at fifteen feet we could mark on the GPS."

"Ain't planning on coming back here, lad," Reg muttered from under his hat. "Enjoy the next dive: should be your last on the Raptor; ain't no point pushing our luck with the lady."

AJ agreed, "Yeah, this is really cool to get to see her before she shoves over, but I don't see us coming out again."

AJ looked over at Thomas, who nodded, and she shifted her gaze to Hazel, who smiled. "Really appreciate you guys letting me do this dive with you," Hazel said softly. "This is really special."

AJ beamed back. "Glad you pushed me to do it."

"I owe you all dinner," Hazel said to the group. "You need to let me pay you back, at least in food and drink."

"Not sure you'll be allowed to buy," Reg said from beneath his brim, "but if you want to join us tonight, we'll be at the Fox and Hare for dinner." He lifted his hat up a little. "It is Friday, isn't it?"

AJ laughed. "Hell if I know."

Thomas helped out. "Yup, Friday it is. I only know cos it's pay day." He grinned at AJ.

"Depends on how you behave next dive," she retorted with a laugh.

Thomas burst out laughing in his infectious way. "Ohhh, sorry Big Boss man, mister Reg, I gotta side back with the lovely Miss Bailey cos she signs my pay cheque these days." Thomas waved a hand at AJ. "Go ahead and check that door out all you'd like, just make sure you come back up to sign my cheque and all."

Hazel looked around the group. "Pretty funny, the islander, the one that's not supposed to care about the time of day, is the only one who knows what day of the week it is."

AJ looked over at her with a chuckle. "That's the thing about Thomas, he'll make you think he's a laid-back Caymanian without a worry in the world, and then you figure out he's the one really running this operation; don't let him fool you."

Thomas busted up again. "Ohh, that's the real deal? I don't think so, Boss!"

Carlos stared around the group. "It's gotta be time to get back in by now?"

39

JUNE 1974

Whitey clambered over the short railing around the bow of the SportCraft and sat precariously on the edge of the boat at an awkward angle with his air tank skewing him against the railing. At least he was above the anchor line and didn't have to swim like a floundering cat along the side of the boat. Ainsley stood next to him with a mesh bag containing the lantern, the filter with rag-wrapped key, the tub of grease and the crowbar. Whitey dropped into the water with a heavy splash and immediately grabbed the rope. Ainsley reached over and handed him down the mesh bag of goodies.

"My brother's going to be mad at me for losing his crowbar," he reiterated, again.

"I'll buy him another one. As I told you, twenty times already," Whitey replied, taking the bag and making sure he had the top secured in his grip. "I don't see how anyone can be so emotionally attached to a damn crowbar."

Ainsley held his hands up. "You don't know my brother, man."

Whitey started to pull his mask down and paused for a second. "You sure it doesn't have more to do with you never bringing back stuff you borrow. Is that it, Ainsley?"

The Caymanian looked down at him with his best insulted expression. Whitey laughed, finished pulling his mask over his face, popped his reg in his mouth and dropped under the surface.

The current hadn't abated any and Whitey was pulled against the crook of his arm wrapped around the rope as he descended to the stern of the Raptor. He took a quick look at his pressure gauge which he realised he'd forgotten to do before leaving the boat. Fourteen hundred psi. He'd used more air than he'd anticipated getting back to the boat and chided himself for not switching tanks to be safe. For a second he contemplated going back up and changing his tank, but he was already halfway to the wreck and decided it would be a quick job to return the filter. In and out, slap some grease around, no problem.

He looked back down at the wreck looming large below him. It really was an impressive site. The fish had already fully embraced the addition to their reef and cruised the decks, hallways, and rooms as though they'd always lived there; which many of them had. Looking towards the bow angled upwards on the sloping sea floor, Whitey picked up the weaving movement of a solitary grey figure. He chuckled to himself, thinking of Ainsley: he couldn't wait to tell him a shark was guarding the wreck this time.

Reaching the stern railing, which was more like a sheet metal low wall with drainage holes along its base, he glanced at the anchor to verify it was still well secured. One fluke was wedged through a drainage hole and with the strain the current was putting on the boat above no way was it coming loose. Whitey actually wondered if it would come free when they needed to leave. He pulled himself around the side of the cabin structure and wasted no time diving down to the door at the back of the hold. It was still wedged wide open where he'd left it. He fished the crowbar out and dropped it on the deck of the hold in front of the door then retrieved the lantern and shone the beam inside the engine room.

Kicking into the cramped space he moved quickly and efficiently to the top of the motor, wriggled into position and pulled the filter from the bag. Popping the lid off the grease tub he slathered the open side of the filter and exposed rag in large quantities of waterproof grease. Adding a little more to the mount threads and rubber seal around the outside edge he reached down and screwed the filter back in place, securing the safety deposit box key in the best hiding spot he could dream up. If someone stumbles across this, they deserve a couple of million dollars he thought. He picked up the strap wrench from the floor where he'd left it and threw it in the bag, deciding hand tight was good enough and should negate the need for the wrench next time. Whitey took a scoop full of grease from the tub and turned around, moving back to the door. He smeared grease on the door hinges and shoved as much as he could into the latch mechanism. Maybe he could stave off the corrosion for a while. He hoped he didn't need to hide the key for long; if all went well, he'd be out of this mess within a month, two at most. He took one more look at the hinges and something barrelled into him from behind, shoving him against the door. He half turned as he caught himself and saw a large grey mass disappearing into the engine room. He swam back away from the doorway and took a few quick, deep breaths through his reg. Bugger me, he swore to himself, maybe Ainsley's right about the bloody sharks.

Still inside the engine room was the filter wrench, his lantern, which he had left pointed at the filter, and the mesh bag. Peeking inside he could see flashes of grey as the reef shark circled the room, illuminated twice each lap by the open door and the lantern beam. He looked at his gauges. He was hanging around at 103 feet with 560 psi of air left. He needed to leave. If there'd been some training along the way on how to remove a shark from a room at a hundred feet under the sea, Whitey had missed it. He floated outside and stared at the predator cruising around the engine room like Jackie Stewart pacing the streets of Monaco. He was about to give up and leave when, as fast as he'd entered, the shark shot out the doorway, straight towards Whitey, who thought about leaping out the way, but the shark was in his face before he finished the thought. With a flash of razor teeth, the shark turned abruptly, inches from Whitey's mask and swam away effortlessly, in complete disregard for the current that Whitey fought.

He floated a few moments longer, his pulse racing, taking gulps of air through his reg in stunned amazement. A quick glance at his tank pressure showed him he needed to move, and move quickly. He shot inside the engine room and wriggled over the diesel motor to grab up the bag, wrench and lantern. He put the lid back on the grease and dropped the tub beside the engine for later use. Backing out the way he'd come, he pulled the door closed against the crowbar he used as a stop; in case the hinges seized, he'd still be able to slip through. Bag in hand he kicked hard up out of the hold and let the current whisk him to the stern, where he grabbed the line and went up as fast as he dared. Looking up, he saw Ainsley's cuddy cabin brightly lit by the sun and a figure peering over the side into the water. His reg breathed heavy on his next inhalation but he knew he couldn't ascend any faster, he was already risking the bends. Next breath he felt the agonising clunk of the second stage closing and his air supply was done. He let the air left in his lungs slowly ease out as he rose. With the surrounding water pressure reducing as he neared the surface, the air left in his lungs expanded so he knew to relieve that pressure as he ascended. He broke the surface and threw his reg aside to grab a sweet lungful of air.

"Everything go okay?" Ainsley looked down at him with an innocent smile.

"Like clockwork," Whitey managed in reply.

40

NOVEMBER 2019

They decided to pair up; Hazel and AJ were hoping to investigate the mysterious door, whereas Thomas and Carlos were staying as shallow as the current would allow. AJ led and, as planned, she released the line when she reached a depth of 70', letting the current take her towards the cabin structure as she continued to descend. Hazel followed suit. They figured they'd gain a minute or two from taking this shortcut... provided they timed it right and didn't get pulled off the wreck. With no air in her BCD, AJ dropped swiftly as the air in her wetsuit was crushed to nothing by the water pressure and she became less buoyant. The plan worked perfectly, and she was released from the current as she reached the rear of the cargo hold at deck level. With a quick okay sign from Hazel, the two continued straight down the back of the hold towards the door. Hazel shone her powerful, compact dive light ahead and AJ carefully watched her dive computer.

It read 131 feet as they settled upright before the door. It was wedged open somewhere around forty or fifty degrees and the base blended to the floor of the hold with a carpet of silt and coral debris. AJ could just make out a coral-encrusted rod of some sort apparently used to hold the door ajar many moons ago. Maybe while they cleaned the wreck after it was sunk, she thought. Hazel shone her light inside the room and AJ peered over her shoulder. It was clearly the engine room. Inside, away from the sunlight the big diesel engine was free of coral growth but covered in a layer of fine silt and a green, sinewy algae that looked like underwater cobwebs. Hazel ran her light around the door frame to size up the entry and AJ was pleased her friend was concerned about not disturbing the living coral on the wreck.

AJ watched Hazel carefully slip through the doorway and, taking her own light from her BCD pocket, turned it on and did the same. The inside was cramped with lines and plumbing from the motor, running in all directions like a dark jungle full of vines. Hazel moved to the port side, so AJ went the other way. The room was narrower than the width of the boat so there had to be rooms either side, but there was no sign of another doorway in or out. An eye glinted in the edge of her light beam, and bringing the illumination carefully back in that direction revealed a large grouper, looking rather unsettled by their presence. AJ was careful not to blast him with light, but he still decided to bolt for the door in a haze of silt that clearly startled Hazel, causing her light beam to flash around the room. They both looked across the engine room, keeping each other in the soft light at the edge of their torches. AJ could tell Hazel was smiling behind her reg.

AJ checked her computer. They indeed had gone a little deeper when they entered the engine room, 135 feet. They were at the very limit of safe depth. No-deco time was nine minutes. They'd barely spent any time inside the wreck but at that depth the volume of gas they were consuming was significant. She decided they could spend three more minutes inside and then they needed to get out quickly. She held up three fingers then pointed down indicating she meant in here. Hazel gave her an okay sign. AJ softly finned towards the back of the room, careful to stay higher in the angled room so she didn't go any deeper. Below her the drive train extended from the back of the engine through a bulkhead towards the stern and the props that were hanging in mid-air over the drop-off. In fact, she wondered, are we far enough back where we are, to be over the edge of the wall? The idea that straight below them was nothing but water for close to a thousand feet was unnerving and she decided to stop thinking about it.

After a few more minutes exploring and enjoying watching a tiny nudibranch inching its way along a corroded steel tube, she checked her computer. It was time to go. She shone her light over the port side to see what Hazel was up to. She could see her light beam but couldn't see Hazel. AJ eased to the top of the motor amongst the myriad of lines, carefully picking her way through the mess. Now would be a bad time to get all strung up and entangled. As she made the port side, Hazel rose up and pointed to the door. AJ nodded, figuring she'd snare some lines if she tried to signal okay with her hand. They both squeezed back through the doorway and immediately ascended to the cabins, allowing their no-deco time to gain a few more minutes with the depth decrease. AJ looked around until she spotted Thomas, watching her from the walkway across the upper cabins. She signalled they were heading to the line, and he confirmed they'd follow. Carlos was just behind Thomas and saw the exchange.

The four divers kicked firmly towards the bow trying to minimise their time below a hundred feet to get there. AJ let the three of them start up the line before she joined them. As they pulled themselves up, hand over hand, they all looked back down at the magnificent wreck. She'd once been a small cargo vessel, nondescript and indistinguishable from a thousand other small boats moving man's goods from place to place. Now she lay in her grave as the core of an ecosystem that bristled with life, from AJ's nudibranch to the school of large jacks they now watched circling above the cabins. Her whole outer shell had become a living entity of coral. AJ felt a stab of sadness as she remembered the precarious position the wreck held. Next storm she'd almost certainly be gone. Her sadness swiftly changed to appreciation that she'd had a chance to explore the Raptor before she left for deeper waters and became the host for another set of life forms.

She looked at Hazel hanging on the line with her strong arms and noticed the sleeves of her wetsuit had a brown hue. Curious, she thought, she must have really dug around in there. Looking back down she saw a large reef shark slowly weave its body back and forth, cruising across the wreck. AJ idly wondered how long that shark had been patrolling the wreck of the Raptor. I bet he's seen a thing or too, she thought with a smile.

41

JUNE 1974

Whitey stood knee deep in the gin-clear water with his Voit fins in one hand and his flat-lensed, oval mask and straight tube snorkel in the other. The warm water lapped gently around his legs before rolling slowly up the pale sand of Seven Mile Beach. Isabella stood on the sand adjusting the rubber strap of a similar mask with her fins laid by her feet. The morning sun shone brightly from behind her in the east, making Whitey squint to see her perfectly tanned figure barely covered in her black bikini. His attraction to her was certainly physical, but it was much more than that. He wanted to hear the words from her lips. Whatever she talked about he was interested in; if it affected her world, he wanted to know about it. With the majority of women he'd frequented, he'd wished they'd stop talking.

Satisfied her new mask was adjusted right, Isabella walked towards him into the water.

"Okay, I think I have it like you said. How far out are we going?" she asked, casting her view across the open water.

He let her walk straight to him and kissed her as her body pressed against his.

"To the reef. I don't know exactly how far it is off the beach here, I'd guess about half a kilometre." He sat back in the water and pulled his fins on while he floated on his back. She watched then did the same. Whitey kicked away from shore until the water was deeper then stood on the sandy bottom and put his mask in place. He kept the very top of his moustache, under his nose, shaved so the mask would seal. Once she'd put her mask in place, he gently swept away some of her long black hair from under her mask seal.

"Okay, just swim using your fins and keep your hands still, nice and calm so we don't scare the fish; we'll see more that way. If you get too much water in your mask, or down the snorkel, pop up and clear it. Later I'll show you how to clear them without coming upright."

She nodded, her beautiful big green eyes gazing at him from behind the glass lens. She put the snorkel's rubber mouthpiece in place and glided across the water with her mask submerged. With a few strong kicks he was beside her and they settled into a gentle rhythm heading west towards the shallow reef. They passed over the occasional small patch of coral and Isabella lingered to watch the juvenile fish busy themselves in their isolated little world. Whitey chuckled to himself, knowing what was ahead of them. If the coral patch was Isabella's tiny hometown of Mojácar, they were about to visit Madrid, Barcelona and Valencia combined on the reef ahead. The depth slowly increased until around fifteen feet, where a dark shadow appeared ahead of them. Isabella sat upright, finning gently to keep her lean body afloat. She took her snorkel from her mouth and Whitey could see her eyes were concerned.

"What is that?" she pointed ahead of them.

He laughed. "That's what we came out here for. Trust me."

They put their snorkels back in and he took her hand for reassurance as they continued. The shadow quickly came into focus and the colours of the reef began to reveal themselves. The overhung ridge of the edge of the reef sprang magically from the sandy flats like an oasis in a desert. Soon the reef was only eight feet below them, and Whitey heard a squeal through Isabella's snorkel. Carpets of gorgonian soft corals gently tickled the water around them, and sea fans and plumes swayed with the almost imperceptible surge. Sponges in bright yellows and pinks stretched towards them and barrel sponges, two feet across, looked like pairs of open-topped tom-tom drums. Isabella's hands became animated as she pointed at one thing after another and Whitey drifted along beside her, letting her soak up her first experience on a coral reef.

She watched a pair of longnose butterfly fish shimmy in and out of a small coral head. She was fascinated by the brilliant blues and yellows of a queen angelfish that shyly hid behind a purple sea fan. Her hands clutched together nervously when she saw the head of a spotted moray eel waving back and forth from a crevice, its mouth opening and closing as it pushed water through its tiny gills. Whitey waved a hand under her mask to get her attention and pointed to his right. Isabella turned to look and her hands clasped together in delight when she spotted the baby hawksbill turtle clumsily taking nibbles from a brown sponge.

Whitey heard her splutter and they lifted their heads up.

"I turned too much," she laughed between coughs. "I swallowed some water down my tubey thing."

He laughed. "That's a snorkel, my dear."

"I swallowed some water down my snorkel," she corrected herself with a big smile. "This is amazing! There's so much to see. I can't believe I've been on the island all this time and never come out this far."

"I'm happy to be the one to introduce you," he said, brimming with joy at her instant love of the world he adored. "Wait till I teach you to scuba dive." He grinned.

"Really? You'd teach me? I want to go down there!" she said, looking into the water excitedly.

"You can go down there right now," he said and taking a deep breath he ducked under and swam down to the top of the reef. He kicked around and rolled over to look up at Isabella, staring wide eyed through her mask at him, her perfect form silhouetted on the surface.

He could get used to this. He knew right then that he wanted to spend forever on this island. Or maybe it wasn't just the island. Maybe it was Isabella.

42

NOVEMBER 2019

The Fox and Hare wasn't a fancy place and it was tucked out of the way enough in West Bay that it catered mainly to locals. An occasional tourist stumbled across it by chance or recommendation, usually Brits looking for a traditional-style pub on the British overseas territory. The only advertising they did was for their Friday night live music, so by the time AJ had picked Hazel up and they walked in, the place was packed. Thomas waved to them from a table in the corner and the two made their way through the crowd and joined the group. AJ felt a little self-conscious in her new, form-fitting summer dress but the compliments flowed as she passed people she knew. She noticed with a smile the eyes lingered on Hazel a little longer in her short denim skirt and vee-neck blouse unbuttoned seductively. Carlos and Sydney were already there, and Reg was helping his wife, Pearl, set up her gear on the small stage. Pearl was the entertainment a couple of Fridays a month and brought in a good crowd of ex-pats and locals alike.

"Hey guys," AJ started, "this is Hazel," and turning to Hazel said, "and I think the only one you haven't met yet is Sydney."

Sydney, a tall, beautiful, Caymanian girl hugged AJ and shook hands with Hazel. "Hi, I'm Thomas's sister and Carlos's fiancée."

"Bonsoir," Hazel replied. "And you go to university in America, correct?"

They both sat down. "I do, Miami, I'm only home for a long weekend visit," Sydney replied.

"Who needs drinks?" AJ asked, still standing.

Hazel went to get up again and AJ touched her shoulder indicating she should stay put. "You'll have plenty of chance; what can I get you?"

Hazel protested, "Okay, but remember I'm supposed to be buying. I'll have one of those ciders you like."

Everyone else had a drink so AJ headed for the bar leaving Hazel being blasted with questions from the others. She detoured to the stage and gave Pearl a big hug. The woman was a little shorter than AJ, and with her busty figure, AJ was always surprised how far she had to lean her head in to rest cheek to cheek when they embraced. Pearl, like her husband, was a keen hugger, so she'd knock the breath out of you if you weren't prepared. AJ loved them both dearly and Pearl's hugs had the warm, unrestrained affection that AJ's mother never quite managed. She could stay in her embrace forever. Well, until she ran out of breath. Tonight, Pearl wore stage make-up, which was a little heavier than her usual eyeliner and lipstick, but still subtly done. They finally released each other, and Pearl looked her over approvingly.

"Lovely dress," Pearl noted in her thick London accent. "Thanks for coming tonight, my dear."

"Wouldn't miss it," AJ replied. "You'll have to meet Hazel when you take a break, she bought me the dress; she's the French woman who's been diving with us."

Pearl smiled. "Reg told me you lot dived that old wreck off the point here. You're always up to something crazy, my girl."

AJ laughed. "It was fun, but maybe don't mention it to Bob and Beryl." Reg and Pearl stayed in touch with AJ's parents, as they had since the Bailey family first came to Cayman on holiday when AJ was a young girl. She knew all four were just looking out for her but there was no point unduly worrying her parents back in England.

The bar was packed but a couple of regulars recognised AJ and let her squeeze in to make her order. Frank was down the far end but looked her way and she held up two fingers to which he nodded back. After a few minutes he made his way down her end with two bottles of Strongbow cider.

"Evening AJ, anything else?" Frank said, his forehead beading with sweat.

"Better get Reg one," she replied and Frank poured bourbon over a couple of ice cubes and set it on the bar.

"Thanks Frank." AJ took the drinks and made her way back through the crowd, saying hi to everyone she knew on the way, and receiving a few more compliments on how nice she looked. As she sat down, the house music cut and she heard Pearl's voice over the sound system welcoming everyone to the Fox and Hare.

They all stood to try and see the stage through the hub of people, as Pearl started strumming her guitar for the intro to Sheryl Crow's 'If It Makes You Happy' to the applause of the crowd. As Pearl got into the chorus Hazel leaned over to AJ. "She's really good!"

AJ smiled back. "She's just getting warmed up, wait 'till she takes on some Heart, she'll go toe to toe with Ann Wilson any day."

Hazel smirked in approval. "I love Heart."

By the time Pearl had finished her first set, the table was littered with empty food plates, the contents devoured by the hungry divers. Pearl and Reg had joined them, and they packed around the small table intended for four.

"Okay, please let me buy a round of drinks," Hazel begged, having been denied several times.

The group relented and AJ accompanied her to help carry the drinks. Hazel started towards the bar but then veered off towards the door and stepped outside. AJ followed and wondered where they were going. Once outside and clear of the door, Hazel stopped and turned to AJ with a serious look.

"There's something I need to talk to you about."

AJ was taken aback, her first thought wondering if she'd said something wrong to her new friend.

"Sure, what's up?" she replied tentatively.

"I need to go back to the wreck," Hazel said firmly, looking AJ straight in the eyes.

"The Raptor?" AJ asked, confused. She tried to read Hazel's expression but in the dim light outside the pub she couldn't really tell.

Hazel had her hands on her hips and replied without hesitation. "Oui. I need to go back inside the engine room."

43

JUNE 1974

Whitey and Isabella spent an hour over the reef before finally swimming back to the beach. The sun was now overhead and they spread out their beach towels they'd left in a bag on the sand. He smiled at her cheap tourist shop sunglasses as he slipped on his Ambermatic Aviators. Moving here would mean giving up such luxuries; a dive guide's wage would be a far cry from the handfuls of cash the Caveros paid him. He couldn't keep count of his income as Gabriel would always slip him money, especially when he was out on the town and drinking in Miami. He knew it was a lot. He didn't know exactly how much he had hidden in his apartment on the mainland; he'd been stuffing cash in there for two years now, so he assumed quite a bit. Probably enough to buy a small house on the island and have some fall-back money left over.

They lay back on their towels and let the bright sun dry their bodies to the sound of the ocean lapping gently up the sand. Whitey's hand found hers and his mind wandered over what he needed to arrange and put in place if he was to disappear. But he'd be disappearing in the second place the Caveros would look, after Miami.

"What was it like here during the war?" Isabella asked quietly, her eyes still closed.

Whitey thought for a moment. "Quieter. None of these hotels were here." He sat up and looked back and forth along Seven Mile Beach. He could see three or four two-storey hotels from where they sat, nestled amongst the palms, seagrapes and ironwoods lining the top of the beach. A few dozen people scattered along the beach front, sunning themselves, as they were.

"I'm guessing there's twice as many people here, I think there's over ten thousand these days, plus all the tourists, which has to be a few thousand at any given time," he added.

She sat up as well and looked towards George Town as Whitey pointed towards the town, a few miles to their south.

"The port was similar but a lot less building around it. The town was mainly homes, and a few businesses. They had a home guard and a small military station here, so we'd stop in for fuel on our way back to Jamaica."

Whitey thought about his early days in the British Navy and the crew of the Motor Torpedo Boat he'd been assigned to. It was only thirteen men, so he got to know everyone in short order, their good and bad traits.

"I was a kid really," he reflected, "but I thought I was Jack the Lad. This bloke Arthur took me under his wing a bit; he'd been around for most of the war, mainly off the English coast in a similar boat, so he'd seen some things. Anyway, he sat me down after my first patrol with them and asked me all about myself, you know, where you from, where'd I grow up, all that. He was a quiet spoken man, had a way of calming things, calming people down. He says, 'Son. You're a small cog in a big wheel and if you don't line up proper with the cogs next to you, the wheel won't turn properly. This may seem like a lark and an adventure but don't forget what's at stake. Have fun, be yourself, but just remember, one day you may need that bloke next to you on the wheel, and best he feels he needs you too.'" Whitey smiled, picturing Arthur Bailey and the rest of the men on the patrol boat. Somewhere in his apartment he had a picture of them all, taken in George Town harbour in 1945. He reminded himself to dig that picture out when he was home.

"After that I made sure I was a bit nicer and not so cocky around my shipmates. Sure enough they started accepting me as part of the crew."

"Did you learn to dive in the Navy?" she asked.

"Later, after the war I did, they trained me, but it was hard hat stuff, the big brass helmet and goofy-looking suit. But I started skin diving and snorkelling over the reef when I was here in '45. Fell in love with it in Cayman. Scuba gear didn't really become available much until the late fifties, which is when I got a kit in Australia and started diving with an air tank."

Whitey could hear Queen's 'Seven Seas of Rhye' getting louder and looked around to see where the music was coming from. Ainsley was walking down the beach, a big, white, toothy smile on his face, a fedora on his head, and a transistor radio hanging in his hand. He waved as he shuffled through the soft sand towards them.

Whitey turned to Isabella with a smile. "Picked this character up during the war too, been my best mate ever since."

Isabella laughed. "Really?" she asked, surprised. "You're a..." She paused to find the right words. "An unlikely pair."

Whitey nodded. "That we are, my dear." He waved back to Ainsley. "But this bloke would do anything for me, never had a friend quite like him."

"Look at you two," Ainsley greeted them, his smile broadening even wider, "two beautiful lovebirds on this fine beach of ours." He reached into the pocket of his tartan bell-bottoms and produced a Kodak Pocket Instamatic 60 camera.

"Let's get a picture of you two looking like James Bond and his Ursula Andress," Ainsley said, waving to them to stand in front of the ocean.

Whitey was reluctant – he hated having his picture taken – but he looked at Isabella and decided he'd really like a picture of her in her scant bikini. They walked into the water carrying their fins and masks and turned when they were ankle deep. Isabella put her arm around him, and Whitey smiled the most natural smile he'd ever managed in a photograph.

44

NOVEMBER 2019

AJ's mind raced with scenarios in which she'd missed something on the dive. She was sure Hazel had come out of the engine room with her light. She'd understand her wanting to go back if she'd lost it, those things were expensive, but she had seen it in her hand.

"What did you lose?" she asked.

"Here, sit down," Hazel said and led AJ to a bench outside the pub where they both sat. "I have some explaining to do."

AJ's concern grew, and her brain was in overdrive trying to figure out what was going on.

Hazel took a deep breath. "Hear me out before..." she struggled for the words in her second language.

"Before what? You're scaring me Hazel, what on earth is going on?" AJ's voice cracked a little.

Hazel held up her hand. "There is something in the engine room of the Raptor that I came here to get." She let that sink in a moment and gathered herself before continuing, "I owe you an explanation, I know, and I can explain it, I promise."

AJ was stunned. It slowly unfolded in her mind until she fell across the crux of the situation.

"You've been lying to me the whole time," she said, not

phrasing it as a question. "All this bullshit about diving some interesting wrecks was a lie to get me to take you to the Raptor." She looked down at the dress she was wearing and wished she could tear it off and throw it at Hazel.

Hazel put her hand on AJ's shoulder, but AJ shrugged it away. "No! You lied to me, Hazel. You've been playing me this whole time and I've been stupid enough to fall for it," AJ spat back, desperately trying to keep from crying. "Why the hell didn't you just tell me up front that you wanted to dive the damn wreck?"

"I couldn't," Hazel said softly, her own voice on the edge of breaking, "I couldn't, there's so much that's been a secret. I didn't know you, I couldn't just come out with the whole story." Hazel placed her hand on AJ's. "But now I know you, I know I can trust you completely, so I'm telling you everything."

AJ wiped her face with her other hand; the tears she didn't want to shed were creeping down her face in complete disregard of her wishes. She rarely cried and it made her angry when she did. She pulled her hand from Hazel's and looked her square in the eyes. "Why should I believe a word you say now? Just because you say so? Once you've lied Hazel, you're a liar – why should I even begin to trust you again?"

Hazel shook her head and in the pale light AJ realised tears were coming down Hazel's cheeks too.

"I know, I know, I've given you no reason to believe me now, but hear my story before you decide, I beg you, please hear me out, and then decide?"

AJ looked at the ground. Her normal reaction would be to tell her to go to hell and walk back inside. People had one shot. If you can't be trusted, then be damned with you. She wouldn't be one of those fools that gets duped and lied to over and over. This is why she didn't let people get close this quickly, she scolded herself; if I'd kept her at arm's length, this wouldn't be happening. But she'd so enjoyed being around Hazel – was she such a bad judge of character? The idea that she'd misread the woman completely, and everything they'd done and talked about since she'd arrived, was nothing but a calculated plan? The thought was unbearable.

"Please AJ, I can't stand for things to end this way between us." Hazel took her hand again and once more AJ allowed her. "Hear me out, and then if you decide to have no more to do with me, I'll understand. I'll be devastated to lose you, but I'll understand." Hazel shuffled closer and sniffled as she spoke quietly, "You don't have to help me at all, I'll figure something out, but please hear what I have to say so you understand why I couldn't be straight with you from the beginning."

AJ's hope that she wasn't the worst judge of another person barely outweighed her anger and feeling of foolishness. Hope was a powerful drug. The scales imperceptibly tipped and she nodded, but kept her eyes on the ground. If she looked at Hazel, she'd either punch her or hug her, and neither would be a resolution.

Hazel took another deep breath and started. "I met a man on Corsica about five years ago. An old French man. He was in his late eighties and couldn't get around much anymore. He would sit in the port at the old town of Calvi in the north, and watch the boats come in and out. We would dive the B-17 aeroplane that was shot down there in the war; it's a few minutes' boat ride outside the port, and the old man would see us off in the early morning and greet us when we returned. I started talking to the him. Most people just ignored him or said hello in passing, but I started spending a few minutes with him each time. He was fascinating, he'd been in the war and had been a diver in his younger years, so the wreck interested him."

AJ looked up. "My grandfather fought in the war. He patrolled these waters, in fact," she said before she could stop herself.

"You said. He rescued the submariners from the U-boat, right?"

AJ could tell Hazel was relieved she was engaged so she just nodded in response and Hazel continued her story. She wasn't ready to be nice.

"After a while I would take the man to one of the little cafes in the old town and we'd chat for ages about all kinds of things. He said he had no family anymore, so he was delighted in the company. One day he says he's going to tell me about something he'd never told a soul before. He said he couldn't tell me how he knew but he swore every word was the truth. I wasn't sure what he meant but he became very serious and spoke quietly so I listened, and listened carefully. 'On Grand Cayman in the Caribbean, there's a shipwreck on the north-west corner of the island,' he said. 'It is the wreck of the Raptor. In 1974 a man hid a key on that wreck and it's still there today. The key is to a safety deposit box in a bank. In that box is four million US dollars less thirty thousand dollars.' I asked him why it was less thirty thousand dollars and he said it wasn't important. The money belonged to no one anymore, everyone that had anything to do with it was dead, or had long since disappeared. The bank had instructions that anyone who showed up with the original key, which had a unique security code stamped on it, would be granted access to the box and its contents. He told me he was too old. Once he'd planned to go and get it, he'd been a keen diver, but he'd never had much money, not enough to jump on a plane and fly halfway around the world. So, time had worn on, he'd never made it to the island, and now he was too old and frail to make such a journey, let alone think about the dive. He took my hand and looked me in the eyes and said, 'Hazel, when you have a time of need, not a time of greed, go to Grand Cayman and get that money.'"

AJ didn't know what to say. The story drew her in and captivated her, but she couldn't let her guard down and simply believe Hazel just because she told a good story.

"What happened to the man?" she asked tentatively.

"I don't know. The day he told me that story was the last time I ever saw him." Hazel looked pained. "I didn't know where he lived or what his real name was, so I looked, and asked around the port, but no one knew him or where he was from."

"You spent all that time with him and didn't know his name?" AJ asked incredulously.

"He told me he went by Père Noël, that's all I ever knew him as," Hazel explained without becoming defensive.

"Father Christmas?" AJ asked, checking her meagre grasp of the French language.

"Oui, Father Christmas," Hazel replied. "So I never saw him again, and honestly I forgot about the story for years until my life starting coming apart. My mother died, then a few months later I lost my job, as I told you, and on top of that I had my identity stolen. In France we have what's called an INSEE code, it's France's social security number system, like they have in America. Mine was stolen and all my credit cards, my house mortgage, my car loan, they were all compromised, and my accounts were locked down. It was like my whole world collapsed within two months, everything turned to shit right in front of me. For a few weeks I couldn't buy a coffee, I had to borrow cash from friends until my bank account was unfrozen. But my credit was destroyed so the credit card companies all wanted the balances paid off and raised my interest rate through the roof. It was then I recalled Père Noël and his crazy story. I thought, what the hell, maybe he was telling the truth, what do I have to lose? So, I booked this trip and persuaded you to take me to the wreck, which honestly, didn't take much persuading, and I looked where he'd told me in the engine room, and I think his story is true."

"So you think the key is still in the engine room? Where exactly? I saw you'd been digging around in there – where do you think it is?" AJ asked, still torn with mixed emotions.

Hazel looked around to make sure no one was close enough to listen, "On the port side of the engine there's an oil filter. There's no actual filter inside, there's a rag wrapped around the key. I found the filter, but I couldn't get it to budge."

"And just because there's a filter on the side of a diesel engine you think Father Christmas was telling the truth? If you check every boat on Grand Cayman, there's an oil filter bolted to their engine." AJ sat back pretty sure she'd shot a big hole in Hazel's story.

"He told me there'd be a crowbar holding the engine room door open and he told be there'd be a tin of grease below the filter; both were true. The grease was used to keep the threads from seizing and corroding," Hazel shot back. "But it's tight enough it won't budge. I think we need a wrench or something."

AJ frowned at her. "We nothing. I still don't know if I should let you back inside the pub with my friends, let alone help you."

Hazel held her hands up. "I'm sorry, I understand. It's a crazy story. Imagine if I'd told you this when you first picked me up from my hotel? You'd have made me get straight back out the van."

AJ had to admit that's probably exactly what she would have done but she wasn't about to give any ground back just yet. She ran through the story again in her mind. There were so many questions.

"Why did he choose you? Why tell you?"

Hazel shrugged. "I was nice to him. I think that was it, I genuinely enjoyed chatting with him."

"Whose money was it? It wasn't his. He said everyone who knew about it, or owned it, was gone?" AJ asked pointedly.

"He would never say exactly but he was adamant they were long gone, and it was just sitting there," Hazel replied.

"So, the money could be drug money or a hitman's life savings? A Nazi's war stash?" AJ wondered aloud.

Hazel nodded slowly. "I guess. I have no way of knowing. What I know is he told me I should turn to it when I have a time of need, not a time of greed. Believe me, this is my time of need. I'm about to lose my house and I've lost all my savings paying all the balances off. I'm forty-four years old, I've worked my arse off my whole life and I'm about to lose everything through no fault of my own. This isn't driven by greed. If it was, I would have come here the day after he told me."

AJ sighed and rubbed her eyes. She was drained and couldn't process this improbable tale anymore. She needed a drink and she needed some sleep.

"Let's go back in. They'll have given up on their drinks." AJ managed a weak smile.

"Are we okay?" Hazel asked hesitantly.

"I don't know, Hazel. I have to think about all this, it's a lot to take in. I'm sorry you've had such a hard time, and I'm awfully sorry about your mum, but I don't know where we are. I get why you held back the story to begin with, but you manipulated me to dive the wreck and that really hurts." AJ stood. "I need to sleep on it. Tomorrow's my day off, Carlos and Thomas are working so you'll be diving with them if you still want to go out."

Hazel stood too. "Maybe I should stay off the boat until we've worked this out. I'll be at my hotel if you want to talk."

AJ nodded and walked towards the door. She didn't feel much better, but she didn't feel like she'd completely misread Hazel either. Unless, of course, she was making all this up. Some imagination if she is, she thought, and pushed the door open to the pub. Pearl was into her next set, belting Sass Jordan's 'Make You a Believer'. AJ shook her head and rolled her eyes.

45

JULY 1974

Gabriel Cavero's villa was a mile from his father's, on the same mountainside overlooking the Río Huallaga and the town of Huánuco. They owned most of the mountainside and Gabriel's brother had a home on the other side to their father's. July was the coolest month in the valley, the nights dipping into the forties, but the sunny days still reached the seventies in contrast to the snow rimming the surrounding mountains. Whitey had arrived late the night before, brought there by the family's driver, and stayed in one of the guest rooms. He'd been glad Gabriel and his wife were already asleep, but now he could delay their meeting no longer, and he walked into their dining area to join them for breakfast.

Gabriel stood as he walked in, wiped his face with his cloth napkin and stepped around the table with his arms open wide. Whitey embraced the man who enthusiastically slapped him on the back.

"Whitey, mi hermano, so good to see you."

Gabriel stepped back but kept a hand on each arm while he studied Whitey with a big smile. "You look good my friend, I think all this time on an island might agree with you, no?" He laughed and released Whitey, offering him a seat.

His wife, Marisol, a slight woman with a pretty smile, didn't stand but warmly greeted him, "Good morning Mr Snow, very nice to see you again."

"Good morning," Whitey said with a forced smile as he took a seat. He wondered how many men Marisol had entertained in their house who had disappeared one day and stopped being a guest. He was sure she didn't ask, and her polite distance was a good indication she considered Gabriel's friends to be temporary. Or maybe he was just reading too much into the whole situation. Deceit was not a natural gift of Whitey's, despite his career in illicit endeavours, so his preference would be to come out straight with Gabriel and tell him he was getting out. But he doubted that would be acceptable to Gabriel, and was certain it wouldn't be for Mariano.

Whitey congratulated Marisol on her pregnancy, and the three chatted casually over breakfast as they often had, and Whitey began to relax. Once they'd finished and the maid cleared their plates, Gabriel kissed his wife and invited Whitey to join him outside on the patio. They poured fresh coffees and moved to a small wrought-iron table on the deck, which stretched to a steep drop towards the valley, protected by a railing. The view was stunning, and the cool air and chilly breeze felt refreshing, but Whitey couldn't help but shiver, his blood used to the balmy heat of Miami, and now Grand Cayman.

"The Cubans and Colombians are all fighting in Miami, Whitey, it's a damn mess." Gabriel switched to business and his easy manner and tone from breakfast disappeared. "I need you to meet with our Colombian contact, just to reassure him we're not switching our allegiance. They're buying everything we can supply and right now it's a breeze moving the goods across the border. We own the border."

"What happens if the Cubans take over the Miami market?" Whitey asked, wondering what mess he was walking into.

Gabriel laughed. "The crazy Cubans have no idea what they're up against." He waved a hand at Whitey. "They're a pain in the arse in the Miami market but the Colombians have the whole of the

US locked up. Their distribution is nationwide, LA, New York, Chicago, everywhere. The only reason they're getting wound up is because Miami is their main port of entry and the Cubans keep shooting people down there. Meet with our man and tell him the Caveros are dealing with one family, and it's them, okay?"

Whitey nodded. "No problem, I'll call him when I land and set up a meet." Whitey sipped his coffee, the smoothest coffee he'd ever tasted, and considered the new twist he had to contend with. He was hoping he'd have a short stay in Miami before getting back to the island; now he had to wait on the Colombian's schedule to meet with him.

"What's your take on the Cayman bank? You think the island is stable enough? None of this Jamaican nonsense?" Gabriel asked, looking at Whitey, seemingly gauging his response.

This was the opening Whitey had been waiting for and he paused to seem casual in his response. "The place is perfect in my opinion, Gabby: no trouble with the people, government's stable and forward thinking. They know banking is their future and they've got their arms open wide, no questions. We should put the cash into the bank and quit shoving it in a safety deposit box."

He hoped he'd been convincing; he desperately wanted to move the money into a bank account in the Caveros' name so he could step away cleanly. He'd evaporate, and they'd have access to their money, so they'd have little reason to pursue him for long.

"I believe you, my brother, and I would agree but father is caught in the old ways, you know? Like I told you, he's got cases of cash buried all over this mountainside," Gabriel swept his hands over the property, laughing. "I swear the gardener is probably a millionaire and father wouldn't know." He leaned over to Whitey. "The next trip you'll have double the cash; use the safety deposit box for one more month, give me time to convince the old man."

"Sure, no problem," Whitey complied, thinking how he could back himself out of this mess he'd created. Hiding the key seemed like a great security measure if they ever turned on him, but now it was a complication he needed to get out of. The volume of cash might be the answer.

"I think I have the biggest box the bank had available, but I'll ask, may have to get two, either way I'll have a different key for you after this trip, okay?"

Gabriel stared at him and Whitey felt the man searching his face, for what, he didn't have any idea. He thought over what they'd talked about and couldn't figure out what he'd said that would raise any suspicion. But he knew the Caveros were paranoid, who knew what any of them was really thinking.

"You okay, Whitey?" Gabriel asked, looking concerned.

"Of course, I'm great. A little tired from travelling is all," Whitey quickly responded.

Gabriel smiled. "You seem like you have a lot on your mind my friend, I worry about you is all."

Whitey tried his best to look relaxed and smile back. "Just tired, mate."

"Nothing you want to tell me? Or need to discuss?" Gabriel asked softly, sounding like he genuinely wanted to help his friend in any way he could.

Whitey paused and considered telling him he was out. He wanted to tell the man that had been so generous to him the truth, surely he deserved that? Gabriel had shared so much with Whitey and their friendship had extended well beyond the business over the past two years.

"No mate, just want to make sure I do everything right for you, that's all." Whitey stepped back from the precipice of the trap he sensed had been set.

Gabriel smiled and nodded. "Okay then."

46

NOVEMBER 2019

AJ sat on the end of the dock at the yacht club and watched her Mermaid Divers' Newton idle away. It was Saturday, the one day a week she took off, but sleep had eluded her, and her internal alarm clock still rousted her early. She'd helped Thomas and Carlos get everyone aboard and sent them off for the morning. Without Hazel.

Two of Reg's boats were motoring in line with AJ's, and her mentor set his coffee down on the dock, before lowering himself down to sit next to her.

"You think you're getting old? Try getting about with these worn out joints," he muttered.

"Yup, reckon you're headed for the OAP's home pretty soon, old man. Pearl'll be trolling for some young blood to keep her entertained," AJ teased.

Reg chuckled. "She could still land her a young 'un I'm sure; that woman's still as gorgeous as the day I met her."

AJ took a sip of her own coffee from her stainless steel travel mug and nodded in agreement. "That she is."

"I may be old and about ready for the scrap heap," he grinned, "but I'd still manage to throttle any man that lays a finger on her."

AJ sprayed a little coffee in the ocean laughing. "That's true too."

They sat in silence for a few minutes watching the early morning sun cast long shadows from the boats and listening to the mesmerising sound of the water lapping against the dock. Reg finally broke the silence.

"You gonna tell me about it or I gotta pry it out of you?" he said gently.

She looked over at him and he ignored her, staring off into the bay. She was always amazed how Reg and Pearl could read her like a book. It made her mad sometimes but other times it was comforting to feel their support and presence. He grinned.

"That obvious?" she asked, already knowing the answer.

"You two go to get drinks and disappear for half an hour. When you come back it's like you're both cloaked in ice. Yeah, I'd say it was pretty obvious." He turned and smiled at her.

AJ rolled her eyes. "I was pretty mad." She thought about how, and how much, to tell Reg. She felt she'd be betraying a trust to divulge the whole story and then she'd be no better than Hazel. She made an attempt at summarising without certain details.

"So, turns out Hazel wanted to dive the Raptor from the moment she landed here. Well, to be more accurate, it's actually why she landed here."

"Really?" Reg said, surprised. "Why didn't she just ask if we'd take her there in the first place?"

"That was my first question," AJ responded. "She had a reason that kinda held water, but it still feels like shit that she manipulated me to get what she wanted."

"What was her reason?" he asked.

"It's all part of this big story that I can't repeat; I was sworn to secrecy and, regardless of what I think of her, I don't want to be untrustworthy," AJ replied.

"Fair enough," Reg said. "Is what she's up to legit or is she breaking laws?"

AJ thought it over. "I'm not completely sure." She looked at Reg with a frown. "Depends a lot on whether I believe her whole story or not. If she's come clean and told me the truth, then she's an innocent victim, down on her luck and taking a long shot to dig herself out of trouble. If she's still making shit up, then who knows."

She sighed and took another sip of coffee while she knew he was chewing it over in his mind. "I just feel so disappointed in myself, Reg. I'm normally pretty good at reading people or at least taking enough time to figure them out so this crap doesn't happen. I don't know why this was different. Maybe I was vulnerable, or off my game with Jackson leaving. I don't know."

She fiddled with her new watch on her wrist and Reg leaned over, bumping her shoulder with his.

"You're assuming you read her wrong. What if you didn't?" he whispered Reg's version of a whisper which was more of a growl.

"But she used me Reg. I didn't see it," she responded with pain in her voice.

"And you say she had a reason that made some sense. What I'm saying is, what if your read on her as a person was right?" He shuffled a little to turn and face her more. "Everyone does right and wrong things, don't they? Everyone screws up or goes about things backwards, we all do occasionally. The question to ask is whether she's a good person at heart or not. She may well be the great friend you thought you'd found, your instincts were right, she just started things off a bit skew-whiff."

AJ laughed. "Skew-whiff you say? Yeah, I'd say she started off a little skew-whiff."

"Look," Reg said seriously, "I don't know the story she's spinning so I don't have much to go on, but I do know you and her have been getting on like a house on fire and you're right, you're usually a pretty good judge. Can you check any of what she says? Is it Googleable? Try and prove out what she says and if it's BS then tell her to get out of here. If it's not, maybe she's genuinely a friend that needs some help."

"Googleable? You're on a roll." AJ laughed again, and it felt good. "I checked a couple of things she told me. Her mum died earlier this year, I found her obituary; it got a bit more press because she owned a cafe, which she'd also told me. But most of her story isn't traceable, I have to either believe her or not."

Reg reached over and rubbed AJ's back softly. "Tread carefully my dear, but don't throw out the idea you were right all along."

AJ rested her head against his shoulder. "Okay. I'll try not to get too skew-whiff over it."

47

JULY 1974

Whitey sat on the end of his bed in his small Miami apartment. Pink Floyd's 'Dark Side of the Moon' album played quietly from the other room. It was a simple place he'd had for years. It had been all he could afford before he met Gabriel Cavero, and after that, when he had plenty of income, he never got around to upgrading. Besides, he didn't need much and was happy to save the money. The place had one bedroom, a bathroom, and a living area that encompassed a small kitchen that he used for coffee and cereal. He'd never been much of a cook, unless it was grilling fresh fish straight from the boat. As he looked around, he realised his home contained very little he cared to take with him. He thought to himself, somewhat regrettably, forty-seven years old and what did he have to show for it? Some great memories, a couple of photographs, and a stack of cash that sat in scattered bundles on the bed next to him. Two hundred and six thousand dollars was a lot of money. It had surprised Whitey when he'd counted it, he had no idea he'd tucked so much away but often he hadn't counted it when it was handed to him. A pang of guilt hit him as it dawned on him that he was running out on the people that had allowed him to amass a small fortune. It passed quickly when he reminded himself of the millions of dollars passing through their hands; a couple of hundred thousand was chicken feed to these men.

He'd been thinking he'd fly to Cayman, tuck the new cases full of cash Gabriel had given him in the safety deposit box, and mail the real key to Gabriel. But the more he chewed that plan over, the more holes he shot in it. Cayman shouldn't be the last place he could be tracked to as he intended to actually reside there. Although it would be easy to stay off the radar on the island it was also a small place. If Gabriel threw a little money around, someone was bound to talk. No, he needed to disappear in Miami, and the more he plotted, the more he decided the Cubans were his perfect escape. He would fly to Cayman, add the new cash to the money already at the bank, return to Miami, leave the real key in his apartment and a note showing a meeting scheduled with the Cubans for the day he'd vanish. Gabriel would search his apartment when he didn't check in, find the key so he'd get his money, and assume the meeting with the Cubans went south and they'd fed him to the gators in the Everglades. It might start a small war if Gabriel thought they'd hit one of his men, or maybe not if he decided Whitey was meeting with them for his own gain. The important part was the Caveros would get their money and Whitey would vanish from the planet to pursue his new life, free of the gangsters. He'd find the next cargo ship heading to the islands, on which he'd crew for free in return for a paperwork free ride. Whitey, Isabella and a couple of hundred grand would start a new life together on Grand Cayman.

All the pieces of the puzzle had to fall together, and his mind spun through the scenarios and details. He'd requested just one key for the real safety deposit box as he didn't want the added complexity of keeping up with two, especially as he'd considered the hidden key as his security blanket. He sorely wished he'd never concocted that stupid plan, now it just seemed overly complicated. Still, what was done was done and now he needed to step carefully and extricate himself from this perilous web.

He laid back on his bed and looked up at the fan making circles on his popcorn-textured ceiling. The idea that he was a week away from freedom, a week away from the beginning of the rest of his life, was energising and calming at the same time. He felt excited at the prospect of having a second chance in this world, one where he walked on the other side of a line. He'd taken a lot over the years, taken money, taken advantage, taken risks. The idea he could live simply, live humbly and give something back settled in him like a fine wine that permeated his being and soothed his soul.

His apartment phone rang and he reluctantly rose, walked to the kitchen counter and took the receiver off the hook.

"Mutiny Hotel, 10am tomorrow, Mr Márquez will expect you for breakfast," a heavily accented voice said in English.

"I'll be there," Whitey replied and the line went dead.

Chatty blokes, he thought to himself as he stared at the receiver. He'd met Miguel Márquez at the Club with Gabriel who'd introduced Whitey as his Miami representative; this would be his first time meeting anyone of this stature alone. Just when he was trying to get out. At least the man was ready to meet the next day. Whitey had been worried arranging this meeting would drag on, which was the last thing he wanted. He looked at the two Halliburton attaché cases next to his wicker couch. Nothing like two million bucks lying around in a cheap apartment while drug lords and gangsters circled the city. From the record player the Floyd started into their song 'Money' with the sound of the cash register opening and coins dropping. Whitey laughed, shaking his head and wished he could share the ironic moment with Isabella. He wanted to share every moment with Isabella.

48

NOVEMBER 2019

AJ stood on one leg, stretching her left leg behind her with one hand while she scrolled through playlists on her phone with the other. The morning breeze was just picking up, which helped fend off the heat from the sun rising swiftly in the eastern sky behind her. She'd driven back from the yacht club, changed into capri leggings, racerback sports bra and water shoes, and now stood on the beach in front of her apartment at the north end of Seven Mile Beach. Running always helped clear her head. She didn't particularly enjoy the act of running but the scenery, the way it helped her push through conflicting thoughts, and the cardio workout made it worthwhile. She switched legs and scrolled back and forth on her phone. Usually she ran to hard rock or upbeat pop music like Pink, which helped put a spring in her step, but today required something more cerebral, without being sleepy. She settled on a 90s mix and Alanis Morissette kicked her into gear singing about things 'Ironic'.

AJ passed the cemetery, her leg muscles quickly warming up as she searched for firmer sand to run on, close to the water. The beach was quiet this early, the tourists enjoying the luxury of sleeping in on their holidays. She crossed paths with an occasional runner and passed by a few folks enjoying a coffee on the beach out front of their condo or hotel, but otherwise the beach was hers. She was soon passing some of the older, two-level condo complexes like Discovery Point and Christopher Columbus. The Calling took over from Alanis and sang about being 'Unstoppable'; she thought that was appropriate and her pace quickened a little.

AJ hated drama and she struggled whenever her life felt out of control. Or at least out of her control. Her parents were both no-nonsense people who had showed her how to break situations down into elements. Examine the contents rather than lose yourself in the overwhelming chaos of the moment. As the sweat beaded down her face and her calves began to ache from the constant slope of the beach, her mind started to clear and sift through the components of her current challenge.

Jackson. That was potentially the most complicated situation, yet easy to compartmentalise. She loved the man and wanted to be with him as much as possible. Time owned the answer as to how they would get there but for now she took solace in knowing the goal was clear. It felt good to wrap that up and set it aside in her mind; she knew she was missing him terribly and it added stress to the other problem.

Which was Hazel. One of the downsides of being humble, modest and slightly self-deprecating, was she had a tendency to put others on pedestals. Hazel had arrived at the exact moment AJ knew she was more vulnerable: her turning thirty and Jackson leaving. The Frenchwoman had given her new energy and it felt good to have someone around that showed her how to be strong and confident as a woman. Hazel had a striking presence, not loud, not arrogant, simply powerful, and hard to ignore. She was many things that AJ wished she was and aspired to be. As usual, when you set someone up on that pedestal as a hero, there's only one place to go from there. As Reg had pointed out, we all screw up. Was Hazel a caring and reliable friend with a true heart? Better Than Ezra tried persuading AJ by singing 'Desperately Wanting'. Was she just desperately wanting a close friend, a woman she could admire? She had Pearl, and her mother – talk about tough women. She had good friends. But she didn't have a close girlfriend, maybe she craved that and didn't know it?

She really missed her grandfather at times like this. She was only fifteen when he died but they'd been close. More than a young girl loving her grandparent, they'd shared a lot of time together and he had a calm wisdom about him that helped her sort through teenage problems. He never told her what she should do, he simply guided her through the trees of the forest to see an answer. A tear mixed with the sweat on her face and she cursed to herself. Damn, two days in a row I'm crying, I'm falling apart. But shedding a tear for Grandad Bailey didn't count in her mind, the man deserved all the tears the world could cry.

Live's 'I Alone' kicked in another level of determination, and she told herself, indeed, I alone must decide the path this will take. Hazel has laid out her story and now it's for me to decide how I allow myself to be involved, or not be involved, she voiced out loud to the pelican that bobbed in the water, staring blankly at her.

AJ slowed her pace and looked around. She was surrounded by beach chairs and a young Caymanian looked over and smiled at her as he raked the beach. She realised she had run to the Westin hotel, halfway down Seven Mile Beach, where they were setting up for their guests. She apologised for messing up his freshly raked piece of beach, but he just laughed.

"No problem miss, messing things up and smoothing things out is just a part of life, no big deal."

She looked at the young man in amazement. Is the universe giving me subtle messages? She smiled back at the guy. Not very subtle, she thought. Third Eye Blind added their two cents with 'Semi-Charmed Life' and AJ threw her hands in the air as she turned to attempt the three miles back home.

"Alright, I get it, I'm a lucky girl," she shouted to the amusement of the beach raker.

49

JULY 1974

The restaurant overlooked the patio and pool where Whitey had witnessed a man fall to his death a few weeks before. He was already apprehensive about the meeting and seeing the patio through the windows did nothing to settle his stomach. He saw Márquez at a corner table, positioned so he faced the room. Two bodyguards stood in front of his table, one watching out the window, the other scanning the room. A handful of other guests sat at tables on the opposite side of the room, clearly placed away from Márquez. The man had half the restaurant to himself. The goon watching the room walked towards Whitey and indicated for him to hold his arms up. Whitey complied and the man frisked him then nodded towards the table, a sign Whitey took as meaning he could go sit down.

Márquez was a stern looking man in his late thirties with wavy, dark hair and a full beard. He was chewing a mouthful of breakfast, so Whitey assumed the invitation was to watch the man have his breakfast, rather than join him. Márquez glanced up long enough to regard Whitey with apparent disdain, then point his knife towards one of the chairs. Whitey sat.

"Good morning Mr Márquez," he tried, politely.

The man continued to eat, ignoring Whitey, who shifted uncomfortably in his seat. He noticed the guard who had frisked him had now taken an adjusted position to cover Whitey and the room. After another awkward minute, Márquez shoved his plate forward on the table and tossed his knife and fork onto the empty plate with a clatter. He ran his tongue around his teeth and wiped his lips with his napkin before tossing the napkin onto the plate as well.

"Why am I talking to you?" Márquez growled, finally looking at Whitey.

"You requested the meeting, sir?" Whitey answered, somewhat confused, wondering if the man had a poor memory.

"Why you? Where's Cavero?" Márquez asked irritably.

"Mr Cavero is in Peru sir, working hard to make sure your product is supplied as requested. He introduced us last month and told you I'd often be your Miami contact. Is that a problem, sir?" Whitey replied boldly, hoping he didn't overstep the line with one of Colombia's most notorious drug lords. He'd seemed amiable in the club when they'd been introduced but now the man was pissed off for some reason. Of course, in the club he'd had three beautiful women hanging on him which may have explained his better humour.

Márquez stared at Whitey with cold, dark eyes and Whitey figured it was fifty-fifty if he was about to have a conversation, or be shot in the head.

"I need twenty-five percent increase in supply next month," he said as though he was ordering extra staples. "And another twenty-five percent the following month." His voice was even and flat, almost sounding disinterested. But Whitey knew better.

"I'll speak with Gabriel today and see if we can meet that increase; that's not much time, you understand. It is a plant after all, it has to grow," Whitey responded with a smile.

Márquez gave him the same blank, cold stare. "What I understand is I need more product and Cavero can either supply me with it, or I expand my suppliers."

Whitey noticed the man's hands were clenching into fists on the table despite his voice remaining even. "If I expand suppliers, we'll start a pricing war, which is better for me because you'll be trying to undercut each other. How long the plant takes to grow, and how many plants you have, is your problem, mister..." He struggled to recall his name and Whitey let him struggle. "...Miami contact, you can either meet my order or not."

He leaned over the table and pointed a finger at Whitey. "But tell me you'll supply, and come up short, and I'll cut you into pieces while you beg me to end your life." Márquez paused with his finger six inches from Whitey's nose before finally relaxing and sitting back in his chair. Whitey knew he couldn't be seen as weak but equally shouldn't be antagonistic to the dangerous man. It was a fine line of macho posturing that felt like a tightrope walk over a fire pit. At some point the rope would burn and you'd fall regardless.

"I assure you, Mr Cavero will deliver what he promises," Whitey said confidently. "I will speak with him and get you your answer on the increases within twenty-four hours."

Márquez frowned and Whitey saw his fists start to clench again. This guy will never see fifty, he thought, he's wound tighter than a nun's girdle.

"If I find out you're supplying those bastard Cubans I'll burn the whole of Peru down, you understand me?" he growled, losing his even tone. "One ounce goes to those bastards and I'll rain hell down on the Caveros, you hear me?"

"Loud and clear," Whitey quickly responded. "Believe me, we're supplying to you, and you alone, Mr Márquez, you're getting everything we produce, and our goal will be to meet your new requirements I assure you."

The Colombian sat back again and seemed to be appeased. He waved his hand at Whitey who sat there a moment unclear on what it meant. When the guard stepped over menacingly, he caught on he was being dismissed and got up from his chair. He started to thank the man for breakfast, but as he hadn't been offered as much as a coffee, he stopped himself. Deciding niceties were a waste of time, he turned and walked out of the restaurant, happy to leave with his heart still beating.

50

NOVEMBER 2019

AJ pulled her fifteen-passenger van into the small car park for Harbour View Apartments, just before the traffic lights where West Bay Road became North Church Street. The small complex had been there since 1990, run by the same local family and these days the apartments were almost exclusively rented by the night or the week rather than long stay. She walked between the two small buildings towards the ocean and spotted Hazel reading a book under the gazebo by the shoreline.

Confrontation was never AJ's strong suit but putting issues behind her was something she never shied away from, so with a few deep breaths she strode boldly forward.

"Hey," she said, trying to sound neutral in her tone.

Hazel looked up from Dawn Lee McKenna's *Squall Line* and smiled.

"Bonjour," she said warmly, placing the book down. "I was hoping you'd come by."

AJ sat down on the bench opposite the wooden table and took her sunglasses off.

"I don't like leaving things hanging, better to get something like this resolved so everyone can get on, you know," AJ explained. She could tell she sounded sterner than she intended but her guard was up.

"I agree. I didn't sleep much last night worrying about it. About us. I took a run along the beach this morning which always helps me clear my head," Hazel replied and AJ looked at her, unable to resist a smile.

"Me too, I'm surprised we didn't meet halfway along. I turned at the Westin."

Hazel laughed. "Me too, I looked at my distance and I was four kilometres which was plenty on the sand, it's hard to run on."

The exchange broke the ice and helped AJ relax a little, so she dived in while she felt confidant. "I'm not happy about how things have come about, Hazel, and I'm hurt you used me."

Hazel looked at the floor and AJ heard her take in a long deep breath. When she looked back up her eyes looked moist. AJ kept going, "But my instincts told me to trust you and I don't think my instincts were so wrong. So, I'll help you."

Hazel appeared stunned as though she hadn't expected this response at all.

"But there are stipulations," AJ added quickly.

"Okay," Hazel finally managed. "Name them."

AJ held up one finger. "Firstly, you can charter me to take you back to the wreck so it's on the books. That way if there's any foul play involved, I was a hired dive boat, nothing more."

She held a second finger aloft. "Number two, I need a hundred percent honesty and transparency. If we're doing something wrong, I need to know so I can decide if I'm okay with it." AJ pointed across the ocean. "There's a hundred dive and fishing operations on this island: you can find one that won't ask questions if you try; I'm not that one. If you prefer to find someone else, no problem, I won't say a word to anyone about your story."

Hazel started to respond but AJ held up a third finger, so she stayed quiet.

"Lastly, we involve Reg. We need a third person for the boat, and I don't want Thomas or Carlos wrapped up in this in case I'm making a mistake, so it has to be Reg. If he won't do it, then I'm out too."

"You didn't tell him already?" Hazel asked, seemingly surprised. "I thought he would be the one you'd go to right away."

AJ shook her head. "No. You told me your story in confidence. Doesn't matter where we stand between us, it was still in confidence so, yes, I talked to Reg, but he doesn't know anything about the key, the money, or Père Noël."

"Wow," Hazel said softly. "You really are a strong woman. I don't think I would have the fortitude to keep all that in."

AJ shrugged her shoulders, but the compliment felt good.

"Well, those are my terms, do you want some time to think about it? Maybe check with some other dive boats?" AJ asked, the sternness fading in her tone.

"No. Of course, I accept all three of your conditions." Hazel looked her straight in the eyes. "But I want to know where we stand? I hurt you, and of course the Raptor is very important to me, but you're just as important." Hazel reached across the table but didn't touch AJ's hand. "Look, my mother raised me to be cautious with people, careful trusting anyone until I know them well. Especially as my life has crumbled around me lately it felt like everyone was out to get me. But right away I let my guard down with you. Believe me or don't, but everything I did, we did, meant a lot to me, and I did from friendship, not from trying to get you to do something for me. As you said, I could find a boat to take me out anywhere here, that's not why I chose you in the beginning and not why I want to go back to the Raptor with you. I trust you as a diver and I trust you as a friend."

AJ swallowed hard, she had a lump in her throat and wished she'd left her sunglasses on as her eyes moistened.

"I... I want us to be friends," AJ stammered and fought to find the right words. "I want us to be the friends I thought we were... but we can't undo what's been done and pretend everything's like it was. Maybe we can get back there again, but I need some time." AJ tentatively placed her hand on Hazel's and gave it a light squeeze before pulling away again.

Hazel smiled at her. "That's more than I have the right to ask for."

51

JULY 1974

Whitey set the two aluminium attaché cases by the door to his apartment and placed the newly released 'Tinker Tailor Soldier Spy' hardback on top of them. He was eager to start reading the latest John le Carré novel and figured it would be a good way to clear his mind on the flight to Grand Cayman. He'd felt jumpy and nervous since his meeting with Márquez the morning before, and not being able to reach Gabriel over the phone was not helping. Having promised an answer for the Colombian in twenty-four hours he was about to be made a liar, unless Gabriel answered now.

He dialled the international number and waited while the connection was made. The strange ring of the Peruvian phone system echoed and sounded distant. He let it ring for a while in case Gabriel was in another room, or outside, and just as he was about to give up, someone answered. He heard Marisol's voice on the other end.

"Hola, residencia Cavero."

"Mrs Cavero, it's Whitey Snow. I'm calling from Miami, I've been trying to reach Gabriel."

Whitey waited through the silence, knowing it would take a moment with the delay on the international line.

"Hola Mr Snow, Gabriel is not here I'm afraid, can you call again tomorrow? Or perhaps he can call you when he's home?" Her voice sounded strained, but the line was crackly and he figured maybe he'd disturbed her in the middle of something.

"It's really important I talk to Gabriel as soon as possible please, Mrs Cavero. I'm leaving my flat for the airport now and flying to Grand Cayman. He can reach me at the Royal Palms Hotel there." Whitey tried to stress the urgency without worrying the pregnant woman.

"Okay," she replied after an extended delay. "He knows your hotel, he'll call you there. Adiós Mr Snow."

The line went dead and again Whitey was left staring at the receiver. He wondered what it was with the South Americans and abruptly ending phone calls. Why the hell did he tell Márquez twenty-four hours? He could as easily have said forty-eight but like an idiot in his eagerness to appease the arsehole, he'd said twenty-four, and now he was a liar. Best thing he could do, he decided, was get on a plane and leave Miami as fast as he could. Maybe his note could be about meeting the Colombian again – Márquez may have more reason to put him in concrete boots than making up a Cuban angle, if Gabriel didn't start answering his phone.

Whitey locked his apartment door, took a Halliburton case in each hand with the book tucked under an arm and headed down the stairs. He'd left his clothes and toiletries in bag storage at the Royal Palms. It seemed pointless bringing them back and forth from the island and with two heavy cases to lug, he was glad he had. With no bags to check he was confident the airline personnel at the gate wouldn't worry to look in the cases; they'd never yet checked his bags going to Cayman. If the rumours and articles in the press were true, the Air Transportation Security Act might be passed later this year, meaning all bags would be x-rayed and that would change everything. He couldn't imagine the lines at the airport while every single bag went through a scanning machine, what a mess. Cavero would have to find another way to transport his money, avoiding America all together, or flying a private plane to avoid questions about the cash.

The taxi he'd called was waiting by the kerb and he slid into the back seat and requested the airport. The driver pulled out into the city traffic and Whitey noticed a man folding a newspaper away, who was watching them depart. He glanced over his shoulder out the rear window and saw the man get into the passenger seat of a black Mercedes. He turned back and looked at the two cases next to him on the seat and his heart rate rose several points. He spent the next few minutes checking behind the taxi to see if the Mercedes was following them, before finally calming down and convincing himself he was being paranoid. He couldn't see any sign of the car.

Whitey paid the taxi driver and with a cautious scan around the airport entrance he proceeded inside and studied the departures board for his gate number. Finding his Cayman Airways flight, he started walking towards his gate but, as he turned, he dropped the book from under his arm. He put one of the cases down and picked up the book, tucking it back under his arm. As he did, he looked outside past the revolving entry doors, and saw a black Mercedes parked at the kerb. He slowly straightened up, retrieving the attaché case and tightening his grip on them both. He stared at the vehicle, trying to decide if it was the same car he'd seen earlier. The Mercedes slowly pulled away from the kerb and blended with the circulating airport traffic. Whitey breathed a sigh of relief and continued towards his gate. How do these guys live like this? he thought, checking the time, relieved he only had twenty more minutes before he boarded the plane.

He couldn't wait to order a rum and start his new book; he just hoped the flight wasn't too smoky, it made his eyes sore. He'd made sure he had a seat towards the front, so at least it took longer for the smoke to reach him. He wished they could stop people smoking on planes. But he knew that would never happen.

52

NOVEMBER 2019

AJ led Hazel past the outdoor bar at Macabuca in West Bay and spotted Reg at the farthest table overlooking the cut in the ironshore they often used as a dive entry. Reg looked up from under the broad sun umbrella and nodded as the women took their seats. The bar area was quiet in the mid-afternoon, just a few people at tables away from them, and a couple of divers who were carefully negotiating the metal steps into the water. Three Strongbow ciders sat in the middle of the table. AJ handed one to Hazel and took one for herself.

"Cheers Reg," she said and tipped the bottle towards him before taking a cool, refreshing drink.

"Cheers," he replied, picking up the third bottle, returning the gesture, and taking a sip. "So, AJ tells me you want to go back to the Raptor?" he said, looking over at Hazel. "And there's a bit of a tale to tell about it?"

Hazel nodded and glanced around to be sure they weren't in earshot. "There is, yes, and I owe you an apology too for not being straight right from the start."

Reg held up a hand. "You two have hammered that out, I'm told, so let's just get to the meat and potatoes of this thing, alright?"

Hazel didn't bat an eye at Reg's direct manner, she just nodded again and told the story just as she'd told AJ the night before. Reg let her get to the end before he tried to ask any questions, slowly spinning his cider bottle around on a beer mat as he listened carefully. AJ watched them both. She knew Reg well enough to know he was playing it hardheaded to see if Hazel would get intimidated and slip something she didn't intend. She figured she'd been around Hazel enough to know the woman was too tough to be intimidated by a grouchy old sailor.

When Hazel was finished, Reg sat there a minute and gathered his thoughts before finally asking, "So where did the money come from? The bloke had to know, right?"

Hazel didn't hesitate. "South American drug money."

AJ was taken aback. "Wait, you never said anything about that; in fact you said he avoided telling you!"

"Rule two," Hazel said pointedly. "You said full transparency, that was rule two, you're getting it."

AJ couldn't argue and sat back in her chair and Hazel elaborated.

"The Cavero family were prominent cocaine suppliers in Peru. Most people don't realise Colombia was late to the party at the beginning, the coca plant wasn't common in Colombia and they originally started in the drug business by buying product from Peru, where it was. The Caveros were one of the biggest suppliers to the Colombians. The father, Mariano, ran the business with his two sons, Gabriel and Gustavo." Hazel pointed to AJ's mobile sitting on the table. "Do a search for those names, you'll see."

AJ picked up her mobile and had Hazel spell the father's name for her and hit search. Sure enough, a bunch of hits came back all leading with 'drug lord' in the title.

Hazel continued, "The younger son, Gabriel, went missing here on Cayman, in 1974."

"Wait," Reg interrupted. "Was he one of the guys who went missing near the wreck? Boat and all disappeared?"

"Oui, that's him," Hazel replied quietly. "The older brother was killed by the Sendero Luminoso, the Peruvian radical communists who tried to start a revolution in Peru in the early eighties. Shortly after, Mariano died of a massive stroke. That was all of them. Gabriel's wife and young son disappeared after he went missing, probably escaped the drug trade while she could, and the older brother never married."

"In the mid-seventies money poured into Cayman, most from something illicit," Reg added. "It's how the islands got their reputation as the best place to hide unreported money. Now everything's above board and legit and they still can't shake that stigma."

Hazel held her hands up. "So, that's it, the money has been in a Cayman International Bank and Trust safety deposit box since 1974, just sitting there. At least according to Père Noël that is, I won't know until I walk in there with the key and ask to see it. Maybe they'll laugh at me."

Reg looked over at Hazel. "And you're going to charter AJ to take you out there, right?"

"Oui." Hazel leaned in closer. "I think you guys realise I don't have much money, so hopefully I can pay for the charter after I get into the safety deposit box? I can give you a deposit before then, say two hundred dollars?"

"It's not about the money," AJ quickly intervened. "What if you walk in the bank with the key and they call the police and arrest you? Maybe they've been waiting for someone to try and collect this money since 1974?"

"I doubt that, honestly," Reg spoke up to AJ's surprise. "There's been all kinds of banks go out of business over the years with unclaimed money in boxes and accounts from them days; I don't think they're bothered about what happened in 1974 at this point. It's odd that anyone with the key has access to the box though; usually it has to be a named person or persons that have access, show ID and all that."

"Guess I'll find out when I walk in," Hazel offered. "But that's a risk for you on the charter AJ, you okay with that?"

"Like I said, it's not the money," AJ said. "We just need to be able to say we didn't know what you were up to; if things go wrong, we were simply chartered to take you diving."

Hazel looked from Reg to AJ. "I'm happy to pay whatever you want to have you guys help me through this, I don't need four million dollars to fix my life. We can split it however you think."

Dollars flashed through AJ's mind before she could even process what Hazel had said. Jeez, she thought, we're all so programmed to think about money and getting more of it. She wondered if Jackson's mind worked that way. It seemed in today's world everyone's did at a subconscious level. But she doubted his did, and scolded herself for being so shallow.

"Maybe some of the money could be donated to do some good? Keep kids off drugs on the island here, or something like that?" AJ suggested.

Hazel smiled. "I think that would be great."

"Let's see if there's a key first. Then we'll see if the key is even a box key. Then we can go from there," Reg said calmly. "One step at a time."

AJ nodded. "Tomorrow afternoon then? Plan to leave after lunch?"

The other two agreed and AJ felt strangely excited, with a sprinkling of apprehension thrown in.

53

JULY 1974

With the key hidden in the wreck, and Whitey confident there was no local threat landing with the money, he'd called Ainsley and told him to waive the police escort. He stepped outside the front doors of Owens Roberts Airport terminal and looked around for the familiar Ford Capri. Terry Jacks' 'Seasons in the Sun' assaulted his ears before he saw the bright red car and he knew it had to be Ainsley. Sure enough, he appeared from behind a tour bus and steered to the kerb with his huge smile greeting Whitey out the window.

"Welcome home, man," he said as he jumped from the car and hugged Whitey, pinning his arms to his sides as he still held a case in each hand.

"Good to see you Ainsley," Whitey said honestly. It indeed warmed him to see his effervescent friend and to feel the hot sun tempered by the island breeze once again.

Whitey manoeuvred the cases into the tiny back seat of the Capri and sat in the burning hot, leather passenger seat. First thing he did was hit eject on Mr Jacks, to Ainsley's dismay – which turned to a smile when Whitey produced a new cassette tape from his pocket.

"Here you go mate, brand new album from Tower of Power,"

Whitey announced, and slid the tape into the deck, "This'll get your funk on, my musically misguided friend."

The horns kicked in for 'Oakland Stroke' and Ainsley looked over at Whitey with wide eyes.

"You don't like 'Seasons in the Sun'? It's a huge hit according to Radio Cayman, I thought everyone liked it."

Whitey shook his head in disbelief. "Seriously? You do know you're a black man, right?"

Ainsley laughed and put the Capri in gear. "I'm a culturally international man of diverse taste and experience, my friend," he said and held his hand out. "Give me some skin, man."

Whitey obliged with a hand slap and they both laughed. "Royal Palms you bloody fool, let's get these cases tucked away before I lose my mind worrying about 'em."

Whitey checked in at the front desk of the Royal Palms and asked if he had any messages while the bell boy retrieved his stored suitcase. The young Caymanian lady checked and told him there was nothing waiting for him currently. Whitey had her double-check, but she assured him there'd been no calls for him all day. Ainsley helped Whitey carry everything to his room where Whitey wasted no time changing out of his jeans and putting on some swim shorts and a tee shirt. It was late afternoon and too late to dive, so they walked down to the pool and found a shady table where they could talk while Whitey soaked up the ocean view. They ordered drinks from the waitress and settled into their chairs. He couldn't believe Gabriel still hadn't contacted him; it was starting to feel like something might be really wrong. Surely Marisol would have said if Gabriel was in trouble or he'd gone up the valley for an extended trip. It would cost a fortune to call international from the hotel, but Peru was in the same time zone as Cayman, so he decided he'd try calling again when he went back up to the room. He attempted to clear his mind and think about seeing Isabella tonight. It took visions of her in his mind, and two robust sips of his rum over ice, for Whitey to finally feel relaxed for the first time in weeks.

"So, the good news is, I brought more cash this trip, so you get your fee, mate," Whitey started. "Bad news is, that's the last lot I'm bringing down."

Ainsley's smile broadened and then turned to a frown. "What's the problem man, did I screw something up?"

Whitey held a hand up. "No, no, no, it's all on me, I'm getting out of this gig mate, but it's going to take some doing. The Caveros aren't the sort to let you just walk away, know what I mean."

Ainsley nodded knowingly but Whitey knew he really had no idea how these men operated.

"Tomorrow we need to go out to the wreck, and I'll get the key so we can put this cash in the bank. When I head back in a few days I'll take the key and leave it in my flat in Miami." Whitey checked around to be sure no one was within earshot. "Then I'm going to disappear."

Ainsley looked at him, surprised and a little confused. "Disappear? Like I won't see you again?"

"You will, but the Peruvians, the damn Colombians and the crazy Cubans won't. I'm gonna stage a disappearance in Miami and then sneak back here on a boat so I can't be traced. Lay low on the island till the dust settles, then I plan to stay here, make a proper go of it on Cayman."

Ainsley's expression slowly turned back to his usual smile. "You gonna move here? To live?"

"Yeah, but I gotta give these guys the slip first," Whitey emphasised.

"What about all that money?" Ainsley asked, his eyes getting wider, and Whitey pictured a cartoon character with dollar signs in his eyes.

"That's why I'll plant the key in my flat; they'll go looking for me there and find the key so they can get their money. Believe me, I don't want the Caveros hunting me thinking I've nicked their cash – they'll never stop until they find me." The thought of it ruined Whitey's freshly found relaxation and he felt his shoulders tighten. "They can have their damn money; I just want clear of them."

Ainsley seemed unsettled and Whitey could tell he still had questions. "What? You've got ants in your pants over there, ask it already."

Ainsley fidgeted some more before stumbling out with it. "All of it? You sure you need to give them all of it?"

Whitey slid his Ambermatic Aviators down his nose and peered over them at Ainsley. "Yes, I'm completely bloody sure."

54

NOVEMBER 2019

On Sunday morning AJ and Carlos took the Newton out on the north wall with new clients on the boat, the Davis and Freeman families having finished their trips. Both dives went smoothly, and afterwards AJ hustled from the yacht club into town to get four fresh Nitrox tanks with the same custom 29% oxygen fills they had used before. She picked Hazel up from Harbour View on the way out of town and patiently sat in the midday tourist traffic along West Bay Road.

"What do we need to take down with us in the way of tools?" AJ asked, her mind checklisting through the upcoming dive as it had been all morning.

"Reg said he was bringing a wrench for taking filters on and off, right?" Hazel replied. "Hopefully that will undo it. Apart from that, just lights I think."

AJ nodded and grazed over the edge of her lip with her teeth, the way she did sometimes when she was anxious.

"You hungry?" she asked.

"Starving," Hazel replied quickly.

AJ indicated right and pulled to the centre lane and waited for a gap in the traffic. A local car coming the opposite way in the line of traffic stopped and waved her across. She drove into the car park of a small strip mall with a toot on the horn to thank the courteous driver. AJ pulled to the far end of the car park and found a spot in front of a shop called 'Treats'. Five minutes later they pulled back out of the car park onto West Bay Road with steaming hot coffees and a scone each in a bag. Another car halted to let them exit and turn right and AJ honked a thank you.

"Polite around here aren't they?" Hazel commented, seemingly surprised.

"Helps if you have local plates," AJ replied.

"Huh? What do you mean?" Hazel asked as she tried carefully sipping her coffee.

AJ pointed to the car in front. "See that licence plate is yellow?" Then she pointed to a car coming the opposite way. "And that one is white?"

"Okay, I see now." Hazel looked at the assortment of cars around them, picking out the two different coloured plates.

"White is a hire car, yellow is a resident's car," AJ explained, "so the locals know if it's a white licence plate it's almost certainly a tourist, who'll probably be confused about which side of the road to drive on, and won't know the rules and courtesies. Yellow plate is a local and everyone's happy to let you merge, will stop and let you pull out – you know, the lost art of being polite when driving."

Hazel laughed. "So true; whenever I had to go to Paris, I felt like I was in a race where they all bash into each other."

"Try driving in Florida," AJ added. "Indicating is a signal for the other cars to speed up to prevent you merging or turning."

It felt good to laugh and feel relaxed around Hazel, something AJ had enjoyed so much before Friday night. She wasn't ready to let her guard down, but sensing some of the tension evaporate was a relief. She knew only she could control that; she was the one with an axe to grind, but she was starting to see a way they might get back to how they were. Time was a catalyst.

They finished their snack as AJ parked the van by Reg's West Bay dock and saw the big man had already brought AJ's RIB over from its mooring. They carried two tanks each down to the boat and handed them aboard to Reg, who stowed them in the racks.

"Afternoon ladies," he greeted them, and AJ handed him a coffee. "Thanks girl. We ready to shove off?"

"I think so," AJ replied, looking around the boat. "Did you bring the wrench for the filter?"

Reg held up an oil filter strap wrench. "Got it."

AJ fired up the outboards and Hazel freed the lines to the dock before stepping aboard as they idled away from the jetty. Conditions appeared to be on their side again. The water was flat calm, a gentle breeze brushed their faces, and a few clouds had begun forming to take away some of the sun's intensity. Once clear of the shallows, where the boats were moored and snorkellers might be bobbing unseen on the surface, AJ opened up the throttles and the boat leapt up on plane and skimmed across the Caribbean Sea.

AJ brought the saved locations up on her GPS screen and after a few minutes slowed as she approached the two dots.

"Let's try running across the wreck this time, I think our best chance is hooking the side railings rather than the sheet metal rail around the bow. What do you think, Reg?"

Reg rubbed his beard and thought for a second. "I marked the line at the length we used last time, want to stick with that?"

AJ nodded. "Yeah, it hooked the railing so it should be about right. I think we got lucky last time though, I'm surprised it didn't just drag along the side all the way back. I hate we're having to grapple it and damage some of the coral, but I don't see another way unless we anchor in the sand farther in."

Reg scanned the waters between them and the shoreline. "I think that's how they used to do it years ago when the wreck was shallower, but now I don't know how you'd swim against the current that far. Only way is to hook the wreck or do a live boat and pick you up wherever you surface."

Hazel had been listening while she squeezed into her wetsuit. "Why don't we do that then?"

AJ thought about it. "Biggest reason would be the safety stops;

we'll be hanging at thirty then fifteen feet for a total of six minutes just drifting, and it'll be hard to see our bubbles. If Reg loses us, we could be half a mile away when we surface."

Hazel agreed. "Right, that wouldn't be good."

"Unless we run a hang line," Reg offered. "We could drop a tank and a reg with a weight like we do sometimes anyway. You guys hang on the line and we'll drift together?"

"That would work," AJ said as she motored towards the shallower end of the two dots. "I'll deploy my inflatable signal when we're at thirty feet, if it's just behind the boat you'll know we're on the line; if it's somewhere else and drifting you'll know to follow us."

Reg took the helm so AJ could get ready. "Alright, that's the plan then." Before she stepped away, he asked quietly, "Are you sure you don't want me to dive? Been in a wreck or two doing this sort of thing."

AJ smiled at him. "No question you're the better man for this job, but I dragged you into this so I'd rather you stayed at arm's length. Just in case anything goes sideways."

He still looked concerned. "I've done a few 'sideways' in my time too."

She punched his burly arm softly. "I know. We'll be fine. Quit your worrying, papa bear."

Whitey waited out front of the Holiday Inn in Ainsley's Capri he'd borrowed for the evening. Isabella was getting off work at 5pm and said she'd change at the hotel before she left so they could leave for their date from there. Whitey had told her he had a surprise that involved the sunset and to dress casual. He looked at his watch; it was 5.04pm and he was giddy to see her. Whitey had tried calling Peru again from his room with no answer at all; even Marisol wasn't home. He was beginning to worry about Gabriel and stabs of guilt kept returning when he considered the possibility that the man who called Whitey his friend, and brother, may be in trouble. The list of potential perils was endless in their line of work. The government or police could have turned on him, rival coca growers, the Colombians, who knew, but the longer he was unable to speak with Gabriel, the more agitated he became.

He glanced out the window and saw Isabella walking towards the car. All thoughts of Cavero, coca plants, and Colombians vanished as he returned her excited smile and soaked up the vision of beauty approaching. She wore her black bikini with a brightly coloured wrap tied around her waist that billowed as she walked. Around her forehead was a bandana, matching the wrap, from which her long black hair cascaded around her shoulders. Whitey stepped from the Capri and she slid into his embrace, removing her sunglasses to look up into his eyes.

"Hola," she whispered softly and kissed him.

He held her close and lost himself in her beautiful green eyes that seemed to mirror his passion.

"Hola," he returned quietly, before forcing himself to let her go. "Come on, jump in, we have a short drive."

Whitey pulled out of the Holiday Inn and headed south on West Bay Road towards George Town. She chatted about the few weeks they'd been apart and what she'd been up to in his absence as he weaved behind the port on North Church Street. He slowed where the pavement ended as it became South Church Street and continued slowly down the marl road behind a scattering of occasional homes between the trees and mangroves. They passed the newly opened Sunset House dive resort and a few minutes later the Grand Old House restaurant, where they'd gone on their first date. He could see she was getting more curious as they went but she resisted asking. Whitey pulled into a break in the trees on the beach side and parked the Capri. They stepped from the car and he reached in the back and retrieved a woven basket with a cloth covering the contents.

Isabella looked intrigued. "A picnic?" she asked excitedly.

He smiled and took her hand, leading her through an opening to a sandy beach perfectly framed on either side by ironshore. The sun was lowering in the western sky and glistened off the water that lapped gently into the cove. Whitey set the basket down and unfolded the cloth which he spread out over the sand. Isabella keenly examined the contents of the basket and began laying them out on the cloth.

"Ooh, my favourite wine," she cooed approvingly, setting the bottle of Rioja down.

Whitey rummaged for the corkscrew and began to open the bottle while she continued setting bread, cheeses, and fruits out.

"This is a beautiful spot; you bring all your girls here?" she teased him.

He laughed. "My first time actually," he said honestly. "That old romantic Ainsley told me about it, said the locals come here to swim but it's usually quiet in the evenings."

He looked around at the trichilia trees and silver thatch palms providing the backdrop to the oasis of sand amongst the limestone shoreline of the south-west corner of the island.

"It's called Smith Cove; a bloke named Webster, a shipping tycoon apparently, owns a bunch of this land and keeps it undeveloped so the people can keep their beach."

He poured red wine into two glasses he'd carefully unwrapped from a small towel and handed one to Isabella.

"Cheers. Here's to Mr Webster and his family."

"Salud." She clinked her glass to his and they both sipped the wine.

They lay on the cloth and ate slowly, talking about Spain, and about Cayman, as the sun settled lower and lower, losing its intensity. As it reached the horizon and glowed the sky above the ocean with orange hues, he leaned over and kissed her.

"I've decided to move here, to the island," he said softly.

She reached over and caressed his face. "You mean it? You're going to leave Miami and your work and come here?"

He nodded slowly and smiled. "I am. I want to be here. It's time I made a change."

"I kept thinking about it after you said something last trip," Isabella said quietly. "But I didn't want to get my hopes up. Men say things they don't mean sometimes." She grinned and he chuckled.

"True."

He thought carefully about how to phrase what he wanted to say. He wanted to be completely honest with her, but he was terrified of scaring her away. He'd already realised moving to Cayman was a lot less appealing if Isabella wasn't in the picture.

"I haven't always made my living in a way I'm proud of," he

stumbled on his words but she hadn't pulled away so he continued. "Lately, I've been working with some people that are not good men, and I want to change that."

She smiled and while he knew she didn't know the gravity of his situation, he was relieved she was not demanding an explanation, or telling him to take her home. But he'd said enough; there'd be plenty of time for revealing more if things went the way he hoped. They'd have a lifetime to tell each other everything they wanted to share.

"I just want you to know I may be off the radar for a week or so when I leave here, but I promise you I'm coming back."

She looked concerned for the first time. "You won't be able to call me?" Calls to the island were ridiculously expensive but he made a point of calling her every four or five days, for a few minutes at least, when he was in Miami.

"Just for a few days or so, a week at the most," he reassured her. "While I wrap up everything in Florida. My phone will be disconnected so I won't be able to call," he added, landing on a legitimate reason.

She rolled over on top of him, her body pressing down on his. She leaned in and kissed him passionately as he wrapped his arms around her and held her even tighter. She left his lips and kissed his cheek, and then his neck, and then his ear, where she whispered softly, "Then we should make love, so you'll know what you'll be coming back for."

Whitey Snow felt a sensation he'd never experienced before in his life. For the first time in forty-seven years, he was pretty sure he was in love.

56

NOVEMBER 2019

Once the two women were ready, Reg lined up the two dots on the GPS and eased the RIB against the current towards the island until they were well forward of where they estimated the bow of the wreck lay. Shutting the throttles down, he waved a hand to the divers and they back-rolled into the water with a splash.

With no air in their BCDs, neither surfaced; quickly inverting, they kicked down to clear the boat as the current immediately grabbed them. AJ orientated herself, spotting the dark apparition she knew was the bow of the wreck. They descended rapidly to avoid being blown away from the target, and she cleared the rapidly changing pressure in her ears often. They planned to angle down and land on the wreck as close to the rear of the hold as they could to save time at depth, similar to what they'd done from the line before. Hazel rolled to her side and signalled to AJ, running her hand through the water quickly to say the current was strong. AJ returned an okay sign. She'd recognised the same thing and kicked down a little harder as they whipped over the open hold. Now she wished they *had* grappled the wreck, so they'd have an ascent line. With this current, if Reg missed them, they'd be in Belize for dinner.

They reached the base of the cabin structure at around 110' and AJ stole a few seconds to gaze across the wreck. The Raptor was alive with fish of all shapes and sizes. The rusting hulk was like a town centre on a Saturday morning with schools of snapper, jacks, and barracuda patrolling the upper reaches, several large grouper making laps around the hold, and scores of angelfish, butterflys, parrotfish, and Spanish hogfish weaved in and out of the railings. Above her, under the walkway that spanned between the two cabin doors, three fat lionfish hovered stationary, fluttering their plethora of brightly coloured fins.

Hazel started down into the hold and AJ focused back on the task at hand. The door was as they left it, held partially open by years of growth and debris and, as AJ carefully examined, a crowbar placed there in 1974. She followed Hazel into the engine room where the French woman wasted no time heading straight over the big diesel to the port side. AJ waited for Hazel's fins to clear and then followed, picking her way between the cables and lines. She shone her torch down the side of the engine and saw the filter Hazel had described, while Hazel got situated to try and undo the cylinder. There was so little room to manoeuvre and it took Hazel a few moments to find the best position to get leverage with the wrench Reg had provided. AJ lay patiently on the enormous valve cover and kept her light on the filter so Hazel could have both hands free. Hazel finally settled enough to slide the strap over the filter and she pulled the handle tight. The handle ran into a line running from the sump below the filter; she had to release it, and shuffle the strap around to a different position. Getting reset, she pulled the handle tight, cinching the strap tight on the filter again and pulled hard on the handle. The filter didn't move, but Hazel was pulled forward by her efforts, into the lines ahead of her. She needed to brace herself against something and AJ saw she was looking around for options as silt and small debris floated all around them from all the movement. AJ spun her light beam in circles to get Hazel's attention. Hazel looked up; her eyes looked calm but determined. Not bad for 130' underwater inside a shipwreck's engine room, AJ thought, a surge of the respect she'd previously felt returning. AJ pointed a finger to her feet and made a flicking motion. Hazel immediately understood and reached down to remove her fins. Just getting her arms to her feet was a struggle; she had to bump and wriggle off various pipes and cables. Some would give way a bit, but others were steadfast and didn't budge, making it more difficult. Hazel managed to slip out of her fins and handed them to AJ so they wouldn't be searching for them when they were finished. AJ pinned them under her own legs, keeping her torch on the work area.

Hazel pulled her knees up tight to her chest and extended her feet until she found a rigid pipe she could push against. Taking the handle, which was now between her legs, she pulled with all her might, pushing with her strong legs as she pulled with her arms. The handle began to slowly move towards her until it was too close to pull anymore. She released and started to move the strap for another go when AJ tapped her shoulder. AJ reached down the side of the engine and slid the strap on the filter then pointed to the filter itself and waggled her finger. The filter hadn't moved at all, the strap had slipped around it making it seem like it had moved, but AJ had been able to see from above they hadn't made any progress. AJ shone her beam on her computer, holding her wrist so they could both see the small screen. They'd been in the water for twelve minutes and had four minutes no-deco time left. Hazel nodded and looked back down at the obstinate filter. She drew her hand back and forth on the cylinder, indicating they needed a saw. She looked back up at AJ who nodded and pointed to the door.

Taking Hazel's fins in one hand and holding her torch in the other, AJ shuffled backwards off the engine a few inches at a time until she slid off the front of it. Hazel pulled herself over the engine to follow and they both eased through the doorway into the cargo hold. AJ handed Hazel her fins, which she slipped back on, and the two wasted no time pushing off the floor and heading for shallower water. They cleared the walkway and stayed close to the front of the cabins to protect themselves from the ripping current. AJ wished she had her spear as they passed the lionfish, but they had more important matters ahead of them. She removed her safety sausage, or surface marker buoy, which she kept clipped to a ring on her BCD, and attached it to the end of her reel. They reached the wheelhouse and scanned the surface for the silhouette of the RIB. Reg had positioned perfectly, above the stern, but they still had 70' of open water to ascend to reach the 30' line hanging under the boat. AJ nodded at Hazel and the two kicked up, clearing the roof of the wheelhouse.

The current immediately tore them west, across the top of the cabin structure that fell away from them as they kicked upwards and into the current. They had to be careful not to ascend too fast and get the bends, but too slowly and they'd be so far from the boat Reg would never see them. AJ was breathing like a sprinter which wasn't helping their deco situation but stealing a glance above she realised Reg was letting the boat drift with the surface current so it was staying above them. She grabbed one of Hazel's fin tips and held up a hand indicating she should stop. Hazel frowned through her mask but looking up she quickly figured out why AJ had paused her. They settled into a gentler ascent and let themselves be taken by the water heading for the open ocean. AJ looked back at the wreck now well behind them. The Raptor was hung precariously over the wall that fell dramatically away to the black below. She looked like a toy boat hanging over the rim of a bathtub as she started to become hazy, before finally disappearing beyond their visibility. The two women had nothing but ink black depths below them as they were rapidly swept out to sea. Above, their lifeline hung like a precious oasis in a vast desert and with great relief they grabbed the tank at the base of the line and held on tightly. Removing her reg AJ exhausted air into the bright orange, soft, inflatable tube of her surface marker buoy. Careful to only partially inflate the tube so it didn't burst as the water pressure decreased when it went up, she began playing out line from her reel until the marker broke the surface about twenty feet behind the drifting boat. Reg would now know they were on the line.

57

JULY 1974

Whitey walked onto the beach in front of the Royal Palms with his dive gear over his shoulder and was happy, but surprised, to see Ainsley already moored off the shore. Ainsley wasn't known as a morning person, another reason he'd struggled to take up the family's fishing profession, so Whitey hadn't expected him to be ready at 9am sharp as planned. The ocean was flat calm, a gentle breeze brushed his face, the morning sun warmed his back and Whitey was happier than he could ever remember being.

He stepped around an anchor lodged in the beach sand, followed the line extending to the stern of the SportCraft, and noticed a second line off the bow leading to deeper water.

"Ainsley, you've moored your boat securely. It's like you know what you're doing," Whitey joked.

Ainsley beamed with pride. "I had my brother show me a few things man – I'm a professional driver now!"

"Helmsman, Ainsley, helmsman. You drive your car, you pilot a boat," Whitey corrected him with a laugh as he waded to the stern and dropped his gear in the boat.

"So, it should be piloter then?" Ainsley challenged.

"That's not a word, Ainsley. Hey, I'm impressed you moored it securely so stop talking cos you're ruining my newfound respect for your boating skills." Whitey hoisted himself up on the swim step and slapped Ainsley on the shoulder with a big smile. He listened for a second and caught Elton John's 'Bennie and the Jets' playing from Ainsley's transistor radio laying on the second seat up front.

"Diggin' your tunes this morning, brother," Whitey complimented.

Ainsley's expression changed and he cautiously eyed Whitey up and down. "Wait a second here," he said, scratching his chin thoughtfully. "I sense a change, man. Something's different with the Snowman." Ainsley threw his hands in the air dramatically. "Whitey closed the deal, man! That's what it is!"

Whitey shook his head and really wanted to keep a straight face but the sight of Ainsley dancing around the boat in front of him was too much and he burst out laughing.

"You plonker, have some respect, you heathen, she's a lady," Whitey said between laughs, trying to deflect the conversation.

Ainsley stopped dancing and turned serious again. "Hold on, man. This thing that took place; it didn't take place in my car did it?"

Whitey frowned at him. "No! You idiot, she's a lady damn it, she's not the quick-shag-in-a-car type."

Ainsley started dancing again. "Thank the Lord for that, wouldn't be able to drive my beautiful Capri anymore without worrying about the seats and all, you know?" He burst out laughing once more and Whitey gave up and moved his gear to the dive tank Ainsley had brought along. He attached the Scubapro pack to the tank with its strap and cinched it tight before fitting his Aqualung regulator to the valve and laying the assembly down on the deck. Ainsley had settled down and watched Whitey put his rig together.

"So, we're gonna go back to the wreck and get the key you just hid in there?" he asked, still clearly confused with Whitey's change of plans.

Whitey looked up. "Yeah, we'll grab the key, head to the bank, put the cash in and then when I'm back in Miami I'll leave the key where I know they'll find it."

Ainsley was still unsure. "And you say you can't just tell this guy you want to resign? Give him the key and say you don't want to work for him no more?"

Whitey stood up and laughed with little humour in his response. "If you met Gabriel Cavero you'd understand, mate. Or even worse, his old man. The family doesn't understand 'I don't want to work for you anymore'. That's not in their lingo, mate."

Ainsley shook his head slowly. "You know these people, man; just seems crazy to me they wouldn't be happy you've found a nice lady and are moving to this beautiful place."

Whitey wagged his finger at Ainsley. "No, no, no, they don't know anything about Isabella and they certainly don't know I'm moving here." Whitey put a hand on Ainsley's shoulder. "Listen my friend, I've worked for them for two years, and in that time, I know of several people that worked for the family and left their employment. They're all dead." He leaned back against the side of the boat. "This one bloke, Miguel, great guy, I met him a bunch of times. He managed their crops in the valley. His second in command goes to the old man and tells him Miguel is stealing from them, taking some of the product and selling it on the side. Bang!" Whitey held up his fingers like a gun. "Bullet to the back of the head. A month later they figure out it was the other guy that was stealing, and Miguel was a loyal worker who had been set up, so this bloke could take over his job. Bang! Another bullet to the head, and now they're scrambling to find someone who could run their operation. Believe me mate, they're paranoid as hell and they'll pop someone just cos they suspect something, leave alone telling them I don't want to work for them anymore."

Ainsley was wide eyed. "That's crazy, man. I hope I never meet a Cavero."

Whitey stepped off the stern into the waist-deep water and started towards the beach to get the anchor. He looked back as he walked. "You won't have to. This will be our last trip out to the Raptor. If I ever dive this wreck again, I hope it's simply for fun."

Whitey noticed Ainsley was staring past him to the beach and didn't seem to hear what he'd been saying. He turned as he reached the sand and looked up to see a familiar, slender man standing next to the anchor wearing white linen pants and a loose cotton, button-down shirt.

"Hola, mi hermano," Gabriel Cavero said without a smile. "Perhaps you can explain why the key you gave me opened an empty box at the bank."

58

NOVEMBER 2019

AJ knew they would drift quite a way, but when she and Hazel surfaced after their safety stops, she was still stunned how small the island looked in the distance.

"Damn, six minutes on the line, maybe another minute ascending from thirty to fifteen, then to the boat, that's seven minutes and we must have gone nearly half a mile. What's that Reg?" AJ pulled herself to the stern using the ropes strung along the inflatable sides of the boat. He looked down as the two shuffled themselves to the ladder.

"Hell if I know, you're the one that likes doing lots of math."

Reg took their fins as they climbed aboard and dropped their rigs in the nearest rack. Hazel looked at the island, noticing it was a lot farther away than when they'd left the boat, as AJ had pointed out.

"Wow, must be over a kilometre."

Reg looked from one to the other with his hands on his hips. "Well? When you're done mentally masturbating the distance to the shore, you gonna tell me what happened?"

Hazel looked up at him. AJ could see she was still unsure when the man was acting mad, or indeed was mad. AJ laughed. "It was a bust. We need something to cut it with, threads are seized up."

Hazel dropped the filter wrench on the floor and stared up at Reg. "Yeah, your fancy tool didn't work," she said sternly.

Reg took a beat before cracking up laughing. Then again, maybe she has figured out the big man, AJ realised, as Hazel broke into a big smile.

"We have a good saw aboard?" Hazel asked. "If not we should head back and pick up something."

"I have a small hacksaw in the toolkit but it's not great," AJ said, pulling her wetsuit down and tying the arms around her waist.

Reg pulled the ladder up and started the outboards. "Nah, let's go ahead and run the 1.216 miles to the dock." He rolled his eyes at AJ. "I got a real saw that'll rip through that tin like butter, I'll grab it from the house. We'll be back out before you've finished your surface interval."

Reg piloted them back to his jetty and AJ tied them in to the cleats of the empty dock. She watched Reg march up the dock and head out in his Land Rover towards his house just a mile away. She glanced at her watch before turning to Hazel, still sitting on the boat.

"Come on, let's grab some fruit and a juice, we've got fifteen minutes before he's back."

Hazel didn't need asking twice; she jumped to the jetty and followed AJ to her van. Two minutes later they parked by Heritage Kitchen and walked briskly to the counter. A full-figured Caymanian woman in a blue chef's hat greeted them with a broad smile as they stood there, dripping water on the pavement from their wetsuits.

"Afternoon, Miss Grece," AJ said warmly.

"Hi there AJ, how can I help you two?" Miss Grece asked politely in a thick Caymanian accent.

"Could we get some slices of fruit to share and three juices – whatever you have going today is fine," AJ replied.

"Hi there girls," Josephine's voice echoed from the kitchen. "Want some barbecue? It's our Sunday special."

"Just getting some refreshers between dives, Josephine; some fruit and three juices please," AJ answered without bothering to explain she didn't eat meat.

Josephine gave her a thumbs-up through the serving window from the kitchen. "Sounds good, Miss Grece will get your drinks, I'll see what I can put together back here."

AJ waved back and Miss Grece rang them up before pouring out three fruit juices. A few minutes later, after furious chopping sounds emanated from the kitchen, Josephine handed a tupperware stuffed full of fresh mango, pineapple, and guava through the window. Miss Grece passed it to the women. "There you go."

"Thanks Miss Grece," AJ said, taking the fruit and scooping up two of the drinks. "I'll bring your container back tomorrow, Josephine," she called to the kitchen.

A hand waved back and after leaving a generous tip with Miss Grece, the two returned to the van.

As they closed the doors and AJ started the van, Hazel looked over at her. "I love this place," she said softly. "You're a perfect fit here, I see why you've made it your home."

AJ smiled warmly. "Yeah, I wake up every day and thank my lucky stars." She turned the van around and glanced over at Hazel as she pulled away. "Maybe it can be your home too."

Hazel smiled broadly and started to reply but something stopped her, and she stayed quiet, looking out across the water.

AJ parked the van, noting Reg's Land Rover wasn't back yet. They walked down the jetty, sipping on the refreshing fruit juice and chatting about the next dive. They both knew they needed to get the filter off, or at least get into it, this next dive. They couldn't keep making these risky dives on the wreck without running into trouble at some point. The odds dictated it, no matter how careful they were. They sat down on the end of the dock and let their legs dangle over, their feet hanging just above the water. AJ opened the tupperware and they eagerly dived into the fruit slices. As they sat there, drying in the warm sun enjoying their refreshing snack, she realised she hadn't thought about her issues with Hazel all afternoon. The feeling was warm and comforting. She was reminded of why she fell into friendship so quickly with this woman; she simply enjoyed being around her.

The jetty vibrated with footsteps, and AJ was relieved Reg was back; she was eager to return to the wreck. She turned and saw it wasn't Reg approaching. A man in his forties with thick, dark hair and wearing beige chinos and a pale blue guayabera shirt strode confidently down the dock. As he closed, he removed his wire-rimmed designer sunglasses and spoke in a heavy Hispanic accent.

"Good afternoon, you are the owner of this dive boat, yes?"

AJ stood and ran through her current bookings in her mind, trying to recall if she had any openings. "I am, I'm AJ Bailey; can I help you, sir?"

The man looked down at Hazel, still seated. "And this is Hazel Delacroix, I believe?" the man said casually.

AJ was completely taken aback and confused. Hazel slowly stood up and turned to face him. The man reached to the back of his shirt and when his hand returned it was holding a gun. He held it close to his body, pointed at the ground, out of sight from everyone except the girls. AJ gasped and Hazel stood motionless.

"I am Gabriel Cavero, Junior. I believe you have something that belongs to my family."

59

JULY 1974

Whitey didn't need to see it to know that Gabriel had a gun tucked under his shirt. The man always carried a gun. He scanned the beach to see if he'd brought any of his goons, but didn't see anyone else. Whitey knew, regardless of anything he could say, he was in a really bad situation. A sadness rushed through him as he realised he was unlikely to see another sunset. His first thoughts were how to get Ainsley out of this mess, and how to keep Isabella out of it.

"Hello Gabriel," he said boldly; this was no time to appear weak. "That's the old box, like I said to you. I needed to get a bigger one, you keep making too much money mate, hard to find a box big enough."

Gabriel smiled but his eyes were cold and angry. "You couldn't fit ten grand in the box I opened, my friend. I suggest you stick to telling me the truth."

Whitey kicked himself for his frugal nature; why the hell did he get the cheapest safety deposit box available? That was the only play he'd had, and he'd been called out on the first move. Honesty was the only way to go now. Somehow, he had to get Ainsley out of this. He wished his friend would untie the lines at the boat and just leave. But he knew Ainsley wouldn't do that. He wouldn't leave him.

"Gabby, let's go up to the hotel, grab some coffee, and I'll tell you exactly how I've buggered some things up. All the money is safe; we can go to the bank together and I'll show you."

Gabriel ignored the invitation and looked around Whitey to the boat, and the Caymanian standing motionless at the helm.

"This your island contact? The man you told me that's been helping you?"

Whitey's heart sank. Cavero was too cagey to leave loose ends.

"He's just a local guy with a boat I hire sometimes, Gabby, he's nothing to do with this. Come on, let's go up to the shade and sit and talk. I promise, I'll tell you everything."

Gabriel looked back at Whitey, searching his face like he'd done back in Peru. Whitey felt like the man was scanning his brain, reading his intentions and truths from his expression.

"So is the money in this bank?" Gabriel asked quietly.

"Yes Gabby, it's in a safety deposit box as I told you – just not the one you had the key for," Whitey answered carefully, knowing he needed to be truthful but scared to back himself into a corner.

"All of it?" Gabby asked pointedly.

Whitey hesitated, thinking through the consequences of his answer. He prayed Isabella was out of the room by now.

"No, the latest cases are in the hotel, the other two deliveries are in the bank."

Gabriel's eyes narrowed. "Why is the new delivery in your hotel and not in the bank? You told me you had a guarded escort straight to the bank?"

"I needed to get the key before I could go to the bank," Whitey answered and immediately knew he was now on his way down the rabbit hole.

"Where's the real key?" Gabriel snapped.

Whitey sighed. "I hid it," he said quietly, the boldness gone as he slipped perilously along the slope of the inevitable.

"Which is where you and your accomplice were heading, I assume?" Gabriel correctly speculated.

Whitey searched his mind for a path that didn't lead back to exactly the spot he was in at this very moment, anything plausible that would get Ainsley out of this mess. He couldn't think of any scenario that didn't involve retrieving the key, short of telling Cavero to go to hell. He was confident how that would end. His only option was to buy time. The longer they could stay alive the more chances they'd have to get out of this.

"Correct. It's on a shipwreck off the north-west corner of the island."

Knowing Gabriel hated boats and couldn't swim, Whitey was confident there was no way he'd go out with them.

"We'll go out and get the key, it'll take about forty-five minutes. We'll meet you back here at the beach and you and I can go to the bank, Gabby."

Gabriel sneered. "I wait here on this lovely beach and you two take off in a boat with all my money hidden somewhere on this island, and I should expect you'll be back here in forty-five minutes? You insult me."

Whitey tried one more play. Had he been wrong about Gabby? Were they the good friends the Peruvian had always portrayed? Or was he right to believe that it was all a facade? He was about to find out.

"Gabby, we've been friends for two years: you know me. I'm telling you I made a mistake giving you a fake key, but I was scared, mate. I thought if I had an insurance policy, I'd be safer, but it was a terrible mistake, which I was about to rectify. Literally, today I was squaring it all away and getting you the real key. You and your family have been so good to me, I owe you a lot. There's no way I'd ever try and rip you off, you gotta believe that?"

Gabriel moved towards Whitey so they stood three feet apart, and stared him straight in the eye. The look on Gabriel's face gave Whitey his answer and the man's voice, flat and cold, confirmed it.

"You lied to me Whitey. I called you a friend and I trusted you.

You're right, my family took you in and gave you everything you have. And you repay us by trying to steal from us and feed me all this bullshit. I don't believe a word you tell me anymore."

Whitey expected Gabriel wouldn't believe him, but he didn't expect the words he heard next.

"Get in the boat, we're going to this wreck to get the key."

60

NOVEMBER 2019

AJ stared at the gun in the stranger's hand. She had no idea what kind of gun it was, beyond a handgun, but she was sure it was the kind designed to go bang and kill things. That's what guns are for after all. She wondered how on earth he managed to get a gun on the island; the Caymans had very strict gun laws and there's no way he had brought it through airport security. He must have found a black-market source which would have taken some doing – the Cayman Islands were considered one of the safest destinations in the Caribbean.

The man turned his focus to Hazel, his eyes cold and hateful. "Give me the key."

Hazel answered more calmly than AJ thought she could have mustered. "I don't have it, why do you think we're diving the wreck?"

Junior lifted his chin and sneered, "What do you mean? I've watched you two diving out there," he nodded towards the north-west point. "You saying the key is out there?"

"That's exactly what I'm saying, it was hidden on the wreck; I've been trying to find it," Hazel responded boldly. AJ was glad Hazel was doing all the talking as she had no idea what to say. "I'm pretty sure the whole thing's bullshit and there is no key," Hazel added.

Junior visibly tensed on the gun. "Then I guess I have no use for you," he spat at her, "or your friend here."

Hazel held up her hands. "Wait up. Worth one more look, don't you think?" she quickly responded, less boldly.

He laughed, without a trace of humour in his tone. "You don't want to lie to me, woman."

"She's not lying," AJ blurted out. "We were going back out there now, to try again."

Junior looked around for a moment and then back at the boat tied up next to them. He nodded at AJ's RIB. "In this?"

AJ looked at her boat, confused why he seemed surprised they'd be using that boat. "Yeah, that's my boat."

He kept the gun hidden at his waist, but his fingers were nervously moving on the handle, and he appeared unsure what to do next.

"Okay, we're going. Get in the damn boat and take me out to the wreck. You better come up with a key or this will be your last boat ride."

AJ stepped into the boat and started the engines; Hazel released the stern line before walking to the front and readying to release the bow line. She looked up at Junior, who was still standing there, staring at the boat.

"Are you getting aboard or not?" Hazel asked impatiently.

He gave her a venomous look and stepped onto the boat, unsteadily moving to the stern so he could see them both. Hazel released the bow line and gave the inflatable's side a shove away from the dock before jumping on board herself.

AJ glanced back at Junior, standing behind her, and noticed his brand new docksiders. He's dressed for a fancy boat but he sure doesn't seem at home on a boat of any kind, she noted.

"You might want to hang on to something when we pull away," she warned him and eased the throttles forward.

AJ looked back at the dock and wished Reg would pull in and

see them leave; she knew he'd know something was wrong if they left without him. Especially with a stranger aboard. If he arrived and saw the boat gone, he'd start calling and trying to figure out what they were up to before he raised an alarm. Time they might not have.

"Where on the wreck is the key?" Junior barked above the noise of the engines, burbling just above idle.

Hazel looked at AJ and shrugged her shoulders as if to say 'there's no point lying'. "We think it's in the engine room, hidden in a part of the engine, but we couldn't get it open. We came back in for more tools, but you showed up before we got them. Not sure how we'll do it now."

Junior cussed under his breath in Spanish. "Well you'd better figure something out fast. No key, no trip home."

"We'll try the saw I have," AJ quickly countered, worried Hazel was pissing off the man that happened to have the gun. Damn, she hated guns. This was her second experience being held at gunpoint and it wasn't getting any more comfortable. They had to buy enough time for Reg to come after them. But then what? If Reg came steaming out, on his own in one of his boats, there'd just be three people held at gunpoint instead of two. Still, with Reg involved, she fancied their chances a lot more than she did right now. She kept the throttles barely above idle and noticed Junior was looking around the back of the boat.

"This as fast as this thing goes?" he asked pointedly.

She thought of lying and saying yes, but the two big outboards hung off the back were a bit of a giveaway, so she sided with not further aggravating the man with the gun.

"No, it goes faster but we have to clear all the boats and the shallow water before we can go faster."

He looked at her and growled, raising the gun for the first time. "You're going to give me trouble too, are you? Go faster."

AJ opened the throttles more aggressively than she normally would and heard the man scrambling to hang on to something behind her. She hoped he'd fall out the stern but the gun barrel poking in her back told her he hadn't. She felt his breath close to her ear and he hissed at her, "Your life is nothing to me, you understand, nothing. I've cut the face off prettier women than you."

His words pierced AJ to her core. She'd had the misfortune to be around some bad people, but never had she felt such hate and evil emanating from another human. This man was soulless. Human nature was to have hope, that almost impenetrable feeling that things could still work out okay, even in the face of certain peril. AJ and Hazel's peril came into sharp focus when Junior spoke those words, and for a moment, all hope was wrenched from AJ's heart. Clearly the man intended on killing them both. He hadn't hidden his identity in any way. As soon as he had the key, they were both superfluous.

He stayed close to her, with the gun prodding her all the way to the wreck site. The barrel pressed against her bare flesh, a constant reminder of how close she was to not existing in this world anymore.

"We're close," she said before gently easing the throttles back and slowing the boat. She glanced down again and could see his feet. His brand new dark blue topsiders with perfectly white laces. Hope filtered back into AJ. His shoes gave her hope again.

61

JULY 1974

Gabriel made them bring the boat in until it beached and still swore and muttered as he clambered onto the swim step, his linen pants soaked to his thighs. He threw his shoes, undoubtedly very expensive shoes, onto the deck and finally pulled the gun from his waist band but kept it low and out of sight. Whitey had no intention of trying to run, he'd be leaving Ainsley to deal with Gabriel and under no circumstances could he do that. Whitey dragged the anchor from the sand, shook it clean in the water, and laid it on the swim step before shoving the SportCraft clear of the beach. After climbing aboard, he reached over and brought the anchor and line over the transom onto the deck, shoving it into a corner. He was trying to ignore Gabriel, who was still swearing under his breath.

Whitey had been taken completely by surprise when Gabriel told him they were all going to the wreck. He'd been sure the Peruvian wouldn't set foot on the boat, but the man had remained calm and absolute in his demands. Until the water reached his knees that was, and since then he'd been extremely agitated. The last thing Whitey wanted was an agitated drug lord with a grudge and a loaded weapon. Ainsley had stayed silent and Whitey hoped to hell he remained that way. The situation was a trigger squeeze away from the worst crime the Cayman Islands had seen in decades.

Ainsley started the outboard and idled forward before selecting neutral so Whitey could climb to the bow and pull the other anchor, which was stowed in a hatch up front. Once Whitey was back in the cockpit, Ainsley opened up the throttle and guided the boat north along the coast. Whitey noted his friend was confident and proficient at the helm, a big change from their last trip; his brother must have given him some great lessons.

Gabriel had settled in the second seat once they'd started moving and had swung it to face Ainsley where he could keep an eye on both him and Whitey, who stood behind the captain's chair. The gun remained in his hand but lay in his lap. Whitey could see Gabriel was still tense but seemed to have settled somewhat.

"It'll take us about ten minutes to get to the wreck and then maybe fifteen for me to dive down and get the key," Whitey said calmly, hoping to establish a better conversation.

Gabriel frowned at him. "What kind of wreck is this? Why did you choose this one?"

"It's an old cargo ship about 40 metres long; hasn't been down there long so it's still intact and easier to get inside. But the currents are a bit wicked, so it doesn't get many divers," Whitey said, unsure why he cared but glad he was talking. Conversation meant opportunities; he was building some hope that he could talk his way out of this. Somehow Gabriel's weakness on the water gave Whitey renewed confidence.

"Is it on the beach?" Gabriel asked. "It ran ashore?"

"No, no, it's thirty metres down on the sea floor, it was scuttled by its crew and sank out over the reef," Whitey replied and watched Gabriel cringe at the thought of the wreck. "A bit further out from the wreck the island drops off to hundreds of metres deep; they call it a wall." Whitey poured a little salt on the wound, hoping fear might force a mistake from the man.

Gabriel gritted his teeth and glared at Whitey. "All I care about is getting that key. You don't come back with the real key and your accomplice here gets a bullet in the kneecap." Ainsley swung around, wide eyed, and looked at Gabriel. "That's right," Gabriel continued with a wicked grin. "One at a time." He waved the gun at Ainsley's legs. "The bullet blows your kneecap apart so your legs won't work anymore – never walk again, incredibly painful I'm told."

Ainsley's mouth opened but no words came out. Whitey tried to diffuse the moment. "It won't come to any of that, I'll nip down, grab the key and be back before you know it." He put a hand on Ainsley's shoulder and his friend jumped in surprise at the touch. "It's alright Ainsley, his beef's with me, not you, but we're gonna sort all this out, no one needs to be hurt, it's just a series of misunderstandings." Ainsley's shoulder relaxed under his hand and he squeezed his friend, hoping he believed him. He looked at Gabriel, who stared back, eyes ice cold.

Gabriel waved the gun towards Whitey who managed not to flinch. "You're a very lucky man, Whitey," he grinned. "I told my father you'd lied to me about the safety deposit box and you know what he said?"

Whitey could make a guess, but he really didn't want to hear the answer. "I don't Gabby, but your old man doesn't know me like you do, does he? He may jump to the wrong conclusion, and I'm hoping you'll see things a bit more clearly."

Gabriel ignored Whitey's words. "He told me I should cut out your eyes and send them to your mother," Gabriel said casually, as though he was discussing a grocery list. "But I had to tell him your mother was dead so I couldn't do that." He pointed the gun higher, at Whitey's head. "So, he said, cut out one eye and make you watch me feed it to a street dog. Just the one, you get it? So, you have one left to see the dog eating your other eye." He smirked at Whitey, who could feel Ainsley shaking beneath his hand, which still rested on his shoulder.

"If I don't get you your key, and all your money, then by all means, turn me into Pedigree Chum, Gabby. But I promise you in a short time you'll have them both and then we can sit down and talk about all this. I swear Gabby, I was never stealing from you."

Ainsley eased the throttle back and Whitey quickly looked to the shoreline for his references.

"We're here," he said quietly, and Gabriel peered over the side of the boat at the vast ocean of water around them, and the shoreline clearly further away than he was comfortable with.

"Make this quick," he muttered to Whitey.

62

NOVEMBER 2019

"Where is the wreck?" Junior asked, peering tentatively over the side without getting too close to the edge of the boat.

"It's thirty metres down there," Hazel nodded to the water, "hanging over the drop-off which goes to three or four hundred metres."

Junior stepped back to the middle of the boat and waved the gun at AJ. "You. You go down and get the key." He waved at Hazel. "She stays here."

AJ protested. "But it takes the two of us, one person can't do it alone, we both need to dive."

Junior shook his head. "Not this time. You go alone. Don't come back and I shoot her. Come back without the key and I shoot her."

AJ thought a moment before asking carefully. "And if I come back with the key, what stops you shooting us both?"

He looked at her smugly and then the shore. "I can do many things, but I can't walk on water. I need you to drive me back."

AJ considered pointing out the flaw in his plan, from the girls' perspective, but was scared to provoke him and she knew the answer anyway. He'd shoot one of them out on the water and the other once they reached dry land. The one had a chance as there'd likely be people at the dock, probably Reg being one of them. She looked at the coastline; there'd certainly be someone around from West Bay dock all the way to George Town but if he made them take him farther north around the point, there were plenty more secluded places to land. Maybe that was his plan. Or maybe he was making it up as he went along. He seemed incredibly confident on the dock but a lot less so now they were on the water, like he hadn't really thought this part through. It appeared he'd expected Hazel to have the key already. Her mind buzzed with scenarios until she realised Hazel was talking.

"We'll have to hook the wreck, there's no buoy out here to tie to," she was explaining firmly to the Peruvian.

He looked at her suspiciously. "No. None of your games, she dives down, gets the key, then straight back up to the boat."

"Sir, it doesn't work like that," AJ tried politely. "There's a strong current out here, the boat and the diver will get taken in the current. See how we're moving now with the drive disengaged? Look at the GPS, you can see."

Junior looked nervously from the water to the electronics on the console which he clearly didn't recognise or understand. AJ, seeing his hesitation, continued, "We drag a grapple hook through the water and snag the wreck, that way the boat is fixed to the wreck. I use the line to go down and come back up and the boat doesn't drift into the open ocean."

He looked at her, searching her face, seemingly deciding whether she was playing him or not.

"Okay, do it," he finally muttered.

AJ put the outboards back in drive and, checking their position on the GPS, circled around to come across the wreck.

"Hazel, get the grapple hook and when I say 'go', drop the anchor in the water and play out the line until you get to the mark on the rope. It's a piece of red twine tied to the line."

AJ lined up the boat, gave Hazel the okay sign and watched her throw the hook in the water. She idled slowly forward, using the port side motor only to yaw the boat at about thirty degrees to fight the current as they went across the wreck's path.

"Got it," Hazel shouted back when the red twine reached her hands and then tied the anchor rope off to a bow cleat.

Going slowly, AJ dragged the heavy hook through the water without the rope wrapping under the boat and into the props. She watched the GPS, carefully running perpendicular to the line between the two dots that represented the wreck's position. She was well clear of where they could have expected to hook either railing and she took a wide arc and slowly pulled around for a pass in the opposite direction.

"What are you doing now?" Junior barked at her with another prod of the gun barrel.

"We missed it, I'm taking another pass," she answered as calmly as she could muster.

"Quit screwing around and wasting time," he said impatiently. "Miss it this time and I don't care how much everything drifts you're going in and we'll just have to pick you up..." He didn't finish the sentence as the RIB jerked and AJ steered to starboard with the current to make sure the hook set and stayed. She shut the motors down and the boat spun around until it was down current, taut against the anchor rope.

AJ turned and looked at the man who stared blankly back at her, beads of sweat running down his face from the hot afternoon sun.

"Excuse me," she said, to which he frowned in return. "If you want me to dive, I need to get my gear," she elaborated, and he realised he was standing in front of the dive tanks. Clearly, he didn't want to be between the two women where he couldn't watch them both, but he reluctantly stepped alongside the helm and waved the gun at Hazel again. "Come back here, help her."

Hazel walked to the stern and dropped the removable ladder over while AJ pulled her wetsuit up. She turned so Hazel could pull her zipper up and Hazel leaned in close as she did so. She whispered firmly, "I'm so sorry. Just go straight for shore and get away."

"Shut up!" Junior yelled. "What did you just tell her, damn it?"

"She told me she was sorry and to be careful," AJ lied quickly.

He didn't look like he believed her, but she continued getting her gear on and avoided looking at him.

"I have to get in the water from the bow," AJ said once she was ready.

He shook his head, "Get in back there, I saw her put a ladder over."

"That's to get back on the boat, getting in I need to back-roll next to the anchor line so I can grab it to go down," AJ explained firmly.

"Fine. Both of you go to the front." He waved for them to pass the helm on the opposite side to where he stood.

"Hazel, get the saw from the toolkit under the console please, and the big screwdriver," AJ asked as she shuffled to the bow with her heavy BCD and tank on and her mask and fins in her hand. Hazel opened the toolbox and retrieved the two tools while Junior watched her like a hawk, the gun trained on her the whole time. He kept it pointed at her while she joined AJ at the bow. Hazel handed AJ the two tools which AJ tried to fit in the drop-down mesh pocket of her BCD, but they were too long. She folded the pocket back up and secured it, juggling the saw and screwdriver in her hand figuring out how best to hold them. Hazel leaned over and checked AJ's Nitrox tank valve was on and again whispered to her, "Get away, while you can."

She straightened back up and AJ looked her in the eyes. Eyes filled with anguish, pain and regret.

"He can't swim," AJ whispered back.

Hazel looked confused for a moment then realised what she'd said and nodded, "Okay." She pretended to check AJ's dive computer one last time. "Please, you can get away, this is my mess."

AJ subtly shook her head and back-rolled over the side.

63

JULY 1974

Whitey decided Ainsley was competent enough handling the boat now, he could dive from a live boat, unanchored, and be picked up afterwards in open water. He figured Gabriel didn't have the patience to wait for them to grapple the wreck anyway, so they weren't spoilt for choices. Ainsley was clearly nervous, but Whitey couldn't tell if it was from the gun-toting drug lord and his threats, or concerns about piloting the boat over the wreck. Both, he decided, were legitimate reasons to be uneasy, to say the least. As Whitey slipped into his gear, he ran through the process one more time to try and calm his friend.

"I'll guide you east of the wreck and that's where I'll go in; just remember everything in the water is heading west with the current. Hold the boat at idle where I go in and watch for circular rings where my bubbles reach the surface. My bubbles are carried by the current also, so I'll be back of them, say thirty feet or so, okay?"

Ainsley nodded anxiously but didn't question and chatter like he usually would. Gabriel fidgeted in the second chair and seemed to be on a roller-coaster between calming himself and letting his phobia take over. Whitey hurriedly finished getting ready while

Ainsley piloted them to the entry point. Once there, Ainsley moved to the stern and Whitey stepped over the transom to the swim step.

"It's as easy as that mate," he looked at his friend and smiled warmly. "Stay thirty to fifty feet behind my bubbles. Remember they'll disappear for a bit when I'm inside the wreck, so again, just idle in place until you see them again, and Bob's your uncle, I'll be back up before you know it."

Ainsley passed Whitey his fins and whispered, "Be careful man, but please hurry back, I don't like this guy."

Whitey put a hand on Ainsley's shoulder while he slipped the Voits on his feet. "Be back in ten or fifteen minutes, don't worry about a thing, my friend, Whitey's gonna sort all this out."

"Get on with it!" Gabriel shouted from his seat.

Whitey pulled his mask down over his eyes, glanced at Ainsley's terrified face one more time, gave his friend a wink, and stepped off the back of the boat into the water.

64

NOVEMBER 2019

AJ pulled herself down the anchor line, hand over hand, as the wreck of the Raptor came into view. They'd snagged the railing on the port side, but she could see as she descended that it was on the heavily corroded top rail. In fact, the top rail either side of the one they'd caught was rusted through and incomplete, just stubs of rotten steel protruding from either side of the posts. There was no way to move the hook with the strain of the current constantly pulling, so all she could do was pray the railing would hold for the next ten minutes or so.

As they had done in the past, she left the line halfway down, around fifty feet, and drifted while descending to the rear of the cargo hold. Schools of fish parted and swirled away from her as she glided in, careful not to drop the tools, and in short order she arrived at the base of the cabins. Without pausing, AJ continued down to the open door, and for the third time in a few days she entered the Raptor's engine room. One hundred and thirty feet below the surface.

Her torch beam sprayed around the dark, shadowy engine room. She shimmied on top of the engine's valve cover and tried pulling herself across without dropping either her light or the tools.

Without a free hand to use, she squirmed around helplessly and finally dropped back off the motor to regroup. AJ realised she was breathing heavier than normal, even for the extreme depth, and her heart rate was pounding. She needed to relax and think this through: she couldn't help herself, or Hazel, if she let herself become flustered and allowed nerves to get the better of her. She took a few long, easy, calming breaths, felt her heart rate slow, and some of the anxiety dissipated with it. Okay, fins, she thought and reached down to slip both fins off, leaving them just inside the door. Next, she shone the light over the motor to get her bearings, then switched it off and clipped it back onto her BCD. Blind in the almost pitch black, she slid back on top of the diesel engine, and used her free hand to pull herself over towards the port side where she knew the filter resided. When she ran into a blockade of cables and lines, she retrieved the light and turned it back on. Two feet in front of her a pair of big eyes stared back and she recoiled, banging her head on something hard overhead. Her mask was knocked askew and immediately flooded, returning her to illuminated blindness, and she clamoured to get her mask resealed. Her right hand smashed into more lines and she dropped the tools as her left hand reached the mask and she fumbled to get it righted. Purging the water from the mask, by exhaling through her nose while cracking the seal at the top of the mask, she finally regained her vision and fortunately still had the torch dangling from its tether around her wrist.

"I'm gonna grill that damn grouper," she thought to herself, once more breathing deeply to get her heart rate in check. The eyes had gone somewhere else, likely even more frightened than she had been. AJ shone the beam down and spotted the tools; they were on the floor, not far from where she needed to be to work on the filter. She slid over the edge of the motor and pulled her legs tightly under her until she was squatting in the cramped space, pinned in by various components in a waft of silt and debris. She considered checking her dive computer but decided not to waste the precious seconds. What did it matter? Go into deco? Run out of breathing gas? Nothing mattered except getting into the filter. All other scenarios meant death, the cause of her demise just varied. She reached for the saw and lined it up across the middle of the cylinder of the filter. Her knees were awkwardly in her way and she tried to shift to give herself a better angle. She pushed the saw across the surface and pulled it back while applying downward pressure. The blade slid helplessly around without gaining purchase enough to start cutting. She looked around for a spot to place the light to free up her other hand. Not seeing anything work-able she lined the saw back up then dropped the torch to hang from its tether and blindly placed her left hand around the filter next to the saw blade as a guide. She carefully drew back then pushed forward hard on the saw handle and felt the blade shaving metal from the filter. She worked the saw back and forth and could feel the teeth stripping grains of the old metal away until it snagged on something and hung up. AJ gathered her light back up and shone it on the filter to see what the problem was. The blade had caught a cloth of some sort and shreds of fabric poked through the saw cut that was now a quarter of the way through the cylinder.

AJ felt a wave of relief and joy surge through her at the sight of the rag. Maybe the old Frenchman's story was at least true. She'd held a nagging concern in the back of her mind that everyone was chasing a crazy man's imagined fairy tale and there was no key. The rag surely meant he was telling the truth. She moved the blade around the cylinder as best she could so it was cutting more surface area of the filter, hoping to avoid snagging the rag. It was slow and frustrating; every few strokes the cloth would snag again, and she'd have to pull the blade out and start over. After several minutes, she'd cut around three quarters of the cylinder and traded the saw for the big screwdriver. Pushing the shaft of the screwdriver through the cut, she tried prying the cylinder apart to open the gap. The sheet metal of the filter buckled where the screwdriver pushed against it and mangled around it rather than opening the gap. AJ bashed at the cylinder in frustration which dented the top down on the outer side of her saw cut. She shone the light and could see the rag inside. She bashed it a few more times until the handle slipped and her hand ripped across the jagged metal and she yelped into her regulator. Blood drifted in smoky grey wafts from the wound in her hand and she winced as the saltwater stung like hell. She drew a deep breath and bashed madly at the filter, ignoring the searing pain in her hand. Checking with her torch, she could see the twisted body of the filter had the rag now hanging out enough that she could pull it free. She yanked at it to wrench it clear of the sharp edges. The greasy rag floated free in her hand. She grabbed it with her other hand, checking for the key inside, the torch once again swinging from her wrist. Nothing. The rag was empty. This couldn't be. Everything the old man had said had been true until now. Had someone else removed the key? Her hand throbbed and the weight of the failure folded over her like a heavy blanket smothering the life from her body. And Hazel's. At this depth the nitrogen assaulting her system with every breath made her thinking heavy and confused. She fought the urge to panic as sheer disappointment and frustration threatened to overwhelm her.

She feebly retrieved the torch into her left hand and looked for where she'd dropped the screwdriver, scanning what she could see of the floor around her. When she shuffled to see better, she felt the weight of the tool move in her lap, cradled between her thighs and her stomach where she was doubled over. She looked down and saw the screwdriver lying in the folds of her wetsuit. Next to it was an odd-looking silver key.

65

JULY 1974

As Whitey watched the cuddy cabin disappearing to the depths, his last words to Ainsley echoed around his head. "Don't worry about a thing my friend, Whitey's gonna sort all this out." Damn it, he thought, that couldn't be farther from the truth. He kicked hard against the current and ascended as fast as he dared, trying to stay over the wreck as he went up. All the way to the surface he swore at himself for the mistakes and foolish decisions he'd made that had led to this point. This point, at which he was now sure, he'd got Ainsley, his best friend, killed. How things had gone down he could only surmise, but his best guess was that Gabriel had decided to deal with one man rather than two, and had shot Ainsley on the boat. Probably also shot a hole in the fibreglass hull which would have splintered and sunk the SportCraft. He knew he'd never know, but as his head broke the surface, what he did know was he was adrift, a long way from shore without a single boat in sight.

He could hear a voice and he scanned the water around him as the gentle swell rose and fell. A hundred yards west of him he spotted arms flailing and water splashing. Gabriel Cavero was spluttering and thrashing but Whitey could just make out a few words.

"Help me! Whitey! Keep... money... it all, save..! You know I can't..!"

Whitey had only a few seconds to decide what his next move should be. Drift on the surface and hope a boat would spot him before he was too far from the island, or dive back down and try to make shore underwater. Not for a single moment did he consider helping Gabriel. If he was closer, he wouldn't have helped him, or held him under. Whitey hoped the man took a long, terrifying time to drown. Ainsley was the best friend Whitey had ever had, a beautiful soul that had never hurt anyone. Whitey's rage was torn between himself for getting them into this mess that cost Ainsley his precious life, and Gabriel, for being the man who pulled the trigger. He really hoped it took a while for that piece of shit to finally go under.

He put the regulator back in his mouth and ducked under the water, finning as hard as he could towards the wreck, hoping he could stay over it. He had plenty of air left in his tank as the dive had been brief, but shore was a long way off. If he could hug the bottom, he'd hide from the worst of the current, but that meant deeper where he'd use more of his air. He used Navy tables as a guide for the safe dive time at different depths, but they were on the boat heading to the bottom, and it wouldn't matter at this point anyway. He was in a race that involved the distance to shore, versus air in his tank, handicapped by the current he fought.

Whitey reached the lee of the superstructure at 70' and quickly tried to recover his breathing after the effort. He moved to the port side, which was slightly more sheltered, but knew he had to go deeper to stay in the cover of the wreck, once he cleared the cabins. He kicked down to the railing and pulled himself along the side of the Raptor. When he came to the hold, he looked down at the doorway to the engine room and stopped. He wanted to return the key to the filter. He couldn't decide why on earth he'd want, or need, to do that, but something inside him was urging him to do so. Knowing he was probably burning through the air that may save his life and get him to shore, he kicked swiftly down to the doorway.

When Whitey finished and squeezed back out the door, he looked at his pressure gauge. He'd now used two thirds of his air supply and was no closer to the safety of the beach. He felt a calm wash over him as he finned across the hold to the bow, staying just inside the hold and clear of the current. His fate was sealed now, there was no way he could reach the safety of shore with the air left in his tank – it was probably half a mile away. That was okay, he decided. He'd created this catastrophe that had taken his best friend's life, it didn't seem right for him to be the only survivor. When he ran out of air, he'd simply let the current take him and he'd be pulled off the island to join Ainsley. Until that moment he'd keep heading towards the shore; it gave him something to focus on.

His mind drifted to Isabella as he cleared the bow and dropped back down to the steeply sloping sea floor. Finally, he'd found his soulmate, and now she'd be left wondering what ever happened to him. The pain he'd put her through, the not knowing what had happened and why he disappeared. He'd managed to hurt everyone he cared about. As Whitey thought about the previous night, he reached the shallower reef where the slope lessened at forty feet. He could feel her still in his arms. The beautiful evening they'd shared at Smith's Cove. Watching her drift to sleep in his arms at the Royal Palms. Waking to the morning sun lighting her pretty face while she continued sleeping, her long black hair falling around her pillow. He wanted to wake her, to hear her words, to see her green eyes shine, to hold her close one more time. He'd quietly left her that morning, peacefully sleeping, and asked the front desk to call the room at 8.30am so she wouldn't be late for work. He wished now he'd woken her. He'd give anything for one more minute with the woman. To explain how sorry he was for screwing everything up. To tell her he loved her. For the first time in his life he felt that, and now he was leaving this world without telling her.

Whitey felt his breath become heavier through his regulator and on the next inhalation the diaphragm clunked closed; no more air came. He closed his eyes and relaxed his body, letting the current lift him gently and pull him away from the reef. Away from the shore. Away from life. Probably best, he thought, not to have told her. Would only have added to the burden he was leaving her with.

NOVEMBER 2019

AJ scrambled over the motor, leaving both tools behind, and lunged for her fins. Bowling through the doorway she pushed off the floor of the cargo hold and began ascending while she reached down and slipped one fin on, then the other. Angling towards the bow she kicked hard and set a trajectory for the anchor line, racing depth against current to reach it before being swept away. She clawed at the water with full sweeps of her arms and long-legged kicks; diving etiquette be damned – she needed speed. She glanced at her dive computer as her arm swept by and the flashing screen was enough to tell her she was in deco and needed to get shallower fast. Air wasn't an issue, she knew she had plenty in the tank, it was the massive overdose of nitrogen molecules crammed into her tissues while she was at depth that threatened her life. Currently. She reached the line, still at 80' and hauled herself up, pushing the very limit of a safe ascent. At 60' she finally took a proper look at her dive computer that flashed an 'up' facing arrow with '30 feet' over it. She did as directed, and didn't pause until she levelled off at the target depth, where it began a three-minute countdown.

AJ checked inside her BCD pocket and felt the key; it was still where she'd stowed it. She calmed her breathing after the effort of hard swimming, and weighed her situation as she hung on the anchor line. The rope fluttered and whipped around under the strain of the raging current. If she popped up and presented the key, Junior was likely to shoot Hazel and force AJ to pilot him to shore, where she'd receive the same fate. If she said she didn't have the key, he'd almost certainly do the same anyway. She wondered where Reg was and if he'd raised an alarm, or was coming out to see what they were up to. She looked up at the surface and could clearly see her RIB, alone in the water. Whatever he was doing, he wasn't out here yet. The line tugged so hard in her hand she flailed around like a rag doll and was glad when it settled down so she could check her computer to make sure her depth wasn't changing too much. It showed 25' and she looked up and noticed the boat was farther ahead than it had been, she was trailing it, which explained her rising some in the water. But how could that be? She looked down and saw the grappling hook swinging freely at the bottom of the line, and the railing it had been attached to, now broken away from the post and disappearing behind her as the current took her, and the boat, away.

Her dive computer ticked off the last of the three-minute count-down and showed the 'up' arrow again and '15 feet'. The line was no longer taut against the wreck; it had only the weight of AJ and the hook below to keep it submerged, so it trailed the boat in a long arc. She pulled herself up the line to fifteen feet where her dive computer indicated she should remain for six minutes. AJ wondered what could possibly be taking place on the boat right now. Hazel would have realised the boat was adrift, and almost certainly would have seen the exhausted bubbles from AJ's regu-lator making circular patterns on the surface. But she was sure Junior was scared of the water and avoided boats whenever he could. His fancy yacht outfit probably came from a store at the airport in Miami when he connected to fly here from wherever he's been hiding for over forty years. He undoubtedly wouldn't believe Hazel as she'd try to explain that the hook must have come free, and that AJ was still in the water hanging on the line. He wouldn't understand or care about 'nitrogen loading' or 'off-gassing', she just hoped he'd be curious enough to wait until AJ was back aboard to see if she had recovered the key. All this bought time, and time was what they needed for help to arrive. She checked her computer: four minutes left. How did this Junior guy, apparently the son of the man that went missing in 1974, know that Hazel was here? Or that she knew about the key? If his father went missing, how would his son know about the key? She could only assume the Frenchman must have told more people than just Hazel. Who the hell was this mysterious old man who held this secret for so long? AJ kneaded and rolled these thoughts around in her mind, trying to find an angle that added up and, more importantly, would help her talk their way out of this when she surfaced. Her computer was showing under a minute so it was almost time to surface. She could stay down longer but surely Junior was pulling his hair out in the boat and she was sure he'd panic and take it out on Hazel. The clock ran down and she eased up the line with what she felt was a lousy plan. With anything better evading her, she settled on lousy over the other terrible options, and surfaced quietly at the bow of the boat.

"You're a liar, just like him!" Junior was screaming as AJ's ears cleared the water. "Tell me where he is, or believe me, you'll beg to die I'll make you hurt so badly."

Hazel's voice was a whimper, "I swear I don't know. I can't tell you what I don't know."

AJ couldn't tell if she was already hurt or just terrified, but if what she'd told her and Reg was true, she didn't know where Père Noël was.

"You're going to die out here, alone, just like my father did. The father I never knew. The husband my mother lost, the loss that killed her inside. The loss that tore my family apart." His voice was cracking as he spat out the words with hateful venom. "Now it's turned around. I've been tracking you since your mother died; finally I found the link. Isabella Alonso it said in her obituary. That was her name before she married. My family has been searching for that name to reappear since 1974. Losing your job? Losing your identity? All me. I knew I could flush out the truth if I applied enough pressure."

AJ heard Hazel groan. "She had nothing to do with this."

"Neither did my mother!" Junior yelled and AJ heard a dull thump and Hazel moaned.

"I've got it!" AJ shouted from the bow, hanging on the line, still out of sight of them both. She heard scrambling on the boat and Junior's face peered over the inflatable rubber front. He was sweating profusely and his hair a tousled mess. He pointed the gun at AJ's face and she instinctively put a hand out in front.

"Give it to me," he demanded through clenched teeth.

"Where's Hazel, let me see her," AJ said, as calmly as she could put together a string of words while a gun was pointed at her face.

"I'm giving the orders you little bitch, I have the gun." He waved the gun closer to her to emphasise his point.

AJ was shaking from fear as further doses of cortisol and adrenaline surged through her system. She surprised herself with her firm tone. "Shoot me and the key goes with me. Shoot her and I throw the key in the water. Let me see Hazel."

Junior let out a stream of profanity in his native tongue but disappeared from AJ's view. She heard him tell Hazel to get up and go to the front and then a shuffling sound before Hazel's face appeared. She was a mess. Her nose looked broken and blood covered her face from the wound. Her left eye was swollen almost closed and a cut wept blood from her forehead. AJ whimpered at the sight of her friend but Hazel managed a slight smile in return. "It's okay, I'm okay," she mumbled through cut and swollen lips. "I told you to get away girl." She frowned at AJ. "Go back under and swim away."

Junior reached over and pulled Hazel violently back into the boat. "That's enough! I'm tired of this shit, give me the key now or I'll start shooting holes in her every five seconds until you do!" He leaned over to see AJ but kept the gun pointed back at Hazel in the boat. Rage replaced fear and AJ glared up at him. "And how are you getting back to shore you chicken shit? You sure as hell don't know how to pilot this boat and I have the key to the safety deposit box; *and* the key to the boat."

His face screwed up in anguish and he started to swing the gun back around to point it at AJ. She instinctively closed her eyes, waiting for the world to go black along with the loud crack her ears would never hear. But she did hear the crack. The gunshot was even louder than she'd imagined it could be and a huge splash right next to her threw a wall of water over her head. She opened her eyes and Junior was surfacing a few feet away, his arms flailing wildly, his hands empty and a look of sheer panic on his face. AJ frantically pulled herself around the rope alongside the boat and reached the ladder in the rear. Throwing her fins aboard, she scrambled wildly up and shed her BCD and tank as she stumbled to the bow where Hazel lay slumped on the deck, her right leg dangling over the bow. AJ fell to her side and looked at her friend in horror. Blood covered her chest and a horrific gurgling sound came from the wound with each breath she wheezed through her throat. Hazel's eyes looked glazed, but AJ slid one arm around her shoulders and pressed her other hand firmly into the wound to try and stem the blood loss. Hazel tilted her head and tried to speak, but any words were too feeble and soft to be heard. AJ couldn't understand and leaned in closer. "Hang in there girl, I'll get you back to shore, I'll get help."

Hazel reached up and grabbed AJ's arm. She could feel her friend trembling and her grip was weak like a baby's. Hazel tried again, "Corsica... Père Noël... Everything I said... True... Everything... Except, I know..."

Tears rolled down AJ's face. "It doesn't matter Hazel, I don't care, I just want to get you to the hospital." She looked around for something to pack in the wound and spotted her tee shirt hung over a front deck seat to dry. She reached over and grabbed it; balling it up, she stuffed it firmly in the bloody wound and put Hazel's hand over it.

"Hold this tight, let me radio in for help." AJ tried to get up, but

Hazel let the shirt go and grabbed her again.

"Trois... Rue Saint-Antoine..." she spluttered, "in Calvi... Okay?"

"Okay Hazel," she pleaded, putting her hand back over the wound, "I got it, please let me get you help." AJ jumped up and this time Hazel let her go. AJ grabbed her VHF radio and started a distress call as she fired up the outboards with the key she'd left hidden under the console.

"This is Mermaid Divers, I need an ambulance to meet me at West Bay dock, I have a medical emergency."

She was about to put the motors in drive when she remembered the anchor line; if she took off it would drag under the boat, straight into the props. The VHF blared back at her asking for details, but she ignored it; wiping tears from her face, she ran to the bow, carefully stepping around Hazel who'd curled up in the foetal position. AJ untied the rope, letting it drop over the side. She paused for one short moment, scanning the ocean for Junior, but couldn't see any sign of him. She ran back to the helm, dropped the engines in drive and shoved the throttles forward. As she swung around towards shore, she saw Reg's Newton charging towards her and she grabbed the VHF, knowing Reg would hear her as well as the Marine Police.

"This is Mermaid Divers, we have a medical emergency, a gunshot wound, I repeat, a gunshot wound, I'm two minutes from West Bay dock but please advise closest ambulance."

She knew the hospital was in George Town so there was no point sitting at West Bay dock waiting for an ambulance to come from town if she could meet them somewhere along the way. She saw Reg turning his Newton around to run with her and she grabbed the radio again. She thought for a second. The feeling she had not seeing Junior in the water was one of satisfaction – that evil man deserved to die – but now her conscience cornered her and nagged at her unrelentingly. She opened the mic.

"Pearl Divers this is Mermaid Divers, there's one still in the water... there's a man overboard," AJ trailed off, her voice breaking, unsure what to say, or how to say it.

"It's the man who shot Hazel, Reg," was all she could manage before releasing the mic button again. Saying the words made it feel more real and she didn't want any of this to be real.

There was a slight delay, but AJ saw Reg's boat change direction again and head back towards the wreck.

"Roger Mermaid Divers, initiating search," Reg came back over the VHF, his concern clear in his voice. AJ wanted to tell him everything, tell him Hazel was bleeding on the floor of her boat, tell him not to look too hard for that scumbag Junior.

"Mermaid Divers please be advised West Bay dock, repeat, West Bay dock, helicopter will be there in two minutes."

AJ hadn't even thought of a helicopter. "Mermaid Divers acknowledges West Bay dock, on approach now."

"Hear that, Hazel? Ambulance will be there as soon as we get there, just got to hang on a few minutes and they'll have you hooked up to lots of medical crap and you'll be patched up in no time."

AJ kept shouting to her over the sound of the engines as she stayed wide open on the throttles. A hundred yards from the public dock, next door to Reg's, she slammed the throttles closed and the RIB dropped out of plane and decelerated quickly as the hull dropped deeper in the water. AJ selected reverse and spun the props backwards, stopping short of the pier, and let the wake swiftly surf the boat the rest of the way. Wailing sirens replaced the scream of the outboards and several people waiting on the dock helped lash the boat to the cleats.

"We're here, girl! Hear that racket? That's your taxi, first class ride into town!" AJ shouted, wiping away more tears and trying to ignore Hazel's blood, smeared all over her wetsuit. The thumping sound of a helicopter's blades joined the chaotic convergence of noise on the usually quiet beach, as AJ ran forward to kneel by Hazel.

"Hear that? It's the helicopter, they're here."

But Hazel didn't hear a word.

67

DECEMBER 2019

It was late afternoon by the time AJ walked up the steep hill to finally stand in front of the door to number 3, Rue Saint-Antoine, in the coastal town of Calvi. It had taken her four flights, over two days, to get from the island of Grand Cayman in the Caribbean to the island of Corsica in the Mediterranean. She'd left the warmth of the year-round summer to be met by the surprisingly wet and chilly December of the French region. The rain had stopped by the time she'd driven from the airport to the old town, but she kept her raincoat zipped tight against the cold air.

She knocked on the door and nervously waited. After a while, she looked around and double-checked the already triple-checked address. This should be the place. The home was a narrow, terraced house, sandwiched in a row of similar ones, on a small street at the top of the hill, overlooking the harbour. The view of the lights below was spectacular. She reached to knock again but before she could the door opened a crack. She couldn't see inside but heard an old man's gravelly voice.

"Qui est là?"

AJ had wondered if her French would be tested and considered the problem they'd face if the man didn't speak English at all.

"Je m'appelle AJ, je suis une amie de Hazel Delacroix," she replied. "I'm looking for Père Noël."

There was a brief hesitation before the door opened wider and revealed a very old man, stooped over and leaning on a sturdy cane. His thinned hair and bushy beard were white as a sheet and matched his pallid skin. His eyes looked tired and weary, but he forced a meagre smile.

"You're Arthur Bailey's granddaughter aren't you," he said in perfect English as he stepped back to allow her into his home, after warily scanning the street outside. "You can call me Whitey. Please come inside."

AJ stood in the doorway and stared at the old man. "You knew my granddad?" she asked incredulously.

He waved at her to come in and she finally managed to get her feet to move.

"We served together, in Jamaica. Wonderful bloke your grandfather, straightened me right out he did. And I recognise you from news articles I read." His voice trailed off. "You know, on Grand Cayman, articles about what happened."

AJ walked into a tiny living room with barely enough room for the two chairs, coffee table, sideboard and fireplace it housed. She recognised ABBA, the Swedish group from the seventies, playing quietly from a stereo somewhere in the room. Noticing three photographs on the sideboard she was immediately drawn to them. Whitey closed the door and slowly followed her. She turned and asked politely, "Mind if I look at these?"

He waved a hand towards the pictures. "Please, be my guest, only three photographs I own. Was only two until a few years back."

AJ looked at the frames and the weathered memories the closest two contained. The first was a black and white of a group of young sailors leaning over the rail of a naval Motor Torpedo Boat, their arms draped over each other's shoulders, and cigarettes hanging from most of their lips. She recognised the boat as the type her granddad had served aboard and instantly picked him out. She picked up the frame and held it for Whitey to see.

"Which one is you?"

He didn't have to look at the photograph and answered straight away. "On your grandfather's right, with my arm around him. He weren't much older than me, but he was like my Navy dad, taught me everything."

Whitey's eyes had drifted to the next picture and AJ turned. Putting the first one down, she picked up the second. It was a grainy and faded colour photograph of a young couple on a beach. They were standing in the water with fins and old-style, oval dive masks in their hands. The woman was gorgeous in a black bikini with long dark hair. The man, who she assumed was Whitey, was tall, tanned, and handsome, with broad shoulders and a broader smile. It looked like a promotional picture for a James Bond movie.

"Who is she?" AJ asked quietly.

Whitey swallowed and started to speak but had to stop and compose himself. AJ placed the picture back down on the sideboard, not wanting to upset the man, and as she did she looked at the third photograph for the first time. It was Hazel.

Whitey's voice was broken, and AJ could tell he was crying. "That's my daughter, who you met, and the one you held up was her mother, Isabella."

Off the living room was a small kitchen, and an even smaller table with two chairs that passed as the dining area. Whitey needed a few minutes to compose himself and offered to put the kettle on for some tea. They now sat at the table, sipping their tea from old, weathered teacups and AJ let Whitey take his time starting the conversation again.

"I'm sorry," he said, "I'm not usually the crying type. But this business with Hazel has finished me off, I'm afraid."

"I had no idea she was your daughter, she didn't share that," AJ confessed, still stunned.

"That's my doing," Whitey said apologetically. "I've been in hiding for forty-five years you understand, mainly to protect

Isabella, so I told Hazel she had to make up a story. I didn't want her going to Cayman, but she'd fallen on hard times since her mother died. I told her the whole story about her mum and me, and the mess I made of things with the Cavero family, so she knew about the money and the wreck. I take it you know all this from Hazel?"

AJ shook her head. "Only parts. She started by telling me a story about meeting you five years ago, but she said she knew you as Père Noël and nothing more. She relayed the story about the key, and the wreck, and the safety deposit box. She told me about her mum dying, but never told me about her mum ever being on Cayman."

Whitey nodded. "Again, that's really all my fault. Isabella had taken the name Delacroix when she married the Frenchman and left her Spanish family ties behind. It was all to hide from the Caveros." His head hung heavier. "And it didn't matter after all that anyway, Cavero's son still found Hazel."

"He found her when Isabella died, her obituary carried her maiden name as well, "AJ hurriedly told him, hoping it would help his guilt. "Junior told us that, there was nothing you could have done."

Whitey looked up. "Oh my dear, there's not much I could have done, but there's a lot more I shouldn't have done."

He sipped his tea and AJ wasn't sure what to say next. Whitey helped her.

"It was true, I met Hazel five years ago. She told you as many truths as I'd let her." He smiled weakly. "I never knew she was my daughter, you see. After I survived that day in Cayman, I found Isabella and told her everything, all about the Caveros, the money, everything. Told her to pack up and leave right away, fly away and never come back. It was too dangerous to be with me. She needed to find another man. Live her life and be happy. Broke my heart into a million pieces."

He paused a moment and gathered himself again.

"I gave her some money and told her to never look back, I could never see her again. That was that. I was sure the Caveros would find me, so I bounced around and used different names. Went back to Thailand for a while, where it's easy to get lost. When I saw the old man had died, I finally thought I was in the clear and I came back to Europe. I spent ages trying to track down Isabella and I finally found her. Living in southern France with her husband, Delacroix, and they had a little girl. Ruined me all over again, but still, I was relieved she'd found a happy, normal life. Her girl was a beautiful little thing. I never spoke to Isabella, didn't seem fair to, I just left. Next time I saw her I was staring at her grave in the south of France, almost a year ago now.

Anyway, after a while, I settled on Corsica, worked on fishing and dive boats as the seasons allowed. That's where Père Noël started; my hair had turned grey, then white, and I had a big beard. I liked the similarity it had to Whitey Snow, my real name I'd had to leave behind so many years before. One day, about five years ago, this French woman finds me. I was done working by then, too old to be of any use on a boat. Says she's the daughter of Isabella Delacroix. Alonso, as I would have known her. Told me she'd been searching for me for twenty years. Finally tracked me down from an article they wrote about an old man finally retiring from diving on Corsica, was a silly article in our local paper. Turns out that beautiful little girl I'd seen was my daughter, and she grew up to be this strong, independent woman. Hazel tells me her mum found out she was pregnant a while after she ran from Cayman and was settled in the south of France. She was working for this man Delacroix. He was besotted with her, and told her he'd happily raise the child as his own if she'd marry him. It was the best day I'd had in forty-five years when Hazel told me I was really her dad." Whitey stared off and AJ could see tears forming in his eyes again.

"How did you get away from the Caveros on Cayman?" she quickly asked.

"From the wreck?" he asked.

"The reports said three people were lost along with the boat that day, right? I assume you were one of the three?" she clarified, pleased to get him talking again.

"I can tell you where the boat is," he chuckled, "It's over the edge in the deep, I watched it going down. Believe me, seeing your way home heading to the bottom while you're going up is a bit unnerving."

AJ laughed with the old man, relieved he could still find some humour. But it was short lived.

"There's my best mate, Ainsley, floating on the top – that bastard Cavero had shot him dead – and when I surfaced, Gabriel Cavero was screaming for his life, getting carried away on the current. Served the arsehole right." Whitey waved a hand in the air and shook his head. "I let him go."

He stared at the table for a moment before continuing, "To this day, I've no idea why I did it, but I went back down, you know, cos the current was so strong I didn't have a chance on the surface. So, I went down and managed to stay on the wreck, then I went back in the engine room and put the bloody key back. No clue why I did that, but something urged me to at the time. Now of course I wish I hadn't cos Hazel wouldn't have had anything to go there for."

"Who knows though, right?" AJ said firmly. "Maybe she'd have gone anyway to talk to the bank, or try and find wherever you'd have tossed the key. Or you'd have kept it, and given it to her, and I never would have had the chance to meet her."

Whitey nodded. "S'pose. Anyway, I wasn't going to make it back and I knew it. Figured I'd run out of air and the current would take me off to be with Ainsley, and I was fine with that. Sure enough, I ran out of air and I just closed my eyes and let myself go. But I was over the shallower reef where there was hardly any current, and before I knew it, I'd surfaced and was just floating there. I ditched the dive gear so it would get pulled out to sea and swam to the bloody beach."

"And you never saw Gabriel again?" AJ asked.

"Nope. Bastard was halfway drowned last I saw him, and they never found his body," Whitey said coldly.

"Well, his son's with him now, cos exactly the same fate happened to him." AJ said, matching his tone. "And if his father was anything like Junior, then the world is a better place without them."

"But they both took someone very special with them, and both were cos of me," Whitey said with his old teeth gritted. He took a long, wheezing breath and looked at AJ. "You were with her? Hazel, you know, at the end?"

AJ swallowed and tried to pull herself together. She'd figured this conversation might come around and she wasn't prepared to speak of it yet. It had been a month, but she could still see Hazel's blood on her arms and chest, still hear her gurgled words, and see her pained face. It was all fresh and raw, the moment she ran to the bow when they'd arrived at the dock and held Hazel's lifeless body until the paramedics pulled her away. When would something like this ever fade? How long before it didn't haunt her mind constantly? She didn't know, but this was her father asking and she owed him a response.

"Yes, I was with her," she whispered.

For a moment she thought that might be enough, but after a minute he found the question he needed the answer to. "Did she fight?"

AJ couldn't hold them back, her tears streamed like pain escaping down her face. "Yeah, she fought the bastard. She pushed him out the boat and saved my life, damn it, got herself shot instead of me." Her face fell into her hands and she sobbed like a child. She felt the old man's arms wrap around her and hold her tight like her grandfather used to do. Her body shook as the emotion poured from her soul and she wept uncontrollably. He kept his arms around her and whispered soothing words until she finally could stop. He stood back, his own face damp from tears and watched as she fished around in her pocket and placed the silver key on the table in front of them. AJ looked up at Whitey. He stood there with red, puffy eyes and shook his head.

"That bloody key has a lot of blood and sorrow on it."

AJ wiped her face and looked back at the key. "What do you want to do with it?" she asked through sniffles.

"I don't want the bloody money, I never wanted the money," he said quietly. "There's nearly four million in there you know?"

"That's what Hazel told me, four million less thirty thousand. She said you wouldn't tell her why the thirty thousand."

"Ainsley's cut. I gave Ainsley thirty grand from it. But I had two million in my hotel room when I got out the water; there was two million already in the bank, but I hadn't had a chance to pay the new lot in. I had to sweet talk the lady at the bank into using the master key so I could put it there before I left. Would have been a lot easier if I'd kept that bloody key. Anyway, I wanted it all there. I didn't want any of it. Money I gave Isabella was mine I'd earned; never stole a penny from them."

She looked back at the old man. "How about something good in Hazel's name?"

"Like a charity?" he asked, sounding intrigued.

"Or a scholarship or something. Maybe for young women or to keep the youngsters on the island off drugs?" AJ suggested.

"You've got the key, you can do as you please with it," he said, managing to find a smile.

"I'll set something up on the island with your blessing. We can think about what kind of scholarship Hazel would have liked to see," she replied as he sat down again. He reached over and took her hand.

"Thank you," he said, looking her warmly in the eyes. "Thank you for being there with her, and thank you for coming here to find me."

"I had to," AJ replied, trying her best not to lose it again. "You were the last person she spoke of."

ACKNOWLEDGMENTS

This book would not exist without the continued, unwavering support and encouragement from my amazing wife Cheryl and great friend James Guthrie. I'm never alone on this perilous journey. My wonderful Mum and Dad always encouraged my creative adventures and for that and much, much more I'm forever grateful and in their debt. Dad would have loved this one.

My editor, Andrew Chapman has been a game changer and an absolute pleasure to work with, thank you so much. He can be found at Prepare To Publish.

Thanks to Jen Skrinska of Greenhouse Cafe and Rosa Betancourt and her staff at Heritage Kitchen, for their input and permissions.

Above all I thank you, the readers, it is your kind words that have opened the door to more adventures for AJ Bailey and myself.

LET'S STAY IN TOUCH!

To buy merchandise, find more info or join my Newsletter, visit my website at
www.HarveyBooks.com

If you enjoyed this novel I'd be incredibly grateful if you'd consider leaving a review on Amazon.com
Find eBook deals and follow me on BookBub.com

Visit Amazon.com for more books in the
AJ Bailey Adventure Series,
Nora Summer Caribbean Suspense Series,
and collaborative works;
Graceless - A Tropical Authors Novella
Angels of the Deep - A Tropical Christmas Novella

ABOUT THE AUTHOR

Nicholas Harvey's life has been anything but ordinary. Race car driver, mountaineer, divemaster, and since 2019 a full-time novelist. Raised in England, Nick now lives next to the ocean in Key Largo with his amazing wife, Cheryl.

Motorsports may have taken him all over the world, both behind the wheel and later as a Race Engineer and Team Manager, but diving inspires his destinations these days – and there's no better diving than in Grand Cayman where Nick's *AJ Bailey Adventure* and *Nora Sommer Caribbean Suspense* series are based.

Made in the USA
Middletown, DE
02 September 2022